Stalking Fiona

Nigel Williams was born in 1948 in Cheshire. He is the author of eight other novels including the Wimbledon series: *The Wimbledon Poisoner*, which was successfully adapted for television; *They Came From SW19*; *East of Wimbledon* and *Scenes From a Poisoner's Life*. He is also a well-known playwright. He lives in Putney with his wife and three children.

Also by Nigel Williams

Novels

My Life Closed Twice
Jack Be Nimble
Star Turn
Witchcraft
The Wimbledon Poisoner
They Came From SW19
East of Wimbledon
Scenes From a Poisoner's Life

Non-fiction

2½ Men in a Boat
From Wimbledon to Waco

Plays

Class Enemy
Harry & Me
Line 'Em
Country Dancing
Breaking Up
Sugar and Spice
W.C.P.C.
Lord of the Flies (adapted from the novel by William Golding)

Stalking Fiona

NIGEL WILLIAMS

Granta Books

London

Granta Publications, 2/3 Hanover Yard, London N1 8BE

First published in Great Britain by Granta Books 1997
This edition published by Granta Books 1998

A CIP catalogue record for this is available from the
British Library.

1 3 5 7 9 10 8 6 4 2

Typeset by M Rules
Printed and bound in Great Britain by
Mackays of Chatham PLC

"Truth is whatever is plausibly asserted
and confidently maintained."

TALLEYRAND

Part

1

1

I woke about eleven.

I remember all the events of that seemingly endless April day – Tuesday April 13th – very clearly. It isn't often you go looking for a man who is almost certainly trying to kill you. But, even now, the moment of waking remains as vivid as any of the horrors that lay in wait for me as I opened my eyes.

The first thing I heard was the rain. It had been raining almost every day since it happened, and, for a moment, the rain made me think I was back in the flat. I was standing, naked, in the bedroom. I had just become aware of the rustle of the bathroom curtain – the first sound that let me know HE was there. I was very frightened, until I realised that it was a week since HE first attacked me, and that I had woken up in my mother's house. I was safe.

"You're safe now, darling," she had said to me the previous night, "you're at home."

To her it's something called home. Mine as well as hers. She's always been hoping I would move in with her and, to try and tempt me back, has chosen a particularly hideous shade of green wallpaper. It's almost precisely the shade of my old convent school blazer. To make it even more appetising, she has bought a white rocking chair and placed it by the window. On the rocking chair she has put two teddy bears and a badly stuffed rabbit that, years ago, I loved very much indeed. The whole effect is decidedly sinister.

My father was never at home long enough to be interested in interior decoration. His idea of comfort was the bar of a hotel. I sometimes try and tell myself that if he hadn't died on me I would still have been living with them, like a dutiful daughter. HE would have followed me home and found Daddy at the front gate. Daddy would have made sure I was all right. And then, of course, I realise that

Daddy would have been away on business. He wouldn't have been there.

I couldn't think what had woken me. It wasn't the light at the thin curtains. Everything out there seemed grey and ghostly. I could imagine the roofs, washed clean by the water, and the lawns, unnaturally bright, between the shabby fences.

Could it have been the noise of the rain? As I lay there, listening hard, I heard a gust blow the drops against the window. It sounded as if someone had thrown a bag of iron filings up against the glass. There had been a noise. But it wasn't a noise like that.

Perhaps it was Mum. She had gone out. I could tell from the silence in the house that I was the only person there. Had she called up as she left? "Fiona!"

That wasn't it. Then I remembered, or perhaps that was when I actually *heard*, a dull thump from the front porch. It was the sound of a parcel falling through the letterbox on to the tiled floor.

Who had brought it? It was too late for the post. Just for a moment I entertained the idea that it might have been Paul. I had a clear picture of him, standing out there in the rain – his curls flattened across his forehead, his pale face decorated with beads of water. I couldn't stop myself feeling suddenly, ridiculously happy. The way I can remember feeling when I heard my Dad's footsteps on the path outside and knew he was coming back from a trip loaded with cheap, wonderful presents.

Then I remembered a lot of other things and felt frightened, ashamed and angry. I went through to the hall, looked down at the street, and saw a despatch rider waddling back to his motorbike in the defiant manner common to people wearing a great deal of leather. His helmet's visor was of blackened plastic and, though I studied it fairly carefully as he kicked his machine into life and roared off down the street, I couldn't make out his face at all.

All men want to look the same. That's why they invented uniforms. The only time I got a uniform – at the Convent of the Five Wounds – I put the skirt and blouse on my bedroom floor and jumped up and down on them for half an hour. I took the little wicker boater down to the front garden and drove my bicycle over it several times.

I couldn't remember – for the moment – which of them in the office, apart from Peter, knew where Mum's house was. That made me feel uneasy. You should remember things like that. You should be very careful about what you have said to other people and what they have said to you. If I had been more careful some of these things never would have happened.

I suppose I should have known all three of them a lot better. Because, for the last two years, we'd spent nearly thirty hours out of almost each week of our lives cooped up in the same office, I suppose I assumed I *did* know them. But office workers are like actors in a theatre – they only show what the place seems to require. So this, I suppose, could be called *The Secretary's Tale* – the story of a girl who sits in the corner, her eyes cast virginally down to the keyboard of her computer.

Not all secretaries play that role. Some won't speak to anyone unless they are called Personal Assistant or some other title that is intended to confer status on their humility. But I never minded being called a secretary. I think words should say what they mean – that was about the only thing my degree course in English Literature taught me.

And yet – poor old Fiona – if they had offered me another role – jolly sister, loving mother or even (God help us) beautiful daughter, I suppose I would have accepted. it. The trouble was that none of us in that office had the nerve to step outside the conventions we prescribed for ourselves. Somehow or other – men are so lacking in curiosity – they turned me into the anonymous girl in the corner. I'm not really like that at all. And, by the same process, they became mere shadows to me – suits and white shirts and briefcases and those gentle, insistent, tactfully phrased demands that feminism has taught men how to make.

Do I sound bitter? I don't intend to. I would like to shape myself to your demands and have you believe I am glamorous, wilful, loving, witty or any of the other things you like your women to be. But I am afraid I am one of these people who, in life or on the page, are sadly lacking in charm. All my charm is in my head, waiting to be discovered.

I padded back to my bedroom and peered out at the rain. Then, hugging myself against the cold, I went down the narrow staircase to the hall. There, by the door, was a fat rectangular parcel. Whoever had sent it had used an old envelope that had been wrapped round with tape as carefully as if it was a toddler and someone was sending it out into the snow for the first time.

I knew, almost immediately, that it was from Paul. I don't know why. My name was printed in crude capitals and his writing isn't that familiar to me. But I knew – the way you know, at first glance, whether someone is going to help you or hurt you – that this was from Paul and that this was his side of the story.

If that was the case it looked as if he was sending me the manuscript of his first novel rather than writing me a letter. Unless it was a food parcel. Whatever it was – it had started to annoy me. Ever since this business began, people had been offering me advice and telling me their side of things. I kept wanting to say to all of them, "it's *my* story. It's not yours. It's mine. You'll know that when I find out which of you bastards has been doing all these ugly, horrible things."

I opened the package. There were several separate bundles of papers. There was a letter that seemed to be from Paul. There was a manuscript, about a hundred pages long, written in black ink – in a neat, firm hand that I didn't recognise. And there were some scrappy sheets that looked as if they had been torn out of an exercise book. They were covered with smudged blue scrawl in letters that were all too familiar. The vowels all seemed to have come out the same shape and every consonant looked as if it had been in a multiple collision. Paul had got hold of my diary. How? I had only just given it to Peter Taylor last night. Was I, perhaps, dealing with a Masonic ring of perverts? Were they passing my private papers round between them and giving me marks for sentence construction, moral sentiment and originality in the deployment of paragraph breaks? As I flicked through the pages I couldn't help thinking that I should have typed the thing. People believe things more when they're typed, don't they?

I didn't know what I felt about Paul reading them. I hadn't really minded handing them over to Peter on the previous night. I had believed everything he had said to me. But the morning afterwards, it was different. I couldn't help thinking that the silence in the flat, the darkness outside and those sinister footsteps in the street had made me lose all judgement. At the beginning of that poisonous, frightening day I realised that I just didn't know who to trust any more. Any one of them could have been the murderer/rapist. Assuming that was the limit of his activities. Maybe they were dividing up responsibility for all these crimes equally between them. Maybe it was a team effort. All I could really think about was the fact that, now, two of them had read their way through my private thoughts. Since the first attack I hadn't felt that my thoughts were my own. I didn't have any privacy left. I was as naked as I was that time when HE . . .

Writing that now, the memory of the first assault comes back to me, unbidden. It comes, at first as a confused mass of images – a yellow mask, a hideous noise from the back of someone's throat and two gloved hands outstretched towards me. I consider it quite consciously, and recall, with as much precision as I can muster, the smell of my own fear. Only then can I take possession of what has happened to me and write the next line, in pen and ink, in longhand on virgin paper, in a place of safety.

All the papers were arranged in sequence. The letter from Paul to me came first. After that came my diary. As far as I could make out someone – presumably Paul – had broken it up into blocks and interspersed it with the pages that had been neatly written in black ink. These, I now realised, were all penned by Peter Taylor. What was all this in aid of? I couldn't suppress the crazy thought that these guys were preparing *Fiona's Life Story* for publication.

I upended the envelope and shook it out over the tiles. A blue computer disk fell on to the floor in front of me. I held it up between thumb and forefinger. It was neatly labelled, in typescript, A:/AIR. I put the disk back into the envelope then I pulled out the opening pages of Paul's letter to me. It began, I observed, "Darling Fiona . . ." There are not many men who have preceded my first name with that particular adjective. I couldn't help noticing, however, that his handwriting, large letters, separately made with a thick nibbed pen, resembled that of an anxious-to-please infant.

I started at the beginning. I squatted down on the floor, right there in the hall, and started to read. Outside, the rain beat ceaselessly against the doors and windows. Further down the street, someone was trying to start their car. It made a coughing sound, like an old man trying to breathe. I was halfway through the first page of Paul's letter when the doorbell rang.

I ran back into the kitchen, went to the crockery cupboard and threw the papers, and the envelope containing the computer disk, into it. After I had closed the door, I stood for a moment with my back to it, as if I was defending it against a burglar. I suppose the tone of Paul's letter had got to me. I wasn't crying or anything, but I knew that I didn't want anyone, not even the forces of law and order, to read what he had written to me.

There is someone for everyone, they say, but you don't always find them. And, when you do find them, they probably bring a whole lot of trouble with them. I remember thinking that, as the bell sounded once more and I ran out to the front door, still half-dressed.

When I got to the cheap, gilt mirror in the hall I stopped and looked at myself. I realised I was wearing a pair of Dave's pyjamas. He always maintained I wore them because they made me look sexy, provocative, wickedly demure. But I remembered, as I stared at my reflection, why I had made sure that they ended up in my suitcase when I walked away from his flat. They were warm. Then the bell went for a second time.

I hadn't thought, up to that moment, that the person on the other side of the door might be dangerous. As you will see, I had every reason to think just that, but my hand was almost on the latch before I had the sense to call "Who's there?" I heard my voice echo around the hall. "Who's there?" *If I go on like this*, I thought to myself, I shall end up like a little old lady.

"It's Peter," he said, "It's Peter Taylor. From the office. And someone from the police."

"Give me two minutes!" I said, "I'll make myself decent!"

That's the kind of thing my Mum would say. Although I hate to admit the fact – there are many ways in which I am horribly like her. I may be able to hold my own in a conversation about, say, French Structural Anthropology or Postmodern Critical Theory, but, when people are talking to me, I still hold my head to one side, like a bird, listening for worms. When smoking a cigarette – a thing I try to avoid for precisely this reason – I am still unable to stop laying my left forearm across my stomach, screwing my right elbow into my left hand and waving around the lighted tip as if I was in a forties movie.

I heard a lot of coughing. Then I ran back up to my bedroom. I took off Dave's pyjamas and bundled them at the back of my clothes drawer. That was when I saw the white silk night-dress – the one I had brought with me from the flat on the previous evening. When I'd crammed it into my overnight bag, I don't think that I had thought of it as important. But, as my fingers brushed against the soft material, I saw with sudden, frightening clarity that it was evidence. I closed the drawer rapidly and, uncomfortably aware of my own nakedness, looked behind me.

I groped through my bag for a clean pair of knickers. I had in my possession the only piece of solid evidence in this whole horrible business. "DNA," a small voice in my head kept repeating, "DNA. It's only just over a week since he stained it! Don't let it out of your sight". And then I suddenly saw a pompous barrister holding the shabby white silk above his head and booming out across a court-room – "This, m'lud, is Exhibit A!" It seemed as if he was holding me up inside the night-dress. I was dangling there, from his fingertips, in front of a crowd of curious faces, with my head to one side like a broken doll or a hanged criminal. I had felt like Exhibit A ever since Dartsea.

I was going to pull on my jeans, when something made me open the cupboard next to the window. There, on a solitary hanger, was the black dress that Dad had bought for me, under my supervision, about six months before he died. I can't think why I chose it, apart from a need to put the poor bastard out of his misery. Like so many items of clothing bought with a particular man in mind, it no longer pleases me. It's drab, almost spinsterish – the sort of thing that a girl who doesn't want to be noticed might wear. Before I went back down the stairs I slipped it on. I suspect that even that early in the day, I was beginning to be aware of the fact that my anonymity was a valuable, necessary disguise – one I was going to have to preserve, if I was to stand any chance of getting out of the business alive. One thing was for sure – it's one of the most important lessons I have derived from all this – the policeman was going to be absolutely no use to anyone.

Even now I find myself wondering what would have happened if I had told the police about that first attack. There are times when I try to tell myself that, somehow or other, they might have found him. Or that, if they had found him, he would have been properly punished. Then I remember that, these days, it is the victim who is punished and that, in my case, the punishment would almost certainly have been death.

Back then, I think I was a little more impressed by the law. As I went down the stairs, I think I probably tried to think of how I should behave to this policeman, standing with Peter Taylor on the other side of the front door. It might even have occurred to me to try and trust him, the way I had forced myself to trust my father's endless excuses and apologies for the fact that he wasn't coming home.

'Bit of a problem girlie! Stuck in the back end of nowhere girlie! Love to Mummy!'

I was scared of course. The only thing that makes you brave is being brave. I don't think that there was any chance of that, for me, until some time later when I first looked into his sick and horrible mind laid out for my benefit, like a dismembered machine. I was scared at the beginning of the day. I opened the door and looked at their feet. When I finally raised my eyes past their knees I saw they were both nodding with fatherly concern.

"It's all right," I said, "you can come in."

They both kept on nodding. I heard that croaking, ludicrously deep voice of mine say, "I'm not going to do anything peculiar!"

Peter laughed, then, and the two of them came through to the kitchen. The policeman stood looking out at our tiny back garden. He studied the shed and the tired rose bush. Then, as if he was trying to remember all this for some police exam, he looked across at the row of gardens behind us. There's something sad about the backs of houses, I think, especially in the English rain.

I made them tea. Peter was sitting at the table. He said, "He broke into my house. This morning."

"Oh!" I said carefully.

I was only halfway through the first page of Paul's letter. I had been determined not to start thinking about him when I started to read. I knew that once I had a clear picture of him – sitting in that pizza place, reading out the menu, or grinning at me across the table in Dartsea – I wouldn't be able to stop myself from taking his side against them. I had tried not to hear the words on the page as if they were being read in his voice – because it was his voice that made me start to fall in love with him. But, even though I had not read more than a few paragraphs, Paul was already in the room with me. I could touch him and feel him and hear him and smell him. I was in that hotel room and he was holding me and time had ceased to be of any account.

I looked at Peter Taylor. He has thick, red hair and a slightly plump face. An obvious psychopath. The fact that he's married with young children makes it even more likely that he subscribes to the Perverts' Charter.

"He might", said the policeman, dragging his eyes back to me, "come here."

Then there was a lot of stuff about how I wasn't to be scared and how the law could offer me armed protection. I said I didn't want anything like that, and that I wasn't scared. That wasn't true. Of course I was terrified. But I was as scared of them as I was of the twisted bastard who was after me.

Now, I am almost sure that he was as scared of me as I was of him. That's why he didn't kill me, I think – the way he killed the other girls. I think that there was something about me that brought him dangerously close to real human emotion, and that frightened him. But he liked it. I think he was saving me up, keeping me like a glutton's delicacy. He was trying to make it last. He was behaving – I can't avoid this comparison – like a lover putting off the moment of orgasm, trying to make things slower . . . and slower . . . and slower . . .

Maybe I already suspected that there was something I could do that would make him reveal himself. But I was also absolutely sure that if I did whatever it might be – it could have been a phrase, a word, or it could have been a gesture or a look in my eyes – then he would forget everything, abandon the peculiar rules by which he was playing and try and kill me properly.

"We think," the policeman was saying, "that there may be a connection between what's happened to you and what's happened to those girls in south-west London . . ."

I let him talk. Men talk but you don't have to listen. While they talked I thought about other things. I certainly didn't want to think about what had happened to those poor girls.

I thought about love, actually, if you want to know. I thought about what it was that could make you decide you knew someone utterly and totally. I thought about how some people are lucky enough to glimpse the rest of their lives with another person. How others think they see it but they don't – and end up alone, angry and sad, in rooms that no one visits.

After my Dad died, in his desk drawer I found a letter to my Mum. It must have been written forty or fifty years ago. It said:

"I've been thinking about you and your independent look and how I like you like that. I've been thinking about how it will be after we're married – oh, and what kind of children and how many. A lot I think – four? five? – but the first one will be a girl and we will call her Fiona."

I cried when I read that. Partly because it made me feel as if I was an *idea* of his. One of his few successful ideas. I was the first child, but there were no others after me. And partly because the way he wrote – nothing like the way he talked – suddenly shocked me into seeing him. The moment when I saw Dad's flushed face, and his pale blue eyes flickering nervously behind his glasses, was the exact point at which I started to cry.

While the policeman talked about brutal murders, I thought about Paul. I summoned up a clear picture of me and him in a small, clean house somewhere, with two kids and a garden and a patch of blue sky, like that patch of blue sky in the photograph on Peter Taylor's desk. An impossible fantasy. And one, I note now with sad irony, that had started in the same week that I had been raped and very nearly choked to death.

It was a fantasy of the kind with which children comfort themselves. I was almost sure that even if I should discover that what I wanted to be was the case – that is to say, that Peter Taylor was lying to me – then it would be too late for me and Paul. But, as Peter and the policeman droned on about how he wouldn't get away and how they would make sure he was punished, I found myself drawn back, time and again, to Paul and Paul's mysterious smile.

No, I didn't know him. That was true. I behaved in an unbelievably naive fashion. I had absolutely no right to trust what I felt about him. Why, in God's name, should I have ever decided to trust my feelings at all? They haven't, as you will see, been a very good guide at any time in my life. But they were all I had left, I suppose. I certainly had stopped trusting evidence by that stage.

"So," Peter was saying, "if he calls you . . ." He ran his hands through his shock of red hair, and looked, suddenly, like a worried little boy.

"Yes," I said, "if he calls me I'll be in touch . . ."

The policeman put a fatherly hand on my shoulder. I gave him a not quite daughterly stare in return. I squinted down at the hand. It was the colour of fresh ham. The fingers looked like uncooked sausages. I hate policemen. I'm sorry. But I do. I've hated them ever since Dartsea. Let them go and put their fatherly hands on someone else's shoulder. "We think," said the policeman, as he fixed me with a look that was supposed to let me know that he wasn't as stupid as he looked, "that Paul Jackson may be extremely dangerous!"

I nodded. "Yes," I said. I liked that "may be". I suppose if they admitted to themselves that he *was* the same guy who, this year, had raped and murdered six other women, then their rather limp offer of a bobby at my front door would not be considered adequate. And perhaps the Metropolitan Police just did not have the funds to move me to a safe house in Malaga or freeze me cryogenically until all this was over.

I didn't think, at the time, that the police could possibly have any evidence to link what had happened to me with the girls who had been attacked on the towpath. At that stage, you see, I thought whoever was after me wasn't quite as far gone as the gentleman who had been attacking young women down by the river. One of them – she was a nurse, only just twenty years old – had suffered injuries so brutal the papers said they wouldn't print the details. The trouble was – that made people fall back on their imaginations. And, of course, there's no limit to the horrific things that people can invent. One secretary in the company had sworn that HE had thrust a knife into the nurse's groin and ripped her open, as if he were gutting a fish.

As he talked on I looked at Plod. The other thing I don't like about policemen is the way they try to come between you and your anger. *I am sorry to hear you have been a victim of crime*, was how the law began a duplicated letter to my mother, just after she was burgled, and at Dartsea I had noticed that all the policemen who tried to talk to me about it wore a look of professional concern that was about as helpful as that letter. Even when they tried to look as if they felt the things they assumed I must be feeling – they did not convince. Once or twice I'd said to them that I was going to find him and that after I had found him I planned to beat out his brains with a hammer. They looked pretty sympathetic to this line of approach. Some of them even volunteered the odd sadistic motif of their own. But you could tell they were not serious about it. They thought I was just talking dirty to make myself feel better about things. They didn't understand that I was utterly and completely serious.

Peter Taylor got up. He seemed tired suddenly. He ran one pudgy hand across his forehead and looked across at me.

"I've read your diary, Fiona," he said, "and this man attacked you before? Is that right?"

I kept my face very still. "No," I said.

"Fiona," went on Peter, "you said that you were attacked at your flat. You were attacked. At your flat. Weren't you?"

I thought about the night-dress, upstairs in my bedroom. Safe in the drawer. "No," I said.

Peter ran his hand across his forehead and sighed softly to himself. The policeman looked at him as if he was going to ask another question but Peter shook his head, almost imperceptibly.

After a while they went. They didn't say where. I didn't ask. All I could think about were those papers hidden in the kitchen cupboard. I had to return to them in the same way I remember having to finish a horror story as a little girl, even though I might be reading it, alone, in a darkened house. Suddenly, Paul's letter seemed as sinister as the smudged print on my favourite Gothic paperbacks. "Darling Fiona" because he wants to get back into your confidence. He wants to get closer and closer and closer. He knows you can't resist him even though you want to resist him. And, when he has your confidence again, when he's made you cry and moan and go to pieces in his arms

14

and spent all of one night with him, then he will reach out for the ultimate closeness, which is to take that wicked ten-inch knife and rip your belly open.

I stood at the door as they climbed into the police car. That was when I nearly told them about the parcel. About the papers and the blue computer disk, labelled only with A:/AIR. But I didn't. I suppose I ought to have said something. And if I had, things would have turned out very differently. But, even then, I was starting to realise that I was going to have to look after this business on my own. I suppose I was beginning to understand that rape is a private matter between the attacker and the victim. That's how it feels to me now, certainly. And, even then, I think I knew I didn't want anything to come between me and HIM apart from that black-handled claw hammer upstairs – in what was once going to be my bedroom.

The other reason I didn't say anything to them, of course, was precisely because of that "darling" in Paul's big, unfamiliar, childish handwriting. I didn't want to say anything to anyone until I'd read everything that Paul had sent me. If I had opened my mouth it wouldn't have been to talk about what they were probably already calling "the case". It would have been to scream at the two of them, "Of course he's dangerous! Love is dangerous, isn't it? Love is the most dangerous thing there is, isn't it? And have you ever been in love, I'd like to know?"

As the car drove away I thought about the night-dress upstairs. That was my only hope. What I still didn't understand, of course, was why HE hadn't been back for it. It might have taken me a week to work out how important it was, but HE must have known that all along. I was sure of that. It was evidence. It occurred to me, just then, that HE might be waiting for me to bring it forward, since, to do so, I would have to make it clear to all three men that I knew that HE must be one of them. And, immediately I had made that move, HE would kill me. While Plod was organising lawyers and identity parades and biological tests HE would come after me – him and his wicked knife.

The rain was still occupying the sky and the street. Opposite, old Mr Lacey, from three doors down, beads of water dripping off his sou'wester on to his yellow cape, was wobbling home on his bicycle. My Mum was still nowhere to be seen.

I went back into the kitchen. I took out the parcel and set out the papers on the kitchen table. There, alone in the quiet house, I picked up the first page of Paul's letter to me. I wanted to read it like a love letter but of course I didn't. I read it like a detective, looking for clues and traps. I read it like a critic, trying to understand the hidden meaning of each sentence, and why each word had been chosen. You read it like that. Because this is a story about how things look, about how a tone of voice or a trick of style can betray you and, most importantly, how words on a page can lie as easily and cruelly as the false lover in whose arms you may have fallen peacefully asleep.

2

Darling Fiona,

I am writing this in Peter Taylor's house. Every single word of it is true. I don't know how I will get it to you but, from something you said to me at Dartsea I formed the impression that in "times of crisis" you might well return to the maternal nest. Have you noticed how people who are sick or hurt always want to go home?

I did not write the document you will find on the computer disk. There are things in it that make it look as if I did but I swear to you that it is not my "handiwork". If, as I suspect, it has been written for the purposes of incriminating me, then I have a fairly good idea of who the culprit may be. I want you to read it because they will be sure to show it to you. I'm a shy, clumsy, awkward sort of a person and I know if I called you or tried to see you I would probably make matters worse. But at least by writing I can try to say what I feel.

•

I put the letter down at that point. I noticed my hands were shaking. Of course – one of the things about this case was that I never got to study the evidence unmediated by the vision of some man. And, if I was going to get anywhere with any of this, I was going to have to try and forget that I was in love with Paul. Find something to dislike in it, said a voice in my head, separate the man from what he's saying. Look at the style as if you were a critic and this were a text.

It was certainly true that, on the page, Paul sounded less like a lover than a Civil Servant who wishes to tamper with the minutes of some astonishingly boring meeting. He didn't write like he talked, I thought to myself. Which was hardly surprising because he hardly talks at all. What was going on with those inverted commas? He seemed to feel the need to sling them around the necks of perfectly innocent words, like a Victorian matron covering up her piano's legs in case they gave people impure thoughts.

Not, of course, that this told me much about him, apart from the fact that he can't write. And it still didn't proof me against the memory of that smile of his or the shy way he had moved towards me on that cliff, overlooking the beach at Dartsea. My hands had stopped shaking though. I went back to the letter.

You must believe me. If you don't believe me I really am finished. Yours is the only opinion I care about. And you are the only person I can think of who could make sense of the papers I am sending to you.

How did I get here? Well, if you want to know, I've been going in for a spot of the old "breaking and entering". I broke in through the kitchen window. I say "broke in". It was open. I hauled myself up over the sink, wriggled over the washing up and, picking my way past the plastic tricycles, the jigsaw puzzles and all the other things that decorate this house, made my way up to Peter's study. That's where I'm sitting now, scribbling this on his notepaper, looking out at the endless rain and the peaceful park that starts at his back gate and seems to stretch away to the horizon.

I can't find the words to say what I want to tell you, Fiona. Can you imagine how I feel about the fact that you suspect that I am the man who did these terrible things? I can't imagine how the world can possibly contain people who could even imagine let alone carry out acts so repellent. I am telling you the truth when I say that until my visit from the "powers that be" this morning, I was not even aware that half of them were even happening. But it certainly looks as if one of us three seems to be responsible. A few weeks ago I thought I knew the people with whom I work as well as I know anybody. Now I am not so sure. I think most people in this city – where families don't seem to mean anything any more and where friendships have been eroded by hunger for money or status – live in a kind of twilight world. They go into an office, say, where they think they know the people who share their work with them. But they do not. All the conversations we have had, over the years, now seem to me to conceal more than they reveal. I have to face the fact that either John Pappanauer or Peter Taylor – both people I thought I trusted and respected – is a murderer, a rapist and a . . .

●

I put down his letter. There was something in it, now, that I recognised as Paul's voice. It wasn't the self-conscious slang or the occasional attempt at a purple passage (I was particularly struck with the bit about us all living in a twilight world) but an atmosphere that was what I thought of as him. There is a kind of churchy gloom about Paul and it had got into his sentences. I saw him, now, in his neat, dark suit, standing at the edge of the office, his hands up as high as a hamster's paws and his head at an odd, puppet-like angle. I saw his peculiar formality – the little touches of dress – the elegant red handkerchief or the amazingly neat grey socks. I saw Paul the way I had seen him just as I started to fall in love with him. And, hard as I tried to be sceptical about what he was saying, I found myself wanting him the way I knew he wanted me.

"Could you possibly do a letter for me, Fiona?" The three men in my office shared me – they did actually use that term without blushing. But Paul's requests were always couched with a painful politeness that seemed genuine. I suppose he was the one I would have described as "a gentleman" – another word of my mother's that I cannot stop myself using.

Why didn't he call? Was he frightened something about his face would betray him? That thought steadied me, and once more I picked up his letter.

Whoever it is, my darling, I swear to you it isn't me. I'm innocent. You have to believe that. If you don't believe it then I don't have a chance. But I am innocent. Swear to God.

Peter's wife is out at work. Peter's children are at school. I know enough about his domestic routine to know that I have to find out whether it was Peter Taylor who planted the evidence at my flat or whether it was Pappanauer. It would have been just like "our John", wouldn't it? To get someone else to do his dirty work for him? I haven't found anything, of course, except a document that seems to do even more to incriminate me. It's the one labelled A:/AIR on the blue floppy disk. I want you to see it because I want you to have the chance to "get a weather eye" on matters for yourself. It's for that reason that I've sent you Taylor's journal, as well as your own diary.

I can't understand why he has taken against me in this way and why he should have decided that I am the "guilty party". At first I was sure that he was covering up something in his own behaviour but, having read his journal, I am not so sure. As you will see it is mostly about a topic in which I know you are not at all interested – money. Why did you come to work for us, Fiona?

•

Sheer lack of drive, old thing. Total inability to get ahead. Inbuilt urge towards self-destruction. Deeply held conviction that my natural role is to be the lowest form of office life. I drifted into it, I suppose. After I left university I went – for reasons I still find it hard to analyse – to Thailand. I went with a girl called Cheryl who had long black hair, a deathly white complexion and smoked almost constantly. "I'm not in a relationship," she said on the plane going out, "I just have sex with people!" She gave me a meaningful glance as she said this. I don't remember much about Thailand but I remember Cheryl very clearly. She was one of those people you think you like until you get to know them.

After Cheryl and Thailand there were a few interviews and then – I think through a friend of Dave's – there was the company. I don't know why I came to work with you, Paul. Things just happen to girls like me. Maybe I came because I thought I'd meet a nice man and settle down.

I know why *I* work there. Money has always obsessed me. I am not at all interested in what one can do with it. But I get a perverse pleasure out of watching it accumulate – even when it isn't mine. But you have always been something of a mystery to me. You're one of those people who always seems to be defending her privacy. I don't think it was just me. I think we were all a little frightened of you – even Pappanauer.

I was hoping there would be something in what Taylor had written that would tell me whether it was him or Pappanauer. But there isn't. He seems, on the page, to be exactly the formal, wise-cracking, grim-mouthed chap he is in "real life". He tells the story just as he prepares those reports in the office – clearly, simply and with a sort of "plain man" humour that is quite beyond me. And I know, as I struggle to write this, that what I have to say sounds hollow and badly expressed and sometimes too obvious to be true. I love you, my darling, you see, but cannot find any clever way of putting it, or of trying to convince you that I am not the person who wrote what is on that disk. The awful thing is that the man who did this – this seems a curious thing to say I know – manages to make himself sound far cleverer and sharper and, sometimes, even more amusing than I could ever be. Isn't that a dreadful thought? That a sick and twisted murderer might, under certain circumstances, be quite "good company".

Why did you let Peter have your diary, Fiona? When you had written about us in it so movingly? Did he convince you that I had done those awful things to you? Did you do it to try and blot out all the trust and affection between us? Because if that is why you did it then I am afraid you haven't been very successful. Because I still love you. I love you so much that I don't mind you reading what's on that computer disk, even though so many things in it seem to point so clearly to me. I want you to make your own judgements, calmly and clearly. I won't stand over you. Read the facts and judge for yourself.

I didn't write it, Fiona. Someone else did. And they wanted certain things in it to sound like me. Because, of course, they know things about me that no one else does know. They know things about

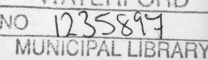

me that I wouldn't dare to say to you and they have worked them into the fabric of this horrible "document", this tissue of half-truths, in order to hurt and humiliate me even more.

•

I put Paul's letter down again. I got out the computer disk and held it up between my thumb and forefinger. Then I picked up the letter and stared at it. He wanted me to be objective. That was fine. I would be objective.

Almost immediately the attempt led me into feeling angry. What was all this stuff about "defending my privacy"? I had spent two years waiting for one of them to treat me like a human being. I was dying for someone to break into my privacy, Paul. Couldn't any of you see that? Do you think I enjoyed watching the three of you breeze out through the swing doors, on the way to restaurants that I'd booked?

I looked down at his letter once again. If I had met Paul through a correspondence course, I thought to myself, there would have been very little chance of my ever wanting to encounter him in the flesh, let alone go to bed with him. He sounded distinctly creepy. Why should going into print shock him into declaring eternal love for me every two minutes?

Somebody had something on him. That much was clear. Someone knew something about him that he didn't want me to know. All I knew was that, whatever it was, I didn't want to know. I was sure that he was going to tell me all about it, because, even on page one, his letter had an almost drearily confessional ring to it. But all I wanted to know, at this particular moment, was whether he was or was not the same guy who has been ripping open those poor young women down by the riverside. I wanted to be completely free of feeling when I looked at what he had to say.

I wanted to know whether it was Paul who had raped me. I wanted to know whether it was Paul who was planning to kill me when the time was right. That was all. I flattened the letter out on the table in front of me and then, as I started to read, all my hard-won objectivity melted away. How can you even think of judging him? You're in love with him, aren't you? You'll believe anything he says, won't you, you stupid little girl? The more clumsily he writes the more you fall under his spell, the way you fell under the spell of his awkwardness and his shyness . . .

Peter came to my place at eight this morning. He was with John Forrester. Do you know Forrester? He's a "high up" in the company and, although he's not Peter's boss, I think he may be in charge of Peter's boss. He's known in the business as the Hoover – because, so they say, he spends his life picking up dirt.

He's a big man. He has a shock of white hair, a belly and an intimidating smile, but the thing I always notice about him is his nose. It's not just a place to hang his glasses. Its veins are broken and jagged with "business lunch", its nostrils carpeted with thick, black hairs and it sits in the middle of his face as if to say "Watch it, boy! I can smell *you*!"

One of the things Forrester does is to sack people. I once saw him walk into an office and order four senior executives to leave the building and never come back. "Nobody take anything with them," he said, smiling as if this was all a practical joke, "just move away from your desks and head for the door!"

I have in the past almost enjoyed some of his performances. I've always thought that he rather liked me. But not this morning. He just walked straight past me into my narrow hall. "We need to search your premises, Mr Jackson," he said, "in order to clarify something. I am sure you have no objection."

I said that I had no objection whatsoever. Since I had no secrets "hidden away" in dark corners of my dwelling place.

•

Unless you count the freezer. There's a headless corpse in there.

I put Paul's letter to one side. It was starting to puzzle me even more than it had at first. I simply didn't recognise the man I thought I knew in its pages. To reassure myself about the fact that, sometimes, people's prose is less revealing than their hair colour or their dress sense, I picked up the sheets that had been written by Peter Taylor. To my surprise, in almost the first paragraph I looked at, I heard, as Paul had said I would, the clear, even tones of our boss. "This is to record the fact that I think someone in the company is on the take . . ." I put Peter's journal back and lowered my eyes to the crumpled sheets of paper in front of me.

Peter Taylor was giving me one of his "odd looks". You know all about those, do you not, Fiona?

•

I didn't actually. I hadn't the faintest idea of what he was talking about.

"May I know what this is all about?" I said. He and Peter exchanged glances.

"Company business," said Forrester.

"And –" began Peter.

"Other stuff!" said Forrester.

I suppose they took my silence as assent. "There's not much to search," I said, as the two of them went into the kitchen and started opening cupboard doors. "There's hardly anything here at all!"

As they went through the drawers and shelves, lifting up plates and pulling out cups and saucepans, I thought at first that they were looking for something small. But, later on, I realised that they were after an object large enough to be easily seen. I assumed they were after papers. As they moved through to the front room and started peering under the armchairs, I thought how pathetic my possessions looked. How temporary everything in my life seems to be. Although I own the glass-topped table, the three bookcases and the Impressionist reproduction on the bedroom wall, it always looks as if someone else had bought them.

After they had finished in the front room they went through to the bedroom.

"If you told me what you were looking for . . ." I said, "I could maybe help you find it!" Forrester gave me the briefest of glances. Then he turned his attention to my clothes cupboard.

'I got rid of the brassière and knickers!" I said. He didn't laugh.

He flicked through my four suits, sifted my socks and unwound my two jerseys. He got very interested in a red scarf at the back of the cupboard. He pulled it out and held it up to Peter. Peter just shook his head.

"There's nothing *in* there." I said. They ignored me. Peter was over by the bed. He was lying on his back scything his right arm through the mess of papers, books and underpants that accumulates in the narrow space between the carpet and the mattress.

It would have made it easier, somehow, if they had been more brutal about it. At least then I could have shouted at them. But they went about their work so quietly, folding clothes after they had inspected them, and replacing the covers on the bed as if they were high-class domestic servants, that they left me with nothing to say.

"Accountants", said Peter with a thin smile, as he got to his feet, "are supposed to be tidy!" Then his face clouded. I could see that he was thinking that this was the kind of thing he used to say to me when I first started at the company. When I was his favourite son.

You see, Fiona, large corporations play "family games". There are black sheep, wicked uncles and obscure cousins of the kind that crop up in Russian novels. Official titles, like the Internal and External Auditing Unit, conceal passions one might only imagine existed between "blood relations". I think that for a long time, in the office, we all went around thinking we didn't know each other while, in fact, we were getting closer and closer to the dangerous moment of intimacy. What happened this last week was horrible But it was also, at times, exciting. Two years of politeness suddenly gave way to crude emotions, violently expressed. And the English are good at suppressing such things, are they not?

I never really told you about the orphanage, did I? I'll tell you one thing. The "seed time of the soul" they talk about . . .

•

When I got to the quotation, I put Paul's letter down on to my knee. I had started to understand what it was about his style. When he was describing things that had happened to him – a guy coming into his room and turning over his things – he didn't appear to feel the need to come on like a maiden aunt. But immediately he was talking to me, or invoking any kind of emotion, out came the inverted commas, the dodgy quotations and what Ernest Hemingway used to call the ten-dollar words.

What he had said about the company was true though. It reminded me, painfully, of how much of my time I have wasted there. That, although I didn't want to acknowledge it at the time, is partly why I split up with Dave.

"We could get married," he used to say, sweet, old-fashioned thing that he was, "you could give up work! You don't enjoy work, Fiona, do you? Even though they make you stay till all hours."

He thought, you see, that because I usually talked about Peter, Paul and John with irritation, I didn't "like" them. As if your feelings about the people you work with could ever be that simple. He couldn't understand that they were part of me – they had entered my bloodstream like some slow-acting disease. All the time I was waiting, waiting, waiting . . .

I suppose I kept thinking I was going to leave. That was why I spent so long sitting staring out of my window, down at the forecourt, or devising ingenious excuses for not turning up for work. Somehow or other I became the bolshy girl in the corner who always has to be asked twice to do the simplest thing. But that was only part of the performance all four of us played. It was understood that because Fiona was a bright girl one day something would be found for her. And if she was difficult, if sometimes she looked Peter Taylor – *le patron* – in the eye and seemed, right up until the moment where she complied, to be about to say "Book your own cab, ass-hole!", well that was because we all understood that, as yet, greatly to his regret, Peter couldn't offer her anything where her talents could be used.

I have to go over and over this, you see, because I want to understand something I never grasped at the time – the exact effect I had on these three men. How far I – what's that ghastly phrase – "led them on". Led HIM on, come to that. Asked him to do the things he did to me.

Yes they humoured me. They gave me that privilege granted to so many women in so many offices – the licence not to care a stuff about the enterprise in which everyone is engaged. The licence to be dim and awkward and unconsidered and gruff and sometimes hysterical or badly behaved, because, like so many women, I was presumed to be waiting, waiting, waiting for all those babies, all that love, all that unimportant business.

The real Fiona, however clever and well educated she was, was just another girl waiting to get married. Which could explain why it took so long for one of them to make a move. I started to read once more.

When they got into the bathroom I could see they were starting to get annoyed. They started to be a little more careless. Peter emptied out a wicker basket, crammed with soap, shaving foam, sponges and towels, and, when he didn't find what he was looking for, left the things where they lay, on the floor. At one point, Forrester even pulled out a tube of toothpaste and started to look at it speculatively.

"The microfilm", I said, "is concealed in the mint gel stripe." He gave me a swift, neutral glance and went on with his search. I went over to Peter who was on his way out to the hall.

"Peter," I said, "I've worked for you for ten years. I think I have a right to know what this is about."

He put on his schoolmaster's face. Did you know his father was a schoolmaster? "We'll go over Harold Porter's place," he said, "you'll have left something there. We'll tie you to him, you'll see."

You've probably only ever spoken to Harold Porter on the phone, Fiona. He's a kind of builder's agent and we have had quite a lot of dealings with him. He's a big, rather loudmouthed man. I couldn't understand why Peter Taylor should be talking about him at all. Although, along with quite a few other people from the company, I have been to parties of his, I don't think I've been near his place for nearly a year. I was saying something along these lines when Peter snapped, "Don't pretend you don't *know*, Paul. Harold Porter was murdered. OK? On Sunday night. And it wasn't very pleasant. OK?"

I swear I had no idea of what he was talking about. Forrester was watching my face as if he expected to find some secret there. But all he could have registered was my blank astonishment at everything that was being said to me. After they went through the hall for a second time I thought that they were going to give up. They were actually on their way to the front door – although perhaps they were intending to take off the panels rather than put themselves on the other side of it – when Peter said, "The briefcase. Of course. The briefcase."

My briefcase stands on a rack in the hall. And my first thought, as Peter said this, was "I've taken Pappanauer's by mistake. This is all a horrible mistake." It would have been an easy mistake to make. All three of us, as you know, have those black, matt plastic briefcases, with the same silver-coloured line on the inside of the lid. I wanted to say something about this to them but, before I could do so, Forrester had picked the case up, jerked up his right knee under it and was wrestling with the clasp. "I'll open it!" I said. They obviously thought they were on to something. They stood on either side of me, as if convinced I was about to whirl the thing over my head and attempt to lob it out through the kitchen window. For my part, I must admit, that as I struggled with the lock, my hands were shaking.

It wasn't until I had got the lid open that I knew that it was mine. There is simply nothing about the exterior of the thing that distinguishes it from Peter's or from Pappanauer's. But only when I was looking at the rulers, the files, the mobile phone and the calculator, all stacked together with the neatness that overcomes me when anything to do with work is concerned, did I know, with horrible certainty, that this was, indeed, my briefcase.

That was when I saw them. They saw them too. I heard Forrester swear, softly, under his breath. He never swears. To the left of the two books I keep in there, was a pair of yellow, rubberised kitchen gloves. There was something, I remember thinking, quite shocking about the colour. The gloves lay together, folded as neatly as the rulers and the pens that lay alongside them. I didn't have to get them out to know what they were. In fact, none of us touched them.

I suppose we were all aware that they were evidence. Forrester closed the lid of the case. I didn't move.

"We'll take this," he said.

"Look −" I replied.

Peter was shaking his head. "Why?" he said.

I couldn't answer that question. Forrester moved his face close to mine. "We'll have to decide what to do," he said, "and we will be contacting the police. Don't go anywhere."

For a moment I thought they were going to try a citizen's arrest. But this is, in part anyway, company business, and the first rule of the company is that you never do anything unless you are forced to do so. Then Peter said, "We have the document."

I just looked at him, blankly. "What document?"

Forrester shook his head. *Liars are bad enough*, his expression seemed to say, *but amateur liars are really not to be tolerated.*

"AIR," he said, "AIR. Isn't that what you called it?" Then he walked across and stood over me. For a moment I thought he was going to punch me in the face. Then he shook his head slightly and stepped back a little.

"You disgust me!" he said. "The document you wrote. About Fiona. And about all of the other things you've been getting up to."

They left me alone soon after that. They told me, once again, not to go out, not to call anyone, but to wait patiently for their next move. I told them, with perfect truth, that I have nowhere to go. That I have no friends, no relatives, no one. What I didn't say, of course, is that I have you. Do I still have you? Will I still have you after you have read this document of theirs? Will you believe that I am the kind of person capable of *thinking* such things, let alone doing them?

•

I picked up the computer disk again. The next bit of Paul's letter, as far as I had been able to tell, was another strenuous denial of the likelihood of his having written the document on it. It was pornographic, he said. It was foul-minded, he said. It made him feel sick to look at it. Then, at the bottom of the page he started to tell me he loved me again.

I wasn't sure I wanted any more of that. I'm really not that interested in whether men love me or not. I think the moment all of that went wrong for me was when I heard my Mum on the phone to my Dad. "You never say you love me!" she said, in a high-pitched, tragedy queen voice. "You never satisfy my tender feelings!" My Mum actually talks like that. "You are never there!" She went on, with amazing perspicacity, "You are not here now! You are in Newcastle. You are drunk!" Can you blame him, mater? I'd be stoned out of my brain in Gothenburg if I was married to you!

One of the most important ways in which we define things or people is by writing about them. Which is, I suppose, why the activity is such an important one. Paul's letter – one of the few I have ever received in my life – had brought me up close to something I had been trying to avoid for years. And, perhaps, am still not honestly facing, even as I break out another sheet of white paper and write this next sentence. How do others see me? What do you think of me? Am I quite the girl you'd like me to be or do I . . . disappoint?

Would you like me to want love more? Like the heroine of a romantic novel? I can remember my tutor at university – a formidable old bat called Muriel – fixing me with an eagle eye and asking me, in the tones of someone who genuinely required information and enlightenment, "Why, Fiona, do you think we like Jane Eyre?" "Actually, Miss Stapleton," I replied, "I don't like her. I think she's a pain in the neck." Love love love. Is that any kind of guide through life? Is that any way to produce better people?

People are capable of anything. You have absolutely no idea what they will do at any given time. And I am afraid that loving them doesn't make their behaviour any easier to predict. As far as I could see Paul's letter was full of the kind of heavily personal stuff that usually only comes out after about ten years of marriage. I wasn't even sure whether I wanted to know all that. If, by some miracle, he wasn't going to turn out to be the villain of the piece, I didn't want to rule out the chance that he might be the hero.

But whether the document on the computer disk was or was not written by the man who raped me, I had to read it for myself. I let the papers lie there on the table and went upstairs to the small room next to the bedroom, which is where Dad's computer now sits, gathering dust, under the window. Mum has covered it with a sheet. I don't think anyone has touched it since he died, and, as I pulled the covers off and switched on the machine, I had the eerie, unpleasant feeling that I was disturbing the privacy of the dead.

"Listen, girly, I've come a little unstuck. I met a couple of chaps at Birmingham Station and . . ."

"And what Dad?"

"I spent the night in the cells in fact . . ."

He always gave me the impression that he looked on prison as simply another career opportunity. A long, long time ago he had done eighteen months for some petty fraud and he always talked about it with a certain, wistful nostalgia. He enjoyed bringing people's attention to it – especially when they were intensely respectable. If they were friends of my mother's as well, that was even better.

"I learned an awful lot in the nick, girly – never tell a porky unless it's absolutely necessary! For example!"

Without even bothering to see what Dad had listed on the hard disk (prospectuses for unbelievably shady companies, I imagine), I punched up on to the screen the contents of Drive A. There was only one document. A:/AIR. As the rain continued to drive in at the window, I retrieved it and started to read.

3

A:/AIR

If I was going to write a book about this (and I may well do so) I think I would probably call it *STALKING FIONA*. It's a horrible, vulgar title, isn't it? Unless you have been far enough away from a newspaper for the last few years to imagine that it deals with red deer.

I was stalking long before the current fad. I was stalking long before the Press picked up on the word. No mere word could ever do justice to what I feel about her. I could never let you know how seriously I take the brown-haired girl in our office. How I dream about her. How I long to have her alone with me. How I . . . well I . . . yearn to see her strip for my benefit. What's that American expression? Butt naked. That's what she has got to be for me whether she likes it or not. That's what the last five years have been about. All of the other women were no more than substitutes for her and all of them were unsatisfactory. You don't really get to know a female by leaping out at her from the trees around the towpath, bashing her on the head, forcing her into the long grass and trying to get her legs apart without even so much as introducing your-self.

And my God they fight! I know all the papers say that I am an inadequate and a coward, but I would like to see some of these journalists try their hand at rape! It is, these days, an extremely hazardous business, for everyone concerned. The women have all been to so many courses and read so many feminist tracts! They kick and they punch and they pull you hair and reach into their handbags for the Mace! Some of them show a working knowledge of the martial arts! The one on the other side of Brentford even tried a bit of kick-boxing, although, after I hit her with the brick she seemed less keen on the attempt to demonstrate the Folding of A Leaf or whatever it was she was working on when I stove in the side of her head.

She was the first one I killed. I didn't, of course, *want* to kill any of them. I wouldn't have killed her if she had simply let me do what I wanted to do. And I don't want to kill Fiona. But she must learn to play the game. She must stop going to the window in that way she has and jutting her bum out in contemptuous provocation. She must stop putting her finger in her mouth when one of us is dictating something to her, or shaking her brown hair over her eyes or . . .

I've tried so many things to make the image of her go away. It was because of her — this may seem perverse — that I started to go to prostitutes. After a whole day spent eating her up with my eyes I had to have real flesh even if I was paying for it. On my way home from the office I went to the cash till, took out a hundred pounds and then went into the first telephone box I could see.

There was a fantastically exciting range of sexual services on offer. London really has improved beyond belief in that department in recent years. In the top left-hand corner was a postcard showing a crude line drawing of a woman's behind, and, next to it, in capital letters the injunction SPANK ME. I wrote down that number first. It looked as if she had designed the card herself and, bearing in mind her obviously limited financial and imaginative resources, done the kind of job that might indicate real enthusiasm for her line of work. I did quite fancy spanking someone that afternoon anyway. I seem to remember that Fiona had leaned over her desk with the kind of wilful calculation common to her type of girl and I had — although I had not wanted to do so — been able to see the line of her panties under her trousers.

I passed over the next card COMPLETE CAPTIVATION BY CHARLOTTE, mainly because I don't like the name Charlotte. And Charlotte's picture suggested, for some reason, that she was a hair colourist, rather than a prostitute. There were two or three next to COMPLETE CAPTIVATION BY CHARLOTTE that were even less exciting. YOUNG AND PRETTY MODEL GIVES MASSAGE. For God's sake! This is a competitive market, isn't it? Some of these girls are openly offering to urinate on your face or tie you to the bedpost and whip you until your bottom bleeds and all she can come up with is YOUNG AND PRETTY MODEL GIVES MASSAGE. Why didn't she come straight out with it and have herself a card printed that read BORING WANK ADMINISTERED BY UNIMAGINATIVE WOMAN OF UNCERTAIN AGE?

I passed over someone calling himself Derek who was prepared to offer what he described as FULL MASSAGE — which I took to be a coy synonym for a sexual act I couldn't even begin to imagine — and hardly bothered to look at I AM CINDY THE MAID! LOOK ME OVER! largely because I genuinely could not work out whether the poor bitch was offering voyeurism, dressing up, bondage or a combination of all three. My eye had been caught by a plain postcard just next to the telephone receiver. It read FIONA WILL DOMINATE YOU — and, next to it, offered a phone number that I recognised as a district no more than a cab ride away. It was entirely possible that this really was the Fiona who works in our office. Considering the money we pay them I am surprised that every single secretary in the company isn't flogging her arse outside King's Cross Station in every spare minute available to her.

Whether she was *my* Fiona or not, she was certainly right for that afternoon. I didn't want to spend too

34

much on travel arrangements. I wasn't sure what the going rate for whatever we were going to do was but it was bound to be prohibitive. And if I was going to start doing this regularly, I couldn't afford to spend more than around a hundred and fifty a week.

In the taxi on the way over I thought about what my starting offer should be. As an accountant I do tend to think about these things. I tried to imagine what I thought it was going to be worth. She probably had a scale of charges that bore no relation to how much her clients might or might not be enjoying her services. How could she know that the pleasure I would get from addressing her as Fiona would far outweigh anything else she had to offer. "Oh Fiona!" I imagined myself saying, all coy and feminine, while the office secretary's namesake was strapping on an enormous dildo, forcing my head on to the floor and tightening her knees round my thighs as if she was the jockey and I the horse.

Was that what she meant by "dominance"? Was that what I wanted? And if it was what I wanted how much was it worth? Wouldn't it be cheaper to do what I had done last year and send the real Fiona a pair of soiled knickers through the internal post? I still remember watching her face when she opened the envelope. And I still get pleasure from recalling her, as cool as you like, closing the envelope and putting it, quite carelessly, to one side of her desk. Oh she is a very strong lady. And I like that.

Fiona lived in a basement flat in Notting Hill Gate and, luckily, there turned out to be a payphone right across the street. She didn't, to my surprise, appear to have one of her cards in it. Perhaps it had been stolen. Or was it, I found myself wondering — carelessness? A market strategy perhaps? Or even something to do with the local police? When I dialled her number I saw a shape moving in the basement room and was almost sure I saw her look up and across at the phone. Maybe her customers always phoned her from across the street. Maybe she always checked that she wasn't about to open the door to a pervert. This thought made me giggle. She spent her day dealing with perverts, didn't she? Very much as my Fiona does.

"Hullo!"

"Hi!"

I was almost insultingly breezy. Look, I tried to make my voice say I've come here to be whipped by a woman in black underwear. There's no need to make a big issue out of this. It's simply something I need to do. So let's get on with it.

On the other side of the street I could see her peering out into the afternoon from behind her net curtains. She was presumably trying to get an idea of the dimensions of the next customer. Maybe there were things about one's stance that would tell her whether one liked "licking wellingtons" or having rolling pins shoved up one's arse. Maybe she really was nervous about the men who came down the stairs to her basement. For the first time since I had thought of this encounter I felt myself aroused.

"Look Fiona," I said, "I'd like to be dominated . . ."

"OK dear . . ." she said. I could see her anxious little head bobbing up and down behind her basement curtains.

"I'm coming over now," I said, "I've got a massive hard-on!"

Although I managed to say this with a fairly straight face, her obvious failure to see the humorous implications of it nearly sent me of into a fit of the giggles. *A fit of the giggles*! As I said those words to myself I saw myself in lipstick and a low-cut dress, swaying across the darkening street in faggoty abandon. And, really excited now, I put down the phone, hard, on

to its cradle and started across towards Fiona's grimy
window.>

When I got to this point in the document I rewound it. I stopped at
the phrase "licking wellingtons" and looked, for some time, at those
two words and the inverted commas that enfolded them. It was the
first moment when I thought I recognised something of Paul's voice
in what I was reading. But of course it wasn't Paul's voice. It was simply a typographical trick. The whole thing was so utterly unlike him
or indeed anyone else I knew that at first I was almost sure it was a
grotesque joke.

I got up and walked out on to the landing. I couldn't bear to be
in the same room as the screen that carried those words. Because I
remembered that envelope with the soiled knickers, very clearly. A
year or so ago. Probably even longer. I remembered the curious feeling I had, as I opened the parcel, that someone was watching me, and
I knew, for certain, that though this man's tone might be mocking, he
meant every word he said.

Or did he? I knew, too, from the first, that there was something
phoney about this document. It was false through and through. But
that detail was from life. Whoever had written it was the man who
had sent me that unsolicited parcel. And once I had decided that
detail was authentic, it was a short step to deciding that every single,
horrible thing the guy had written was literal, accurate testimony. We
do have a tendency to believe what we read. We look for truth, so
desperately, even in the most casual remarks vouchsafed by strangers
that we can't even begin to understand how and why it is that those
closest to us tell us lies.

I listened to the rain on the roof and, suddenly, wanted, very
much, for Mum to come back through the front door. She didn't. So
back I went to what I now was convinced was HIS handiwork.

>A:/AIR.
Fiona opened the door to me with a curious sort of formality. She was dressed, for work, in a flowered
dressing gown which, at this stage of the proceedings,
she kept wrapped fairly tightly around her. Presumably

there was a charge for seeing what was underneath. As she moved away from me into the room I thought I caught a glimpse of black lace around her breasts and leaned forward, a touch too eagerly, in an attempt to inspect the goods. She drew the dressing gown more tightly around her. She was a black woman in early middle age.

"Come on in, dear!" she said, in a light, singsong voice. Then she peered at me suspiciously.

"Have you been to me before, dear?" she said.

I looked around the bare living room for any sign of whips or chains or hoods. I could see none of these things. The only potential aid to dominance in the room, as far as I could tell, was a rolled-up newspaper on the dining table. Unless, of course, she whacked you on the bum with the flat of her hand. She looked a big, strong woman. She went to a door on the other side of the room and turned back to me. When she spoke again her voice had a harsh quality that, I assumed, was part of her professional role. "Come through then!" she said.

As I went after her I was thinking, not about her, but about *my* Fiona. I thought about office Fiona as I came into a room, about ten or twelve feet square, in which the walls had been painted black. There were no windows. It was clear that she had taken a good deal more trouble with the décor than in her living room, and the accessories were quite spectacular. There were hooks sunk into the wall, a couple of chains hanging from the ceiling and, in the corner, what looked like a large wooden crucifix. To amuse myself I crossed myself and did a brief genuflection towards it. Fiona did not appear to notice. On a table in the corner, arranged in a manner that reminded me of a jumble sale in aid of some charitable cause, were a pile of whips, vibrators and, at the far end, a thing that looked like a giant, unpeeled, plastic banana.

Fiona leered at me. "You like that, do you dear?" she said.

I had forgotten about her. When I turned back to her I saw she had let her dressing gown fall open, although it was impossible to tell whether this was, or was not, some kind of sales tactic. She was wearing drearily conventional black underwear and a pair of knickers. Sprouting out, like some sinister, ungovernable plant, on to her left thigh I saw a handful of coarse pubic hair and found myself unable to tear my eyes away from it. Presumably, if she wore the thing I was carrying in my left hand she would put it on over the knickers. I didn't like that idea. It seemed, somehow, like cheating. "No!" I said, coldly, "I don't like it at all."

My every word seemed to have a curious weight to it. I had somehow imagined this encounter without the woman having any sort of real presence at all, and, although she was obviously trying not to let me see anything apart from the things she was selling — her breasts, her legs, her thighs, her large, flaccid buttocks — there were horrible little fragments of her personality coming between me and my pleasure. I put the dildo back on the table and looked straight at her.

I don't look great. I look like any other face in the crowd. I dress conventionally, as we all do in my office, and there's nothing about me that would make you remember me. If I look at myself closely in the mirror (and I do that quite often) there is something about my eyes — a paleness, a reserve — that could be quite frightening, but no one really looks at my eyes. No one really looks at *me*. And I like it that way.

I am not easy with people. Sometimes I can give the impression of being humorous. But I never really surrender to laughter. And though I can be polite and attentive to women I don't really like them. Apart, of course, from Fiona. But this "Fiona" wasn't Fiona.

"You want to get your clothes off, dear?" she

said. She sounded like a gym mistress! Why should I want to get my clothes off? And why — this seemed to me to be the most important point — should she have had the nerve to take in vain the name of the woman whom I intend to carry to the heights of ecstasy? The woman whom I have been watching so carefully for two long years — whose time is only now coming in.

"You're not Fiona!" I said. And, suddenly, and very quickly, I picked up the dildo and struck her, hard, across the face.>

I didn't read the next bit. For a start, as I think I said, I was frightened I might believe it. If only he hadn't made that remark about the soiled knickers! I so wanted to take the whole document as fantasy. This next section did read like the kind of thing you find in Soho porn shops. As far as I could see he had turned the entire contents of this poor woman's dungeon against her.

There, you see? His style is infectious, isn't it? And if I picked it up, it must be because I still don't believe it. After all the things I have seen and heard since that morning — the reality of what HE did and what HE got up to still eludes me.

The bit I did believe was the section about his eyes and how people never looked at him. It sent me back to thinking about Paul and Peter and Pappanauer, and how, of those three, the only one who avoided others' eyes was Paul. I scrolled on down the document until I came across the following.

>A:/AIR
I say, glibly, "average suburban marriage". I have no real idea of what that might be. I was brought up in an orphanage in a remote part of England and I live alone, in a small flat. I am one of those people you see on the train, going home in the evening, who leaves at an anonymous station and walks away down the platform to one more anonymous life on the edge of this vast and lonely city. Yes, I live in a suburb but it really doesn't matter which one. I'm lonely, if you want to know. Feel

sorry for me if you like. It makes no difference to me either way.>

There was only one man in our office — as far as I knew — who had been brought up in an orphanage. And that, too, was Paul. When I went back over the description of what he had done — or said he had done — to the prostitute — I found, to my horror, that the tone of it seemed to have been infected with this knowledge. And though it wasn't how Paul had written to me or how, for the most part, he talked, there was a cadence I thought I recognised. Something about the sudden, surprising switch to emotional directness recalled the man I thought I loved. Could this be Paul's voice?

People aren't consistent. In the way they talk or act or think or write. When they are themselves, alone with you, say, in the dark, or perhaps alone with themselves, they become funny where they should be frightening, or boisterous where they should be shy. When I went back to the document I decided to try and read it without preconceptions. To listen to it as if it were some horrible tale, told by a fool or a madman. If I could get through to the end of it — and I really wasn't at all sure that I could — maybe some light would break through.

>A:/AIR
I didn't regret killing the tart. And I don't feel at all sorry for her. If you are going to deal with sick and twisted bastards like me — it would seem sensible to install some kind of panic button in your soundproof dungeon. But perhaps the police simply wouldn't show for a hooker whose profession is bondage. Anyway — she was the only one of the prostitutes I killed. It was, I tell myself, first night nerves. I got near to it with one of them — off the Edgware Road I think — who started to grope for my flies when we were halfway through the negotiations. Since I have started going to them regularly I have made a few simple rules and I find it, on the whole, an enjoyable and instructive experience.

For a start I always get the money over with first and I make sure that both of us know exactly what we are going to do. How appropriate for an accountant! (I sometimes say that. They never laugh.) I also make sure that I never go to anyone who has the nerve to operate under the name Fiona. It's not a problem these days, since, recently, I have been paying for sex with men rather than women. There's a guy within walking distance who is prepared to wank me off for fifty pounds cash. I quite enjoy going to him. On several occasions I have tried to make our relationship more intimate but although he answers my questions politely I get the impression that he just wants to get me out of there as fast as possible. He says he's a dancer. It occurred to me the other day that he may think I am the kind of person who might suddenly pull out a knife and slash at his neck, screaming, the while, about the vengeance of the Lord. I found that thought curiously exciting. But when I went there last week he didn't answer the bell — although I could see his shadow at the blinds.

Men are good because there is no pretence about wanting them. They are also far more naive. You want "it" and they understand that. The "want" I take to their rooms is something that has been with me since I was very young and it is only now that it is crystallising into something I recognise. For years it was simply a pulse, a word in my head as I walked past clothes shops or women in the street, but it is only now that it has shaped itself into a word that describes something — someone I should say — and drums in my head the same three syllables from waking to sleeping "Fi-o-na! Fi-o-na! Fi-o-na!"

She is wasted on this company. She is far too intelligent. She has a degree! Once or twice she has even tried to boast about it. She has hardly any friends — something I always find very erotic. She is the girl for me! I thought that from the first day she walked in through the door, wearing that green dress, with a red ribbon in her hair. Oh Fiona! Do you remember, my sweetness?>

I had to stop again. I didn't remember. I didn't remember at all. But I found myself going back two years ago to the first time I walked into the office and trying to picture the three of them, Paul, Peter and Pappanauer, each at their workstations. Did their heads turn towards the door as I came in? Or did one keep his eyes down, away from me? And was that one Paul?

>A:/AIR
Fiona and I get on quite well. Once, (I can't quite remember how long ago), just as we were all packing up ready to go home, I passed by her desk, and, looking straight at her, I said, "No peace for the wicked!" She smiled. Although she didn't say anything in reply, I counted this as a conversation. Five words! And one of them two syllables! "No peace for the wicked!" When I was with one of my ladies, a few weeks ago, I said to her, as she was chaining me to the wall of her studio, "No peace for the wicked!"

   "No," she said, strapping on a leather dildo, "there isn't." Then she got on with her job. I squirm with pleasure at the memory.

   What I didn't tell her, of course (she's only a tart, why should I tell her anything?) was that, as my cock grew hard, I was thinking about Fiona. I dedicate all my stiffies to the girl in the office.

   That first, significant exchange was followed by a great many "interchanges" that meant more to me than to her. "Hullo Fiona, how are you?" "All right, mustn't complain and you?" "Oh, not so bad, I suppose!" I grew to love these banalities and there were times when I had to ration them very, very carefully. Just how many times can you ask someone how they are without it seeming, well, kinky? But, since I started going to the

43

prostitutes, it has got harder and harder to contain myself.

Last year (or was it the year before last? Time has no meaning where Fiona is concerned), my desire for her was so strong that it simply wasn't possible to wait until I had the chance to pick up the phone and beat a path across the city to Debbie or Julie or Jenny or Jane. They were no longer enough. And, anyway what these women had to offer was so obviously not what I really wanted not, well, Fi-o-na-ish enough that I was having to ask for more and more bizarre services in order to make my need disappear. One of them was pre- pared to don a leather cloak and urinate on my face, and the first time she did that I recall thinking "Oh! Quite interesting!" But it didn't last. Wet and salty and pointless — at the end of the day.

I think that was when I started to visit the Gents lavatory down the corridor from the office. On one occasion, just before Christmas, I had to go there no less than *four times* during the course of a single afternoon for the purposes of self-stimulation. I came every time, I am glad to be able to report. On the third occasion, when I was absolutely sure there was no one in either of the adjoining cubicles, I moaned aloud as I climaxed . . . "Fiona . . . Fiona . . ." I was rather proud of myself. But, as I walked back into the office I buttoned my lip. I thought of how it would look if I were to, literally, button my lip, with those little grey buttons like the ones we wore on the short trousers at the orphanage. I pictured my mouth, pouted like someone shaping up for a kiss and then I imagined myself carefully undoing the buttons so that I could speak. I almost laughed out loud. But didn't. There isn't a lot to laugh about in accountancy. Especially when several million pounds have gone missing from the company.

There have been moments when I have been able to forget about her. Funnily enough I have never, until

fairly recently, had the urge to telephone her at home
or to follow her out of office hours. It has been as if
my lust for her was something to do with the staplers
and memos and meetings and all the rest of the set
dressing of this weird, twilight world in which we all
seem to live. But, over the last few months it has
reached crisis point.>

Well, I thought, they all go out of the office, all the time. They don't
put their hands up to ask to be excused. If one visited the toilet (his
word) more than the others, it was Pappanauer. I tried to remember
what he looked like when he returned from these expeditions, but
was unable to do so. My eyes returned to the screen.

>A:/AIR
I'd made a resolve, you see, to clean up my act. I don't
like writing this stuff down any more than you like
reading it. I wasn't proud of scurrying off to the Gents
for a wank every ten minutes. If I am honest it wasn't
simply finance that made me want to abandon those trips
across the city in search of sex. I realised that counting the number of steps it takes her to get from her
desk to the door — or any other of the routines I had
been going through to make me feel close to her —
weren't working. A few weeks ago, I had got to the point
where I knew I had to make the sort of approach that
people make to girls when they want to be nice to them.
I had been trying, I think, to feed this horrible, bes-
tial *thing* inside me to capacity. And, finally, I wanted
it to sleep like a lion in its cage so that I could get
on with the business of . . . Lo-ove. A re-lat-ionsh-
ip . . .I had to make my move!
   I waited until Fiona started to clear her desk.
When she tidies things away she is frighteningly
attractive. It is then that her near plainness becomes
compelling. She sits, her bum square on the little
black chair the company has provided for her and rotates

through about 90 to 100 degrees, picking up things, screwing up waste paper into small balls and, (this I find most erotic), repositioning the telephone. I don't know why she does this at the end of every day.

When she has finished with the telephone, she gets up, crosses the open-plan office to the double doors that lead out to the corridor and takes down her brown scarf and her brown coat. Then she turns, very briefly, ducks her head so that the dark brown tresses bounce off her sallow cheeks and allows that wide mouth to crack her face open in a crooked smile. "Byee!" she calls. She never looks at anyone as she says this. She never waits for an answer either. She just jerks her bony shoulders out into the corridor, along to the lifts, down to the foyer, across the wide piazza in front of the main building, up to the perimeter fence and then . . . Where?

Where? It was only then that I realised that I had absolutely no idea of where Fiona might live. I was standing by my workstation, stretching myself, when the thought occurred to me. The double doors banged shut and she was gone. Without thinking, I grabbed my black, hard-topped briefcase and ran after her. I was almost at the door before I realised that such behaviour might incriminate me (I think this was the first time I had had a *criminal* thought in relation to Fiona). I took care to slacken my pace and, when I got to the door, I turned to face the rest of the office as we all do after the end of another hard day. "Byee!" I don't know who answered me as I pushed through the double doors. All I could think of was that there — about fifty yards ahead of me — in the dying London light, was the woman I wanted.

"Wanted" is the wrong word. I had to have her, that's more like it. I didn't want to have to have her. But that was how it was. Looking back over what I have written I can see that I have tried to make myself sound like someone who makes choices. But I don't. The truest thing I wrote was about this animal inside me, this thing that eats away at me and makes me do and think things I don't want to do. I think that's why I started to write this document — in the hope that the feelings and thoughts might go away. I haven't begun to describe the horror of them.

"Dying London light" is wrong too. I don't want to suggest that she was softening me up. Or that I let things like the weather or the light affect my moods. Or that the city in which these things happened matters particularly. It doesn't. The only horizon I have is me and I am completely in control of my life. It isn't everyone who can walk into a furnished room, take off his blazer, hang it over a chair and say to a young man with a moustache, "I'd like a massage please." But there is no doubt that something about the way she was walking, one left arm dangling from one wide shoulder, and one right hip at an awkward angle was, well, attractive. And, at long last, I felt like someone who might be able to talk to her.>

4

That was the point in the document I had reached when the front doorbell rang for the second time that morning. I jumped clear out of my seat. Although, earlier, when Peter Taylor and the policeman had showed up, I had felt curiously calm, I was now just as frightened as I had been last night. Even if I had gone back to thinking that most of what HE had written was fantasy (I couldn't bear to think that the alternative was true) the stuff about me was real enough. And there was a horrible logic to it. As if his obsession could only lead him in one direction.

Up to now, anyway, HE had been a physical but not a human thing – fighting him had been like fighting a disease. Now he was staring out at me from my father's computer, and I was left with the impossible task of matching his tone of voice and his choice of his words to the . . . thing that had done that to me. It had been much, much easier when I thought about HIM as a monster in capital letters. But now he was there in the room with me, whispering in my ear in the lower case. Before I went to the front window to see who was waiting at the door, I switched off the screen.

John Pappanauer was waiting by the front door. My first, slightly hysterical thought was "well, they're all here this morning!" He was wearing that ridiculous little leather jacket that he sometimes affects. It has no possible value as a shield against the weather, and enhances his appearance about as much as a tea cosy or a dustbin lid balanced on his head. He had his hand on his hips and, after he had pressed the bell for the second time, he smirked up and down the street, just in case Mrs Dunlop, the pensioner from 33, should be so overcome by lust that she would be forced to leap out of an upper window and apply herself to gratifying his every need.

There was a time when I found John Pappanauer funny. I don't find him funny any more. I find him as frightening as the rest of them. He has a beaky sort of face with two, very bright, coal black eyes, like the eyes of a rodent. His black hair is as stiff as a fox's brush and, like the other two men in the office, he has small, neat hands. They're all the same build, of course. Same build, same briefcases, same way of moving . . .

Who had said that to me? Who had said "no peace for the wicked"? I simply couldn't remember.

I wasn't intending to answer the door. I was past worrying about how all of them seemed able to find their way here. I must have told all of them more about myself than I ever remember. After you've worked with people for several years, of course you sometimes forget what they do and don't know about you. I held myself very still against the landing wall, frightened to move in case he heard a sound from inside the house. Then, very slowly and carefully I tiptoed to the window again. He wasn't looking up at the house. He was still smirking up and down the street, his hands poised on his hips, pawing the ground with his ridiculously fashionable shoes. I went back to the computer and switched on the screen. Was it Pappanauer's voice I was listening to?

```
>A:/AIR
```
As soon as she had disappeared into the lift I ran along the corridor, jabbed my finger into the button and, when the next lift came, went plummeting down after her through one of the long, dark, cool wells that irrigate our building.

"Going down!" said the lift.

"I know!" I replied.

"Floor 5!" said the lift.

"I know!" I replied. Then someone came in and I stopped talking.

In the lobby I caught sight of her by the glass doors, pushing her way past a commissionaire. I was only about twenty yards away but she didn't see me. Once she was through the doors I hurried up to them and as I reached out my hand against the glass the commission-aire spoke to me.

He hasn't done that before. I've been coming in and out of this building for ten years and he has always given me the impression that I was rather less important than the crease in his trousers. I have always studiously ignored him. To me a man in a ridiculous white peaked hat and a ridiculous black uniform that makes him look like a trainee member of the St John's Ambulance brigade is not to be taken seriously. Why not dress him in a binliner, for God's sake, for all the good he does? But on this occasion, and this is important, he spoke to me. "Good evening sir!"

For a moment I wanted to laugh. Either to laugh or to smash him in the face. I could see from his asinine smile that he assumed that he and I were, today anyway, part of a team. He was an NCO and I was an officer. "Good evening!" I said, in a loud, firm voice, as I pressed on out after Fiona.

There was obviously something different about me. I had crossed a bridge. Fiona was starting to show in my face. I've often worried that the things I do with the prostitutes — and some other things too that I don't want to talk about, things worse than what happened with those women down by the river — show in my face. That there's something unclean about me and that people can smell it. But on this particular evening I must have looked — to him anyway — like a man in control of himself. And that was all thanks to Fiona.

Outside, in the evening crowd on the street that leads towards the station, she became anonymous. There seemed, suddenly, hundreds of young women just like her, in coats and scarves indistinguishable from hers, drifting, in inconsolable loneliness, towards the trains that would carry them out to bleak suburbs like mine. "She needs me!" I said, aloud, to myself. And then giggled at the thought. She so obviously *didn't* need me. There was probably some spotty youth waiting for her in some pub somewhere — a male nurse or a trainee clerk —

some *nothing* who would complement her anonymity perfectly.

There was a Dave, once, but as far as I can tell he stopped ringing. Sometimes I can remember her shouting at him, usually about domestic arrangements. But for more than six months there hasn't, as far as I can tell, been anyone calling for her. Yes, I am sure she is alone in the world. She started to walk faster — big strides and a lot of shoulder work.

What I like about her, of course, are the things that have made her so lonely. Her bloody-mindedness, her lack of social grace, her suppressed anger and energy. I love all that. "Do you want te-ea?" she'll say, as she puts her right hand on her hip and jerks that enticing bottom of hers sideways in a manner that is openly satirical. *Lay a finger on me asshole and I'll scream the place down*, say her eyes, while her tits and ass say, *come on, big boy — let's see what you are made of*!

Why was she walking so fast? Was she on her way to meet someone? I found I was breathing hard. The idea that there was a *Dave* or something even worse than a Dave, a *Kevin* perhaps, lurking somewhere in the background of her life did not please me. The rain lifted and, suddenly, light leaked from the low-slung clouds. The grey sky above the railway bridge was as dramatic as an opera set. I had the sensation that the crowd moving towards it might all freeze abruptly, and that that huge mass would turn like some primitive tribe towards its god. But they wouldn't be worshipping. They would all turn in anger towards one white face, pointed out by some sign, a light or a giant finger from the lowering sky; that face would be bent out of shape with fear, hollow with anxiety and the person who owned the face would be me and everyone in the crowd would know my name and all my secret thoughts.

She had already gone into the station. I ran after

her. For a moment I thought I might invent a reason to speak to her — "You dropped a coin!" "There was a message for you." But as soon as I caught myself out in this thought, I rejected it. It seemed, somehow, obscene. That a great project like this should start with a lie!

The Reverend at the orphanage always used to say, "Tell the truth and you will never be in trouble!" He got quite a lot of confessions that way. And a confession never stopped him beating you.>

That was when the bell went again. I thought — isn't that about the only personal thing he said when we first had lunch? That he had been brought up in an orphanage? And is it that common, Fiona? Is there anyone else in the office who, as far as you know, has been brought up in an orphanage? Although, from the way Pappanauer talks and acts, if you didn't know about his mother, you might assume he was the product of an institution. When I first met him I concluded he had probably been brought up by wild animals. I think I said as much to him — which has always given our relationship a certain piquancy.

The sound of a doorbell always frightens me. My Mum's is a harsh, no-nonsense affair that cuts into the usual silence of her house like a buzz saw. I didn't get up this time. I just sat there staring at the words on the screen in front of me. *"That a great project like this should start with a lie!"* Was that the kind of thing John Pappanauer would say. Well no, of course not. But then, I reminded myself, Wordsworth didn't lounge around the local blacksmith's saying things like "She dwelt amongst untrodden ways . . .."

The private thoughts of others have a shape that none of us should even try to imagine. He would ring one more time and then he would go. I stared at the screen again.

>A:/AIR
As she pushed her way up to the ticket office I was able to get quite close to her. There were three or four people ahead of her in the queue. As they ducked their

heads down to the opening in the wall they looked fearfully around them, like animals dropping their mouths to drink at a river. As they scurried off, Fiona sorted through her purse for the exact change and when it came to her turn she presented her face, foursquare, to the invisible presence in the ticket office. I heard her mention the name of a station. The clerk asked her to repeat it. This time she stood a little way away from the grille, and giving him that slightly contemptuous stare I know (and love) so well she said the word like an actress on the stage of a theatre. Oh that deep, gravelly voice! It's the voice I fell in love with, darling Fi!

I turned then and walked back out to the street. I let her go alone up the metal steps of the bridge. I didn't look back once as I pushed my way through the crowd towards the company car park and my company car. But there was an ecstatic lightness in my chest. I felt that if I pushed downwards with the tips of my fingers I would float up and over the heads of all these homeward travellers, up towards the unexpected light. I thought to myself, over and over and over again, "I know where she lives. I know where she lives. I know where she lives."

I didn't, of course. Unless she was camping out in one of the signal boxes. In fact, once I was in the car and on my way home I had to have quite a conversation with myself in order to let myself know that I had been *fucking stupid*. I repeated this phrase to myself, over and over again, in the way Bill at the orphanage used to say it, as he beat the flat of his hand on one of the desks. "Don't be so *fucking stupid*!"

I could easily have slipped on to the same train as her. I could have got out at her station and, as darkness came on, I could have followed her down past the red wooden boxes of the housing estate, across the ragged lawns that fringe them and towards the bigger houses, close to the river.

Funnily enough I knew the station she had named well enough to visualise it quite clearly, as I drove home that night. When she got out of the train she would have to cross a footbridge back to the opposite platform. Then she would have to walk out past a small shed beyond which are a group of allotments. If someone was waiting for her when she got out of the train, and if that someone didn't want to be seen, they would probably position themselves in the car park, which is just beyond the shed. Once she was on the road she would (I decided) almost certainly walk. There are no buses that run from the station towards the river and I was, for some reason, sure that she lived in that direction. The road runs past scrub grass and rusted wire fences, towards the line of poplars and willows that mark the path of the Thames. There are never many people walking in that direction. There was a good chance that she would be walking on her own.

I waited for that thought to excite me but found that it did not. I felt calm. I simply knew that, at about six or six thirty one evening I would be sitting in the car park when her train pulled in and that, as she clattered her way south towards her flat, I would turn the car, quietly, out into the road, and follow her until I was sure where she lived.

She's my Holy Grail! I thought to myself. *This isn't sex.* As I thought the word I had a vision of Fiona in black panties, a suspender belt and high-heeled leather shoes. She had no bra. But she wasn't, as I half expected her to be, parading herself for my benefit, she was bending over a thick wooden table and she was howling with pain. I was doing something to her (although I wasn't quite sure what it was) that was causing me savage, necessary pleasure.

You see, when that thing inside me starts to sit up and growl he won't take no for an answer. Just a simple word like "beheading" can start him off. Just the picture of the word "scaffold" on the page. Just the bracing thought of Mary Queen of Scots slipping off her outer dress, tipping her arse in the air and lowering her head on to the block and he's off ordering me to the nearest place of safety, commanding me to fish out my John Thomas and roll it out between my flattened palms as if I was testing a Havana cigar.

When I got home I got one of the city maps I keep in a cupboard upstairs and pulled out the page that depicts the place that I was starting to think of as Fiona Town. I have always loved maps, especially maps of the suburbs. I like the way that, as you get to the outer areas of the city, the tangle of roads and houses gutters out into white spaces marked only by words like RESERVOIR or COMMON LAND or sometimes simple, virgin blankness with no indication of what it might be.

Fiona Town didn't disappoint me. There was, indeed, a reservoir. There was the housing estate I had remembered, just south of the station, and beyond the white space that fringed it, the river. A few roads came in from the east, along the line of the river. I could picture the houses there quite clearly. They would be big, Victorian and Edwardian villas divided into flats, each flat with its own entrance. Fiona — I was sure of this — would live at the top of one of them. You would reach her front door by climbing a fire-escape. She would have three big rooms, and her bedroom (I felt my cock stiffen at the thought) would look out over the flat grasses to where the river wound away, westward, in the evening light.

That erection annoyed me. I hadn't wanted that. The animal always does that. He comes when he hasn't been asked and squats on my chest, boasting. I tried to feed him some more. *If that's what you want*, I said to him, *let's give you a whole load of Fiona and see how you like it. Let's feed you Fiona until she makes you gag.*

I thought about what one of the women I go to had done for me — a long time ago now. The trouble is, I couldn't connect Fiona with this kind of scene. She just wouldn't fit. She stood, helplessly, watching me and the tart. She kept to the edge of the room, like a drab, frightened bird, her angular face contorted with something that seemed like shame. She's too good for that kind of thing. She's too precious to be wasted.

I think it was this that decided me against following her home. I could picture, all too clearly now, the expression on her face, if at any point in the journey she should turn and see me. I realised that she would see something in my face that I don't want anyone to see. It wouldn't be an obvious thing. But, if I was keeping even twenty or thirty yards behind her in a slow car, watching her ankles, watching the way her arse grinds into itself under her dress, I could see that it would be almost impossible to keep the beast out of my face. I wouldn't be snarling or showing my fangs. The beast doesn't need to do that. It would just be a slight angle of the head, a flicker in these pale eyes of mine. But it would be enough to send any self-respecting girl tottering off towards the nearest police station, making a noise like a car alarm. I would have to get a mask of some kind.>

I stopped reading, suddenly. There had been a noise outside, I went to the window and looked down into the street. To my horror, Pappanauer was still there. He seemed to have lost interest in ringing the bell. He was standing, his hands still on his hips, looking away from our house. He was staring down the empty street as if he was expecting someone. For some reason this thought frightened me. When I moved away from the window, I did it with extraordinary delicacy, as if the smallest noise I made could be heard from the pavement below. When I started to scroll down the document once more

I was careful to hold myself very still on the chair. There was just me and the blue screen and silence.

>A:/AIR
I was beginning to understand the significance of that commissionaire's remark. Fiona had started to work some magic on me. Just as there was a Fiona Town there was also a Fiona Me that was better, purer than the sad character who spent his lunch break tossing off over her in the gentleman's lavatory and his weekends being buggered by the kind of woman who is so dominant that she even charges for the service.

The mask would hide the beast. I liked the idea of the mask. I could see the expression on her face as I lifted it off. She would be frightened, although I could not quite think, for the moment, *why* she should be frightened. But slowly the fear would change to a kind of radiant surprise. I might even make some kind of humorous remark as I removed it. "Hey guys! It's me!"

I made myself supper and thought about how I could make the mask. Thinking about that was fun. I quite forgot about Fiona. I forgot about the orphanage as well and that was a relief. Like the beast, it comes into my thoughts unbidden and its characters sprawl around the rooms in my mind, sometimes using words and expressions that frighten me. Bill once told me that real, flesh and blood people were hatched in his head and sometimes sprang out of it and hared off down the corridor. But then Bill was a paranoid schizophrenic. Among other things.

I cut myself out a piece of tartan blanket about three foot square and, to get the fit right, stood in front of the mirror and wrapped it round my head. I actually laughed out loud when I realised I had forgotten to make the eyeholes. After I had laughed I spoke to myself quite severely.

"You'll have to do better than that," I said. "We don't want her yanking it off your head! She does know your face, old bean!"

I am clumsy with my hands but always wanted to be able to make things. Not the crude, wooden stuff they made the boys build in the carpentry shop at the orphanage — I seem to recall making a grotesque thing that looked like a primitive fertility object but was in fact a toothbrush rack — but delicate, girlish things.

"Most of you," the Reverend used to say, "will do manual work." Then he would look at me meanly. "Some of you will probably be shopworkers!"

He thought I wasn't strong enough. He assumed, I think, that I was a queer and frightened of being found out. Which was why he was rather surprised when I said I wanted to do sewing classes with the girls.

Later I went out to that weird shop in the High Street, where they sell ex-Army equipment — knives and camouflage jackets — and bought the mask. It was a yellow balaclava with tiny slits for the eyes. I didn't really think I was buying it with Fiona in mind. In fact I let it lie in a drawer for a week before I tried it out — on the girl in Chester park. And after I had done what I did to her I put it away again because I remembered the look on her face when she first caught sight of me. I sort of blamed the mask for that — and for the horrible noise she made in the back of her throat. It was a mistake, a stupid mistake. I didn't want to wear it for Fiona.>

The bell hadn't gone again. Maybe Pappanauer was still out there. Maybe he wasn't. I didn't much care. I was concentrating, so hard now, on what was in front of me, I was scarcely aware of the rain on the window, the ridiculously loud ticking of the clock in the hall or the one-note humming of the machine in front of me.

The ritual he goes through with me is quite different from anything else he does. He may not even be the person who is doing these other things. There's something odd about the tone in which he describes them – as if they had happened to someone else. Unless, of course, that's part of his sickness. He wants me, that's the really frightening part. He wants *me*.

>A:/AIR
I suppose I knew I had *really* bought it for Fiona. And that thought frightened me. It lay in my drawer for weeks, tempting me towards it. Sometimes I would walk into the room, make for the cupboard, as if to fool it into thinking I was on my way to using it, only to veer off at the last minute. But even when I was alone, in the next room, I found I was thinking about it. Of how it would make me look. How it would conceal me so beautifully from the ugliness of the world.

In the end, a week or so ago, I went through to the bedroom and took out the thick yellow thing from where it lay, folded, underneath a pile of clothes. It was even better than I had remembered it being. Made with perverts in mind! The eyeholes so tiny and the material so thick as to obscure the outline of the skull.

I wasn't altogether pleased that I had finally given in to temptation. I felt I was letting Fiona down. And, at the same time, for reasons I still can't explain, I felt as if she was making me wear it. I was angry at her for that.

"Bitch," I said aloud, "you'd better behave correctly or you will be in trouble, my girl!" I put the mask, neatly folded, at the bottom of my briefcase, poured myself a large glass of whisky and sat down with some of the spreadsheets we're currently studying. It was nearly nine thirty by this time, and I needed something to put me in a calmer frame of mind. Numbers have always been able to do that for me.

You should never make pictures of what you intend to do. The pictures acquire a life of their own. Like the creatures in Bill's head, they spring out of you and hurry away to fulfil their own destinies. I suppose I knew as soon as I had pictured myself in that car park up at the station in Fiona Town that I would never find myself there. I had imagined it. It was too, too boring to actually *do* it.

Which was why, a few days later, I wandered down to the Organiser's office and started browsing through the list of the names, home addresses and telephone numbers of company staff. The whole time I had been watching her I had — deliberately — refrained from trying to find out those personal details. It would have seemed the grossest intrusion. But once I had decided that it was fair and right for me to do so it woke all sorts of delicious possibilities. I could get closer and closer and closer to her. I could read her mail and listen to her calls and wait and watch, night after night, under her window, as she stripped off those little white panties and made herself ready for bed!

There were three Fionas in the department. There was Fiona Macmillan, Fiona Malahide and Fiona Hamlyn. Fiona Macmillan lived at:

> Flat 2,
> 1, The Avenue.

It instantly made me think of a big house, set well back from the river, with wide views across the peaceful fields. I noted the address and the telephone number and went back up to the office. I got out a street atlas from my desk drawer and as I studied the route to her flat I looked across at Fiona.

She was typing up a letter. She would look down at it, then put the tip of her index finger to her lips. She would touch them, very gently, with the extremity of her finger, as if she was about to slip her hand's flesh into her mouth. There was the shine of saliva on her lower lip. She took her finger away, typed a few words and then, as she looked down at her shorthand once more, allowed it to float towards her now open mouth. But this time she didn't touch herself. She teased her own hole and then, suddenly fascinated by her own nails, held them out, stiffly, critically, for inspection. They are varnished bright red — the colour of blood.

I bent back to my atlas. I was annoyed and distressed to find that the Avenue wasn't near the river at all. It was in a maze of ugly-looking back streets, to the north of the station. I could tell they were ugly from their names — Gladstone Road, Kitchener Street. They would be mean, two-storey dwellings put up at the end of the nineteenth century. Fiona lived in one half of one of them. A *maisonette*, that was the word. I said it aloud to myself as I looked at her over the top of the street map.

I suddenly decided that she was ugly. Her beaky nose and assertive little chin gave her the look of a crow pecking the ground for food, and her manner at her workstation which, the day before had seemed to me so graceful and precise, now seemed fussy. She looked up and for a moment our eyes met. Although I looked away immediately, I had the unpleasant feeling that she knew what I was thinking.

If anyone could know anyone else's thoughts. Really know them . . . I don't think she did though. I think she's stupid. Stupid and vulgar. She was on the phone to someone called Pam once, I remember, "I kno-o-ow . . . it's *awful* isn't it . . . yeah . . . we-ell byee! . . . *mmm* . . . *yeah* . . ."

She listens with all the busyness of women. But when I pick up the phone no one could possibly have an idea of who or what is at the other end of the line. She is so obvious. I think that what I did to her was right. If I hadn't done it someone else would have bloody done it.

Mustn't jump ahead of the story. I have to put all

this down in order. I want to read it over and read it over so that I can experience it again and again and again, just as it happened. I like to correct my mistakes too, to think of Fiona in the light that wasn't dying or of how nearly Fiona was followed by me, in a dark car, as she clacked her way along the lonely road to the river, where she doesn't live.

A great deal of money seems to have gone missing from the company. Did I mention that? I think I did. When I say "gone missing" you probably assume that it has been stolen but that sort of thing is not immediately obvious, especially to accountants. We have been looking at the problem for what seems like years — and there are some days when I think it literally has just wandered out of the building on its own. The company is so large and its accounting procedures are so complicated — they are completely revolutionised every three or four years — that I am not sure that people here understand the relation between income and expenditure any more.

Does anyone? Does the country?

I mention all this to explain why it was that I was able to leave a little early that afternoon. We are preparing a report for our department head on what happened on a building project last year. The company is building a conference centre somewhere in the country — where tired executives can go and relax from the strain of worrying about how much it cost to build. It cost a lot and, from what I can see, a lot of the money is proving rather hard to trace.

I had an appointment to see one of the contractors — a furtive little individual called Al Hunter — at four, and so at a quarter past three I got to my feet, and nodding to the office, made my way to the door. I was playing a little game with myself. *If she says goodbye*, I remember thinking, *I won't go and see her tonight. But if she doesn't . . .*

When I got to the double doors I stopped. I counted to three and turned back to the office, a big, blue room with four well-spaced desks and on one side a long, grubby window that looks out towards the railway bridge. *Come on, Fiona!*

"See you tomorrow!" I said. But she didn't answer. *Right*, I thought, OK. Right!

I didn't go and see Al Hunter. Hunter is one of those small, ferrety men who is always demanding "meetings". When you get to these "meetings" he just sits on the other side of the table, usually in his shirtsleeves, looking as if he would like to nibble you. Instead I went home and changed.>

When I got to the second mention of Al Hunter, I got up and crept once more to the window. Al Hunter is dead. I know that to be true. Pappanauer seemed to have gone. But, down the street I saw a small, neat figure in a belted grey mac. She hugged the line of the housefronts' fences, hedges and walls, as if anxious not to disturb the street with her presence. Even from this distance I could see that she was biting at her lower lip and her eyes had the shuttered look of someone wrestling with a difficult intellectual problem. I also knew that her mind was almost certainly absolutely blank.

The sight of my mother always depresses me. Why? She's done nothing wrong. She worked hard while Daddy was away. She, too, was somebody's secretary. She performed the role of Norman's slave (he was an estate agent called Norman) with no complaint whatsoever. She's happy being subservient. If she ever felt reproach when I stayed out late or swore in public or drank too much – she only showed it with her eyes. But the fact of the matter is that I always feel as if I am in a Greek play when I see her – that she amounts to a terrible indictment of all my tragic flaws. I think I was probably supposed to do all the things she never did. I was supposed to settle down and be a professor somewhere and have more than one awkward child.

All I could think about, on this occasion, was that if she was in the house and someone rang the bell, it would be impossible to ignore them. Her days are empty enough to welcome interruptions of any kind. And I knew – though I could not have said why – that John Pappanauer was going to come back quite soon. I went back to the computer and read on, with the guilty hunger of one who is sharing a terrible secret.

5

>A:/AIR

I wasn't sure what to wear. Although, by now, I knew I
was going to find Fiona at home, I wasn't sure whether
I was going to reveal myself to her (I liked that
word — *reveal*). At first I thought I might wear something casual — the blue blazer for example, that I
sometimes wear when setting out to get a Turkish lad I
know to wank me off. But the blue blazer wasn't right.
I looked, I thought, like a bank manager.

I tried on a pair of jeans. They felt much better.
I chose a loose grey jersey to go with them, and, over
it, a shabby blue anorak. Once I was wearing the anorak
I got very excited. I looked so unlike the office me! I
went to my bedroom, pulled out a dirty pair of trainers
and pranced around in front of the bedroom mirror.

"You look like a rapist." I said, aloud, to my
reflection.

Once I had said that I couldn't wait to get on the
yellow mask. As soon as I felt it slide over my face I
felt very quiet and calm. When I had pulled it down over
my neck I had a sensation that I often courted as a
child. It was as if I was invisible — as if I could go
into any house I chose, unasked, step up the stairs and
watch the inhabitants talk, eat or make love as if they
were there only for my entertainment. I pulled it off
and thrust it into the pocket of the anorak.

Then I let myself out of the front door and started
the long walk towards Fiona Town. There was no question
of taking the car. The steady rain that had disfigured

the earlier part of the day had slackened; there was moisture still in the grey air, but it seemed to be sewn into the atmosphere in single, stinging drops.

I love walking in the city. Sometimes, at the orphanage, I would go out into the streets behind it, walk down to the gas station and then climb the hill to where the rich people lived. I would stand by the white walls and clematis-heavy fences and stare in at their rooms. The one I liked particularly, I remember, had a grand piano in it and, just visible from the street, at the rear, a picture window looking out at a paved garden, bright with flowers and herbs. There were flowers, too, in the room, on a vase on the piano and on the ornament-laden mantleshelf above it. Over to the right were hundreds and hundreds of books. It looked like the sort of house where people might actually have read some of them.

What I liked about the room was the way it seemed to be waiting for someone to arrive. I sometimes stood in the street for a long time. But no one ever came. I thought there might be a boy in grey trousers and a wistful expression. I thought he might look a little like me.

The empty streets of London are like that house. Around each corner I imagine the stranger who is going to transform me. "We'll all be changed!" Bill said, before they took him away, after the last time he did it to the Carter kid, "We'll all be changed into something beautiful!"

I will be changed! I said to myself, as I struck off the main road and took the first of the many tributaries that wind their way in and out of shopping arcades, motorways and endless one-way systems. *I will be changed!*

I was acutely aware of the mask in my pocket. I started to worry about when and how I would put the thing on. I was worried, too, about the time. For some reason I had decided that it was very important not to get there after dark and though I started early enough, I noticed, when I was about three quarters of the way there, that some of the street lamps were starting to come on.

There is something frightening about a knock at the door or a ring at the bell at night-time. "Who can that be?" you say to yourself, and, as you turn on the hall light, you see a huge, dark shape behind the glass panel in the front door. But, just as you have decided that it must be a despatch rider delivering a book or a package from your office, you remember that nobody ordered a despatch rider. You weren't expecting a parcel or a registered letter. And that bulky form isn't a man in motor-bike leathers. It's something else, and whatever it is, as it weaves and taps at the frosted glass, it seems to want you.

I would break into her flat. I would make myself at home — settle into one of her armchairs, and when she opened the door, I'd just sit there, grinning, glass in hand. "Hullo darling! Good day?"

I didn't know what I would say. As I found myself in the street that leads up to what I had begun to think of as *her* station, I started to think, seriously, about going home. I couldn't quite see the form that the encounter with Fiona would take. And I didn't quite like that. Usually I have a very clear idea of how I will talk and behave in any given situation. When things turn out not quite as I had anticipated I sometimes do unpleasant things.

It was like that with the dancer who I go to just down the road. When he didn't answer the door that time I went back to it and leaned against the bell. If he had come down then I know I would have hit him in the face. And after I had hit him in the face I would have done other things. He's a sensitive guy — maybe he guessed something from the way I was ringing the bell.

On that occasion I walked away from his door until I came to a park — a patch of waste ground, really, with a few drab wooden seats, stained with bird shit. I walked until that horrible emptiness in my chest had gone away and until I was sure that thing inside me was no longer hungry. I thought that, this evening, the feeling would go away. That was partly why I had decided to walk, not take the car. But this time — the more I walked, the worse it got. Oh, I made a pretence of stopping at the corner of the main street in Fiona Town, opposite a chemist's shop, and I made a great performance of looking like the sort of person who *might be about to go in*. But I knew that this "stopping at the corner by the chemist's" was an act done to propitiate the invisible person who always watches me. I wanted to make them think, you see, as I always do, that I am not a wicked person. But it was an act. Inside me the beast was holding his hands up to his mouth and snickering as if to say — "You know what you want to do. Go on and do it.">

I heard my mother come in through the front door. I heard her drop her shopping bag on the floor and sigh quietly to herself. Then she called out to me, once, in her curiously uninflected voice. She spent much of the time she worked for Norman talking to foreign clients of his and she always talks to me as if I was fresh off the boat from Gothenburg, eager to get hold of the few simple English phrases that might lead me to a few simple English boys.

"Fiona!" I didn't answer. I froze in my chair, wondering if she would be able to hear the hum of the computer. Would she sense my presence in the house?

"Did you go out, Fiona?" This is the sort of lunatic question my mother is always asking. Even if I had felt like replying to it, its form seemed to make it almost essential not to do so. I heard her sigh again and go through to the kitchen.

She was worried about me of course. I can see that now. I hadn't explained why I had suddenly turned up on her doorstep the previous evening, escorted by my boss. I think I had got Peter to say I was coming down with flu. But, when she had started to offer all the traditional consolations, I had snapped at her. I do remember thinking, as I heard the kitchen door close, that there was something in me that prevents me from being what I want to be – even with the person who loves me most in the world.

HE seemed to see me as a sad sort of character. In so far as HE was capable of seeing me, or indeed anyone. Sometimes, as far as I could tell, he simply ascribed his own thoughts and feelings to the people around him. And because these were so random and so crude, it was hard, apart from the reference to the orphanage, to connect what he had written with any single person in the office. But, if he was the kind of crazy who borrows bits of other people's personalities, it was quite possible he had simply borrowed bits of Paul's story – the way he had borrowed the hideous attacks on those girls by the towpath and appropriated them himself. I was absolutely convinced (although I still couldn't have said precisely why) that whoever had written this document was not a murderer. What he wanted was power over other people's lives but he wanted to exercise that power in an imaginary world.

OK. I was wrong. I read what I wanted to read, not what was there on the page. You might argue that that is how we read almost everything, and in my case there is a very good excuse for my having done so. I knew what was coming up. I knew what HE (we were back to capitals again) was about to do. To me.

>A:/AIR
So I was moving like someone in a trance as I came up
to a parade of shops — a launderette, a toy shop and an
off-licence, above which was a shabby line of apartments in red brick. None of the windows were open. At
almost all of them were net curtains, grey with city
dirt; as far as I could see the only way of getting in
would be to prop a ladder against the wall. It was only
when I went round the corner and into the street down
the side of the building that I saw there was a black
iron fire-escape, leading to an iron landing off which

was a row of doors even grimier than the windows at the front. By one of these doors, its blue paint blistered and worn, was a sad window box, packed with daffodils that were already moving from Easter yellow to a shrivelled, defeated grey. "That's Fiona's place!" I said to myself, "She's where the window box is!"

I was right. Just as I had been right about the fire-escape. The flowers were by Flat 2, 1 The Avenue. And, although it was now nearly dark, there were no lights on inside. Neither could I remember having seen any from the front of the building. Fiona was out. She had gone straight from the office to meet a man in town. A young man with a moustache. They were going to come back together, flushed with cheap wine, climb the iron staircase and, as she fumbled for her key he would put a clumsy arm around her and get one of those free kisses people seem to manage to get out of other people.

I was suddenly terribly afraid that they might come back *now* and find me there in the street. I almost ran to the staircase, went up it two steps at a time, and, without really thinking about what I was doing, found myself looking at the window to the right of the door. "I'm casing the joint!" I thought to myself, smiling at the peculiar phrase.

The window was divided into two. The upper part was a rectangular strip of glass. It was slightly ajar. I climbed up on to the sill, eased it further open, and managed to get my hand inside. I could just reach the handle of the lower pane. In two minutes I had opened it with the easy, natural manner of someone who is making love to someone who *wants* them to undo the buttons, force up the skirt, peel off the knickers or *whatever*. I felt that Fiona was waiting for me, the way the darkened hall was waiting for me, as I slipped inside, closed the window gently behind me, and, like Aladdin in the cave, walked slowly through her deserted flat.

There was a sink, piled high with dishes, immediately to the right of the front door. *She's a slut*, I thought to myself. There was a half-empty bottle of red wine on the wooden table and on one of the chair arms, a paperback crime novel, its face turned into the upholstery. The furniture looked rented. She hadn't even bothered to put up any pictures on the wall. There was a calendar above the sink, with the abandoned look of something in an office. It seemed to be stuck at October. I went through to the bedroom. She must have left in a hurry this morning. The sliding shelves on the left-hand side — a tangled mass of panties, tights and brassières — gawped at me from out of the cupboard like a row of irregular teeth. She had left clothes on the floor too. Just by the bed was a pair of black knickers. I picked them up between thumb and forefinger and sniffed at them.

There was no Fiona smell. There was no Fiona smell anywhere in the place. For a moment I thought I might have wandered into the wrong flat. And then, on the bedside table I saw a photograph of her, standing next to a small woman with white hair. From the uniquely stupid expression on both their faces I took this to be her mother. No sign of a father. That was the only "personal" thing in the room.

I lay on the bed. The sheets were yellow, and I wondered whether they might have come with the flat as well. The bathroom was separated from the bedroom by a loosely hung plastic curtain. I suppose the estate agent who sold the dump to her described it as "en suite". It was only when I peered around the curtain that I realised a tap had been left running. I don't know why, but that made me think that Fiona had come home and gone out again. And that thought made me very, very angry.

She would move out of this place, I thought to myself. She had probably already bought somewhere with her young man. The one with the moustache. A box house on an estate, a little out of town. She would leave the company and have two squalling babies, with big, round faces, covered in jam. They would buy one of those ridiculous things, like stunted aerials, on which she would drape his washing and the babies' washing. The fence would be low enough for them to see into the next-door neighbour's garden.

I think that was when I decided to put on the mask. I got off the bed and went through to the bathroom so as to get a look at myself in the mirror. The bathroom was as I had expected it to be. A white cupboard on the wall with its door open. Inside, a dirty plastic cup full of toothbrushes. And, on the shelf next to it a round plastic box containing a diaphragm. Oh Fiona! So we like fucky fucky, do we? Oh *Fiona!*

I looked at myself in her bathroom mirror, flecked with stains and scratches. I wondered how I compared with Mr Moustache. Perhaps when she came back with him he would lie on the bed and wait for her while she ran into the bathroom, bent at the knees and hooked the diaphragm into herself. I looked at it out of the corner of my eye and then flipped the lid on it. Then I thought how funny it would be if I went out now, into the street, leaving the flat *exactly as it was* apart from the lid on her diaphragm. She wouldn't notice. Or if she did, she would assume that that was the way she had left it.

I liked the idea of going around her flat, making tiny alterations and then leaving quietly. That might unsettle her. She would wonder — *did I leave my cold cream just there? Surely my knickers were a little to the right, weren't they? Has somebody been here? Why would they do that?*

She would be frightened then. I thought about how she would look, alone in her flat, as she realised that someone had paid her a visit. I thought about how she might look behind her as I pulled out the mask and fitted it over my head. Then I zipped up the anorak. The only things that might betray me, I decided, were my hands. That was when I saw the gloves. They were yellow, rubber kitchen gloves. She had left them in the rack over the bath. I held up my hands, like a surgeon, and worked my fingers into them. I made sure that they went over the cuffs of the anorak and that there was not a single inch of my flesh anywhere to be seen. Then I pirouetted, again, in front of the mirror. I was dressed, I decided, for a very important task. I heard Fiona's key in the lock.

I hadn't turned on any of the lights. That was lucky. The neon of the shopping parade filtered through, ghostly and cruel, into the bedroom and it was in that light that I saw, quite clearly, Fiona Macmillan come in, alone, to her sad little flat. I could see straight through to the hall. She closed the door behind her quietly.

She was carrying a shopping bag. She was wearing the brown coat and the brown scarf. Her head was cast down. She looked, I thought, like a broken puppet on limp strings. One foot followed the other across the tired carpet. One hand let go of the bag of shopping. The brown coat was allowed to fall and to lie, coiled, on the carpet. One foot kicked off a shoe. Another shoe followed. The head shook two or three times, the way a dog shakes itself when coming out of the water, as if Fiona wanted to shake off the dirt and noise and sorrow of the city outside. Then she came through into the bedroom.>

There was a noise downstairs. Just a slight one. But, for a moment, I heard it as a kind of soundtrack to the document – pulsing white on a blue background – that now faced me on the computer screen. It was like the noise of HIS shoes in my flat. I stayed very still for nearly a minute, not even daring to read any further, before I realised it was my mother, moving across the hall. Curiously enough, that didn't make it any less scary. What was she doing?

It seemed very important not to let her know that I was in the house. I felt like a little girl in a game of hide-and-seek. My heart was racing as fast as HIS heart must have been going as he waited for me behind that curtain. Although I was looking at the words, I couldn't, for the moment, make sense of them. Mum went back into the kitchen. Very slowly and carefully, as if each movement of a muscle could be heard, I raised my eyes once more to the document.

>A:/AIR
I didn't want her to come into the bedroom. For a start I could hear my heart beat so loudly that I was almost sure she would be able to hear it. And then the plastic curtain stretched almost to the floor but there were a few inches that, if she looked down, might reveal my trainers. I stepped back, very, very quietly and watched her through the crack in the curtain as she made her way up to the bed.

When she turned on the light I held my breath. I was sure my shadow must be visible through the material. But she wasn't looking towards the bathroom. *Perhaps she'll turn and go back out*, I thought. At this stage, you see, I didn't want her to be there. I didn't want to be watching her. I'd started to think of her flat as belonging to me. It felt as much mine as the lifts, lobbies, streets, stations or cars that I inhabit daily. I was frightened. Would she scream if she saw me? Would the neighbours hear?

I very much did not want her to do something intimate. I very much did not want her to show me that she wasn't the bowed little secretary in the corner of the office, but a woman. As I thought the word *woman* I had that light feeling in the chest. And I had a vision of white flesh, gaping open. There was blood there too, although whether it was in my ears or on the body I could not have said. I had to hold on to my wrist, hard, to stop myself crying out or ripping back the curtain. I knew, you see, that something bad was going to happen. And, sure enough, like the fire-escape or the window box, what I had imagined came to pass. That damned imagination of mine! People can die of mere imagination.

When I looked again she was taking off her clothes. The prostitutes I go to always do this in a sneaky way. Sometimes they do it when you're not looking. Or, if you are looking, they pretend that it has no significance. As if they were going to bed. They remind me of an artist's model I saw once. She was surrounded by twenty or thirty people, nearly all of them men, poised over pencils and paper and, as she walked into the middle of them, there was a little rustle of expectation. She was wearing a loose caftan but, before anyone was really aware of what she was doing — at, I would have said, the precise moment of the crowd's inattention — she had moved from the clothed to the naked with a contemptuous flick of her shoulders. Maybe if you were with someone and she *wanted* you to see her strip and you *wanted* to watch her and then she did, sliding her bra over her breasts, like in the movies, and looking up all innocent and surprised suddenly — oooh did you want to see my bottom . . . did you . . .?

You see, watching her was like that. It really was as if she wanted me to be doing it. Because I wanted it so much. I didn't want it to be like that but that was how it was. First of all she unzipped the side of her skirt. That was OK. I could deal with that. It wasn't even so bad when she stepped out of her tights because that was done, too, like a girl in a boutique changing room — very quick and businesslike. It was bad after that because I could see her white legs. And pretty soon after that it got *really* bad because she crossed her arms over her head and in a way that was as brisk and perky as the skirt manoeuvre, started to pull her blouse over her head. She hadn't, you see, realised that there was a button not undone too close to her neck and she had to dive one hand back down into her blouse just about where I guessed her breasts would be, to free herself. I saw her ribcage then, and the bone of her pelvis, like a shark's fin.

I thought she would stop there, you see. I thought that maybe she would change into something else – jeans, a skirt – and make her way back out to the street. But she didn't. She stood for what seemed an age by the bed – wearing nothing but bra and pants – her eyes as vacant as a cow giving milk. Then she let her hands creep round to the bra strap and let the brassière fall to join the rest of her clothes, on the floor.

OK. OK. Stop *now*, I found myself thinking. But she didn't stop. She put the thumb and forefinger of each hand into the space between her belly and the top of her knickers and then she slid them, quite slowly, over the small hillock of her bum.

I wanted her to put on her clothes. That was why I stepped out from behind the curtain. She was turned away from me, stark naked, and all I could think was that I didn't want to look at her arse any more. I had decided, after a brief flicker of excitement when I first saw those legs of hers, that she was playing tricks on me – like that artist's model or those women whom I pay to do things a lot more intimate than taking off their clothes. Even when people are alone, I found myself thinking, they protect themselves, they shield themselves from unwelcome attention.

In my fantasy that I can step out of my body and go wherever I choose, I look in on couples fucking and I catch their most intimate conversations. I sometimes find myself on the pillows of people that I know or knew – watch the Reverend licking his wife's arse, or one of the orphanage governors taking his boyfriend's cock into his mouth.

Well, there I was. Doing it. And yet, like the sex I pay so much for, it was slightly unsatisfying. Did I say that? At the beginning I was trying to pretend that it was all I needed but of course it isn't. I need something more and the trouble is I don't know what it is. Only the beast knows what it is. But, I want to make it clear, it wasn't the beast that made me step out from behind the curtain — *I* stepped out into her bedroom because *I* wanted there to be more. There had to be more than a thin woman with a big nose taking off her clothes in a furnished room above a parade of shops. Although I had no idea of speaking to her I thought that when she saw me her face would tell me what to do. *Run, you kinky bastard! Run for your life!*

Actually that wasn't what her face said to me at all. Her expression made the whole business come alive. It perked things up considerably. Well, it would, wouldn't it? If you were to turn round, stark naked in your bedroom and see a guy in a bright primrose mask with yellow rubber gloves on his way out from behind one of your curtains you might think — hey! I mean — it's *different*, isn't it?

I thought she was going to scream. She didn't. She just let her mouth hang open like a fish. The way she does sometimes in the office. Her breasts, I thought, were in very poor taste. They lolled about above her scrawny rib-cage without showing any of the charisma I usually associate with breasts. They didn't look in the least bit saucy or pert which is, in my opinion, how breasts ought to look. But I was unable to keep my eyes off them. And there was an almost uncomfortable amount of time available to meet the eye of each pink nipple. The silence seemed to be spreading through the flat in great waves, muffling the distant noise of the traffic and the steady trickle of the rain which had started again out on the iron landing. It was stretching out the seconds like rubber in a strong man's hands until the perspective of the moment was as flat and eternal as a desert horizon. And the breasts, which were now staring me down, reminded me that the mouths of greedy infants might one day clamp over them the way Bill's hand closed over the Carter kid when he . . .

I pushed her, hard, in the chest, and she fell back on to the bed. She fell back, her legs spread in the air. That was when I started to get excited. It was the look on her face that did it. She still didn't scream — perhaps she liked men in primrose masks, perhaps yellow rubber kitchen gloves were what turned her on — but at least she lost the dead fish expression. She looked *alive* for the first time. I couldn't remember seeing that before. I had seen her look patient, resentful, bored, angry, and once or twice I had noticed her come on like a little girl to the other men in the office. But this was the first time I had seen what I would call a real *expression* on her face. It wasn't just that she was impressed by my outfit. She was clearly very involved in discovering how things were going to turn out. What was in this for her?

I got on top of her as she started to scream. I grabbed her by the wrists. Then — I am afraid I have to give you these little physical details because it's important that you get the full picture — my cock started to get hard.>

I think that was the first time that I was forced to confront the person I had been the week before, when all this happened. What was strange was the vivid way this pervert seemed to make my former self come alive. I suppose I had deliberately rejected, not thought about, the horrific events of that evening. And now I was looking at myself, seeing myself the way I can remember doing sometimes in shop windows or mirrors for which I was totally unprepared. Fiona as others see her. Fiona lying down and taking it. I breathed slowly through my nose for about thirty seconds — about the only useful thing poor old

Dave taught me to do — and then, with a kind of dreadful calm, went back to the text.

>A:/AIR
I've never felt so strong. At the orphanage I was considered a weakling. I didn't take exercise of any kind. This strength wasn't coming from me. It didn't really feel as if I was responsible for it although the person who grabbed her arms, turned her over and forced her face into the pillow did seem to be wearing these yellow, rubber kitchen gloves. And the eyes that watched her bony arse buck and twist were deep, deep inside a mask. I had her in a full Nelson — forcing both arms up into her shoulders and the more she shouted the deeper I pushed her into the bed.

That was when I decided, or, rather, when it was revealed to me, that she had wanted it to happen. It wasn't that I suddenly understood that I was inhumanly strong but that her struggles were a kind of girlish display and that each flutter of legs or arms or bum was a kind of come-on, a sort of don't stop it's so good do it to me oh please do it to me don't stop please please ple-ease . . .

I don't know why I spoke. I think it was to make it more exciting. Although, I must say, it wasn't exactly dull. But there was a possibility that, at any moment, I might get *used* to what I was doing. And speaking to her seemed to offer the prospect of making it, once more, unusual and challenging. I suppose if you got your kicks out of killing people, after a while it wouldn't be enough to simply spray them with bullets or push them over the odd cliff. You would have to think of more and more *outré* ways of finishing them off. I was quite aware of what I was doing when I *did* speak. I know that Fiona knows my voice and that if there was the slightest chance that she recognised it then I was in trouble. But that only made it more exciting. I was going to disguise it, of course, and that in itself was a thrilling prospect. I had, also, a few other things in my favour. I don't think I've ever done anything in the office that might suggest that I am the sort of chap who is capable of getting into a primrose mask, yellow kitchen gloves and bursting in on my secretary in order to rape her. She wouldn't be *expecting* to hear my voice.

I produced the voice from the back of my throat. I tried to give it a synthesised quality — laying an even stress on each word of the sentence. And I also composed the one sentence I said to her with very great care. I wanted her to know that she had no redress against me. I thought, at one point, of saying what I had said to her in the office that time: "No peace for the wicked!" But although the symmetry of that would have been amusing I didn't want to take such a risk. I rather despised myself for this.

I said, "If you tell anyone about this I will kill you."

I was quite pleased with this. It sounded like the sort of thing that a guy with a primrose mask over his face and a pair of yellow kitchen gloves on his hands might actually say. It was deep and cracked and even — the kind of voice that comes out of a computer on a spaceship when it wants to tell you you are three million miles off course and that the air conditioning is looking dicey. And, perhaps more importantly, it was obviously not *mine*. It made me feel completely removed from the fact that the person who had said it, was, even as he spoke, getting his cock out of his trousers. I think I said it again.

"If you tell anyone about this I will kill you.">

6

He didn't say it twice actually. He said it once. Mind you – once was enough. Did I read somewhere that psychopaths have no sense of time? Or did I make that up? I remember thinking, when I first dipped into A:/AIR how weirdly faraway HIS account of that first attack seemed to me – although, in fact, it had only happened the week before. But what also struck me was the horrible immediacy of HIS tone of voice. When I ask myself why I didn't tell anyone about what happened that first time I sometimes pretend that it was because of my absolute loneliness after Dave and I finished. I sometimes try to tell myself that it was something to do with the person I was at the beginning of that April day but . . . but I know that neither of these things accounted for my silence for the week or so between the first attack and the day I went looking for him. The real reason was, quite simply, fear. I was sure that he meant what he said. I was frightened to tell anyone because I knew, or felt I knew, that if I did he would find out somehow. I felt he had the power to know what I was doing at every hour of the night and day, that he was watching my window when I woke in the morning, tapping into my calls and opening my mail. All that from one sentence in a weird, cracked voice, like the voice on a computer. Absurd as it seems now, I was frightened to tell anyone because I was sure he would find out I had told them and he would come and find me and kill me.

Why? Why should I have believed him? Just because there was a horrible authority about that voice of his. I just thought I knew in the way one thinks one knows that two and two is four or that Paris is the capital of France. It seems absurd to me now. But then I am not frightened now. I am, at last, myself. But, even on that last day, as I listened to my mother fussing around in the kitchen downstairs, and read on through the document, HE had a horrible power over me. His voice on the page was as believable as it had been in the flat. I found, although I was still putting up an almost conscious fight against it, the more I read of it the more "authentic" it seemed. Every word of this – I caught myself thinking – is true.

I remember Dave telling me about some guy he had met at the prison who had stabbed two children, both under ten. This man claimed to have absolutely no recollection of what he had done. He had been drinking since the morning and, so as to finally absolve himself from responsibility for his actions, had swallowed about an ounce of marijuana and a tab of LSD. I remember Dave saying that he did not want to hear about the fact that the man could not recall his crime. He wanted him to understand what he had done. With HIM I had that feeling – only it was worse. He thought he understood all right. He had it all worked out. He had a system. I have no system. Maybe that's why he found me such a sad character.

The next section was quite a long and involved piece about the orphanage. I found myself hurrying through it. I note, now, with a certain amusement, how that sentence, written at the head of the next paragraph, gives it a . . . hollowness. Do we really believe this man has been through an orphanage? Does any place such as the one he describes really exist?

```
>A:/AIR
```
It was the look on her face that did it. It took me back years. I travelled years and months and weeks and days and hours and minutes and slowed to seconds in a second. And then, suddenly, I was the boy in the orphanage, talking to Bill in the empty classroom with the Reverend beating on the door and shouting something I could not understand.

I did not like that feeling. My cock was out but it was like it didn't belong to me. I could no more take it to any of the places I had been planning on showing it – the guided tour of all her openings, her mouth, her arse and her vagina – than I could somehow apologise for this terrible, ugly, pointless thing I was doing to her. Is that why I started this document? Because I want to give myself absolution the way I give myself all of the other things that other people usually seek from other people. The angry feeling came back in waves. This was worse than the beast. It wasn't something I could dignify with a mere metaphor. It was as if I was running at the end of a long, long race, like the cross-country races they had at the orphanage, with every breath tearing at my lungs. I don't know how they got there but my hands were around her neck, starting to squeeze. Her hands were flailing at me but I was too heavy for her.

I was quite in control when I had the orgasm. My cock pumped out gobbets of stuff that looked, I thought, like melted ice-cream or hair conditioner. And, as it pulsed out on to her night-dress, crumpled on the bed, the words "DNA, DNA, DNA" went off in my head like a police siren.

That was why I let go of her throat. If I hadn't thought "DNA" I might have gone on squeezing until her movements died away in little, helpless circles on that bed and her face turned blue with its tongue stuffed in its mouth like a bolster in a boarding-house bedroom. But I did stop. I lifted myself up to the sound of her choking and ran to the front room.

My only thought was to get out of there. I pulled the door back, clattered along the iron landing and was halfway down the stairs before I realised. I was still wearing the mask. I yanked it off my face, forced it back down under my jersey and, walking slowly now, came out into the deserted side street.

I hadn't really enjoyed any of it. It had all been a bit like a difficult piece of homework, like some task I had had to perform in order to get someone off my back. Although I had made quite a creditable job of it, the actual process — forcing her on to the bed, getting my hands around her throat and so on — was rather tedious. I only really started to feel all right when I was out on the main street, walking, still slowly and calmly towards the station that I had not yet visited. I quite often get an exalted feeling when I am alone in public places nearly (I nearly always am alone) but this feeling was different. There was a great sense of calm, a tremendous relief. As I walked northwards, towards the river, I thought of Fiona, in her flat. She would be gasping back into life. She would be reaching for the phone. She would be giving a confused and inaccurate account of her attacker. She would be . . .

I realised I was still wearing the kitchen gloves. I didn't think anyone had seen me. But I had a sudden vision of a policeman on the television: "Miss Macmillan's attacker was last seen walking towards the station and he was wearing a pair of yellow rubber gloves!" I thrust my hands deep into my anorak pockets. I hadn't been aware of people until I caught myself out over the gloves. Now there seemed to be hundreds of them, all looking my way. I caught sight of myself in a shop window. I looked, I thought, rather dashing.

There were no sirens, no police cars, no sign that in a shabby room somewhere behind me a girl lay, bruised on her own bed, her sheets stained with gobs of my semen. They can DNA all they fucking like, I thought to myself. *Whose* DNA I'd like to know.

Getting the ticket for the return journey was comic. I hadn't found anywhere that was safe enough for me to take off the gloves, and so I had to pull them up into my sleeves and pick out coins from my pocket with pincer fingers through the fabric.

"Did you notice anything unusual on that evening?"

"Well, officer, there was a bloke who didn't appear to have any hands . . ."

"Right, we are looking for a man with no hands!"

They would be looking for somebody. I went to the farthest end of the platform and peeled off the gloves and then I put them deep in my anorak pocket. I didn't want to leave them in Fiona Town. I was sweating. That's unusual for me.

When the train came I chose an empty compartment. I sat in the corner staring out at the dark. The rain was streaked down the glass. As the train rattled on over bridges, through high-sided embankments and then on by darkened suburban streets, occasionally lit up by the brief flash of a high street or a shopping centre, I hugged a thought to myself.

Tomorrow, I repeated, over and over again, to the rhythm of the coach on the tangled miles of steel, tomorrow I will see Fiona. And she won't know. But I will know. Even if it isn't tomorrow, but the day after that or the day after that she will have to come back to the office. She will push through the double doors in her drab brown coat and drab brown scarf. And I will sit at my desk and watch her. I will know what I did to her. But she won't know. And if she ever does know, if by some fluke she should find out it was me she will never dare to say so. She will never dare to let anyone know what kind of person I am. Because, of course, if she does, I will kill her.>

The document seemed to end there. Although someone had opened it beyond that last, chilling sentence, the succeeding pages were blank. I started to scroll down them to see if there was anything on the other side of the empty space. It was puzzling that there should be quite so many of them. I had counted at least twelve when I heard a noise behind me. I turned and saw my Mum, out on the landing. She was carrying a basket of washing. She was clearly surprised to see me there.

"Oh," she said, "I thought you were out!"

"No, " I said, carefully, "I'm in."

This is the sort of conversation my mother and I often have. It can go on like this for hours. It doesn't seem like there is any animosity there, but the deliberately controlled banality may be a way of avoiding any that might be lurking. If there is tension between Mum and myself, it is liable to be of the explosive kind.

"What", she said, after looking at me fishily for some time, "are you doing?"

"Nothing!" I said. This was a mistake. She came into the room and peered down at the computer keyboard.

"This was David's!" she said.

I knew, then, that we were going to get a sentimental speech about him, perhaps to make up for the frozen contempt with which she had treated him when he was alive. That is probably why I let her tap the "up" key and start to work her way back to the document I had just been reading. I knew I didn't want her to read it and I knew I didn't want to talk about it. I was simply powerless to stop her. When she got to the last page of text she read, out loud, in her carefully articulated, neutral voice.

"And if she ever does know, if by some fluke she should find out it was me she will never dare to say so. She will never dare to let anyone know what kind of person I am. Because, of course, if she does, I will kill her." She looked down at me.

"Are you writing a book?" she said.

"Yes," I said.

She pursed her lips.

"A thriller?" she said.

"Yes," I said.

I thought for one horrible moment that she was going to go further back into the document and I reached out to switch off the machine. When she saw my hand go forward she stopped, put her index finger to her lips, like a little girl, and laughed, lightly.

"Private," she said, "Your private book! Like that diary you kept when you were little."

There are many different kinds of assault. My mother doesn't actually put on a yellow mask and leap out at me from the bathroom, but her constant, unyielding interest in my privacy wears me down the way water wears away stone. When she had finished pouting at me and trying to make me feel guilty for excluding her, she carried that artful index finger from her lips to the papers on the table next to the computer.

"That's your writing," she said, "isn't it peculiar?"

"Isn't it?" I said.

She was looking at the diary I had started to keep the day after

HE attacked me. I was, once again, very glad that I had persuaded Peter Taylor not to say anything to her last night about why I was there. Angry with her now I reached my hand out and spread it over the page at which she was looking.

"It's my book," I said, "I don't want anyone to read it until it's finished!"

"You are funny, Fiona," she said, "You and your father. You were so alike!"

She started to hum to herself, brightly, to show me that she didn't really care what I did or said. Then, to show me that she was an independent person with things to do, she picked up the basket of washing and tripped out on to the landing. She turned, just before she left the room and said, "You're feeling better anyway!"

Guilt rose in my throat like nausea. You're all she has, Fiona. Why can't you accept it? It's not her fault Daddy drank himself to death, is it?

Only when she had finished in the bedrooms and, still humming to herself, gone downstairs, did I take my outspread palm off what I had written last week. At the head of the first page were two heavily scored pencil marks. They looked, now, just like doodles, but I could remember how I had felt when I had made them. I had gouged out tracks in the paper as if I was drawing the point of the pencil across HIS face. I could also remember what I had written before I made those marks and why I had thrown it away.

Now, reading what HE had to say for himself, I was struck with how my first private words to myself had sounded. Most of it had been what I wanted to do to him and how I would do it and what he would say and how I would watch him and how he would suffer and how I would enjoy that. I was almost annoyed with myself, now, for having thrown it away. The first pages of what I had written after that had been about my Dad. Not about what happened to him later on, but sentimental stuff about him coming home and picking me up in his arms and swinging me round in our drab front garden until my head swam and my heart raced. I suppose I was trying to hold on to (or possibly invent) those untarnished childhood memories Wordsworth talks about. Those with unsatisfactory childhoods are condemned to invent alternatives.

Reading it now I was almost angry with myself. And I was shocked too, at the way my tone of voice betrayed me. I couldn't believe that I could sound so dumb, so childish, so artfully artless.

If I couldn't recognise myself in what I had written, how was I ever going to get a clue to his identity from the document that called itself A:/AIR? I pushed the chair back from the computer and started to read back in the diary I had started the morning after the first attack, in the flat. Only a week lay between the girl who wrote it and the girl who read it over to herself on the thirteenth of April. But, already – I can see this clearly now – I was quite another person.

TUESDAY APRIL 6TH. 11 A.M. (F)

After Dad died I got on much better with Mum. Sometimes I think that the arguments I used to have with her were really the ones I didn't dare have with Dad. I still remember the things he brought me when he came back from Spain. I still remember the way the room lit up when his face rounded the door, bright red from his last drink, his eyes sparkling. "Hullo girly! Not cross with me, are you?"

I was never cross with him. I didn't dare argue with him because the little time I had him to myself was so precious. I didn't want to spoil it.

He was a spry little man with a small ginger moustache. When I was small I always thought he wore the same suit every day of the year. One day I stole into his room and looked into his cupboard. It turned out he had about thirty suits but they all looked identical – black with charcoal grey stripes. His ties, I remember, were up at the other end of the cupboard. There was an Air Force Tie and a Rugby Tie and an Old School Tie and one extraordinary dark-blue number that seemed to suggest he had once had something to do with ballooning.

His limp was the thing. That and the appendix scar. I think the limp was supposed to be something to do with the Korean War but the appendix scar, which was often exhibited to comparative strangers was always accompanied with a single, two-syllable word delivered with the terse dignity of the true hero. "Shrapnel!"

I think the nearest Dad ever got to any kind of army was watching American films on television. But he really believed the roles he played. And when he was being a loving Dad — watching me unwrap a present or listening with total attention while I read to him — I believed him too. His sudden entrances into our narrow life surprised me into a curious, weightless feeling that I now know was happiness. The mere sight of his handwriting on a postcard — after I hadn't seen him for nearly a year — could bring tears to my eyes. "AM IN TUNISIA!" One of them read, "HOT!" And after that, nothing for another six months. But his absences were part of his charm. For, no matter how bad things were between him and my mother he always came back to see me. I suppose he must have loved me very much.

I am writing about my Dad because I want to keep hold of something that's good and gentle (he was never, ever violent, even when drunk) and pleasurable in a world that has turned out to be worse than anything I could have imagined. I sometimes wonder if I *had* been able to imagine anything as horrible as *that*, whether I could have found a way of foreseeing it, of somehow knowing what was waiting for me when I opened my front door last night. But it's too late, now, to even consider such things.

I've not kept a diary for years. I haven't told anyone you see. So I have to tell this piece of paper. Outside it is raining — steadily. The cars and the buses shoulder their way through huge puddles; on the leaves of the trees in the forecourt, and across the grimy windows of the office where I am writing this, the drops keep rolling down like tears that can't be helped. I'm holding on to things. Even though I can't imagine telling any of this to my mother.

But, although I haven't got anyone to be a sister or a daughter *to* I am going to think of myself as a sister and a daughter. I am even going to think about the good things there were between Dave and me. That only went wrong, I think, because he was too like a brother. There was nothing cruel or horrible about our relationship. When he left we didn't quarrel at all. I think the only time I shouted at him was when he insisted on watching the football on television and taping it at the same time.

I am a sister and a daughter and I am myself. You have to hold on to your self-respect, they keep saying, don't they, if someone harasses you at work? They don't say what to do if some horrible pervert breaks into your flat and rapes you but I suppose I have a fairly good idea what they *would* say. I know what everyone would say, you see – which is partly why I can't bear to tell anyone. Self-respect blah blah blah. Sisterhood blah blah blah . . .

I can't get that horrible voice out of my thoughts. I believe what he said. I believe that, if I tell anyone, wherever I am, he'll come and find me. I have to find all the good things in my life and heap them up, like a sea wall, against him. So that next time he comes – and, yes, I am sure there will be a next time, I will be ready for him.

One of the good things in my life are the people in this office. You see, I said "people" although all of them are men; things like this are supposed to make you hate all men, but I don't hate all men. I just hate the one who did that thing to me. The men in my office are as unlike my father as anything you could imagine. They are curiously formal with me. They arrive at the same times and leave at the same times. Over the years our office routine has become a carefully observed ritual – right down to Pappanauer's blue jokes and Peter Taylor's disapproval of them. They may all be fearfully interesting but I am very careful never to let them have the chance of being so. I glory in the fact that they wear almost identical suits. They even have identical briefcases. That's how safe they are.

Even John Pappanauer was civilised to me this morning. I almost burst into tears. He just came up to me when I was by the photocopying machine, and put his head to one side like a bird listening for worms.

"You OK, Fi?" he said.

It was that "Fi" that did it. Abbreviations can really melt you, can't they? I had to hold on to the side of the machine as it spewed out paper. And I found, without really knowing I was doing it, I had put my hand up to my neck, to where my scarf hid the huge, ugly bruise he had made.

"Fine!" I said.

I know I shouldn't have come into work. I know I should have rung the police. I know all sorts of things I do are wrong and stupid but that doesn't stop me doing them. If you want to know what I think I think none of us know why we do anything.

This is what is making me feel better. Writing all this in my crazed handwriting, like a spider's footsteps. Describing things gives you some control over them. The bruise on my neck, for example, is dark blue, almost mauve and when he came at me I . . . You see? I can start to think about it at least. Even if I can't yet bring myself to start describing it.

It would have to be Pappanauer who nearly made me cry. He's the only one of them I don't really like. The other two I suppose I have come to trust. They are, in their different ways, mysterious to me. They both have pale, reserved eyes that don't let you see what they are thinking. Both of them have, sometimes, looked at me in that curious, cold, speculative way that men sometimes have when they fancy you. But you know – or think you know – that there's a gentleness about them – a quality now I remember and treasure about my poor dead father.

Peter Taylor is the oldest of them. I suppose he is the boss. And though I don't exactly fancy him I think of him as a warm, protecting presence. He has red hair. He is the only one in the office who is married. Although I've never met her, I've often heard her voice on the phone and he once showed me a photograph of her. She looked much prettier than I had expected her to look. She had blonde hair and very regular features and she was smiling in a way that didn't make her face fall to pieces – which is what happens to mine when I express merriment. A few days later I asked to see a picture of his boys and he said, in that rather wry way he has, "This is getting embarrassing, Fi! Only perverts display pictures of their wives and families!" Then he grinned, "Especially on the sun visors of cars!" But he got them out just the same and you could see he was desperately proud of them. They were about two or three and they were standing in a garden, holding buckets and spades. Jimmy, the elder, a serious-looking little boy with a pudding basin haircut was looking at his younger brother slightly warily, and Jonny, the younger, all freckles, was staring straight at the camera, grinning. His whole body was in on the smile.

Peter has very pale freckles on his pale skin, like his younger son.

He also has a rather cute little turned-up nose, so, although he is the father of two and the Head Accountant, whatever that means, he often looks as if he is about to burst into "Oh, for the Wings of a Dove". Once, and this was considered very daring, he came in in a lightweight suit.

Because I've never met his family I often think about what they are like. Once, when he had hung up his jacket by the door and there was no one else around I tiptoed up to it and pulled out the photograph of his wife. She was wearing jeans and a T-shirt. She was standing in a garden, and behind her was a lot of blue sky. For some reason, I decided that if she spoke, in the photograph, she would have an Australian accent, although on the telephone she's got a funny, timid, English little voice. A few days ago I said to Peter, "Has your wife ever lived in Australia?" He gave me a funny look. He didn't look pleased that I was asking about her.

"I don't think so. Whatever gave you that idea?"

"Nothing."

It's funny how describing the small details of office life is making me feel calmer. I suppose that, since Dave left, this place has become the centre of my life. I feel safe here.

I always think that if they were brothers Paul would be the middle one. He is very careful and reserved. When he does say something, which isn't often, it is thoughtful and considered. He has thick, curly hair, which is odd, because he hasn't got the kind of face where you expect curly hair. There was a time when I seriously thought it might be a wig. Paul doesn't talk much about himself and, unlike the rest of us in the office, he hardly ever takes personal calls. And he rarely says anything to suggest that he would have a reason for receiving one. I don't know if he has a girlfriend or even a mother or a father. There's something about him, though, that makes me think he might be unhappy. He doesn't laugh like the rest of us and when we do laugh he looks a little frightened, as if he thinks we might be laughing at him. Peter says he is very, very clever. And particularly clever with figures. I'm hopeless with figures.

He scared me a bit the other week. I was working late and I didn't realise that there was anyone else in the office. The carpets in our office are really thick and if you're busy with something you simply don't hear people coming up behind you. So I wasn't really aware that there was anyone near me when, suddenly, a hand came out of nowhere and touched me very, very lightly, with the delicacy of a child, on my right arm. When I looked up there was Paul, with that serious look of his. When he speaks he speaks very precisely. He puts ·in all the bits of words – paying special attention to the consonants.

"Good night, Fiona!" he said.

"Oh," I said, "Good night!" And off he went.

Although they all look a bit boring, what they do – they keep assuring me – is very important. They're in charge of paying out all the invoices the company makes with outside firms – especially building firms. And, at the moment, as far as I can gather, they are all in *deep shit* as they seem to have lost a few million pounds. I don't know whether this is because they added it up wrong in the first place or whether all three of them have just been taking it home in their briefcases, but over the last few months there has been a lot of head-shaking about the Newsom Project as it is called.

Not from me. I don't understand a word. of it. All I know is that it wasn't my million pounds and I don't think I saw any of it. I type out letters to people I am never going to see. I print out lists of figures that I do not understand. But that, of course, is why I work here. I just can't imagine myself doing something I was supposed to care about. I know that the least sign of hopelessness in, say, a teacher or a critic would set me shaking with rage. But in here all is calm, and level. If my life here had a colour it would be peaceful grey.

It's funny. I do feel better now. It will take an awful lot of time and an awful lot of words about other things before I can really start writing about *that*. But, already, I don't feel that writing it down will make it happen again, that using the expression HIM will conjure him up like the devil. Although I think, if you want to know, that he is the devil or that he was possessed by *him*. I think he was really wicked. There are wicked people and they should be punished for what they do.

To myself, I call the three men in my office the Apostles. Because, of course, the third one is called John. Divine he isn't, I am afraid. He is *flash*. You know the kind of person who has always been to a great party last night and who has to tell everyone about it? He doesn't only tell you about the party, he tells you about how he was sick in the cab home, how he felt when he woke up at three in the morning and, whenever possible, he lets you know who he woke up next to. If he can't remember their names he's always got a few physical details handy – like bust size or any little problems of personal hygiene they might be experiencing. If I woke up next to him I would scream and scream until I was sick.

He's even more gross when he's out with the boys. Once, he told us, he got so drunk with Ted and Mick and Sid and Jim (all these names come up in regular rotation and you're supposed to know who they are and how many more spots they have than Kevin and Dan and Jeff and Ted) that he fell asleep on the *train* and when he woke up it was *four in the morning* and he was in *Southend*. Amazing!

"I chatted up the guard," he said, "I have always got on with Turkish men!" Then he winked at me. I just raised my eyebrows. You never smile with men like John Pappanauer. They always get the wrong idea. Actually you might as well smile because they get the wrong idea anyway. He leaned over my workstation and winked again, "I go for Turks, Fiona!" he said, "How about you?"

"They're better than spotty Englishmen!" I said. But it had absolutely no effect.

He always has two or three women on the go. So he says anyway. And, as far as I can make out – I don't always listen to him when he starts – they are quite often other people's wives. He seems to think there is something amazingly clever about this. He never says their names. They are always just Mrs.

"So," he said once, "I'm in the bedroom giving Mrs one when I hear her hubby coming up the stairs. He is one tough *hombre!*" Pappanauer is always using words like "tough *hombre*". "The stairs are *shaking!*" he goes on. And he looks across at me. I am supposed to be interested in this, you see, because I am a female.

"What did you do?" I say finally.

"Out the window!" says Pappanauer, "I am outta da window. Leaving Mrs at the Gates of Heaven!"

Of course! You would, wouldn't you?

Actually John isn't spotty. He's the kind of person you wouldn't notice in a crowd. He has a neat, hatchet face, and smart, rather stiff black hair. Although he talks about his women a great deal we never hear anything of his family. I sometimes wonder if all this talk is fantasy – it is quite possible he lives alone in a furnished room, staring at himself in the mirror. I quite often catch him studying his reflection in the windows and, at least two or three times a day he disappears to the Gents to preen himself. At least I assume that is what he is doing in there.

Like all three of them he loves talking about routes and maps and drink and machines and numbers and all the other things that men seem to love discussing. When he wants to look sincere he screws his eyes up really small and does a horrible sort of chewing thing with his mouth; if he is absolutely desperate to impress you he'll try and sound American. I'm making him sound worse than he really is. He's like one of those puppets people hang in the back windows of their cars as mascots. He's not *supposed* to be in perfect taste. If you didn't mind people who practise bottom wiggling in the office at nine thirty in the morning or say things like "I'm having a total personal re-think!" you could probably get to like him. His eyes, though, have an absent quality. You don't notice the colour or the expression and then, when you try and do so you wonder why it is you hadn't noticed.

•

That was when the doorbell went again. Before I could get to my feet and try and think of a convincing reason for my mother not to answer it, I heard her footsteps in the hall. The Yale lock clicked and, with frightening clarity, I heard John Pappanauer say, "Mrs Macmillan? My name is John Pappanauer. Is your daughter in by any chance?"

I started to pull my papers together, as if he, too, was going to climb the stairs and start peering at them the way my mother had just done. But before I could put them in order, she was calling up the stairs to me, and I was walking to the head of the stairs and saying, in the awkward squawk that I recognised as belonging to the girl who wrote the diary, "Mr Pappanauer! What brings you here?"

7

It was almost exactly a week since the first attack on me and the first, desperate diary entry that followed it. And I walked down the stairs with a curious calm that probably resulted from the fact that I had told absolutely no one about the first rape in the flat. As far as HE was concerned – even if HE was Pappanauer, I was playing by his rules. I had learned, you see, to give nothing away.

If you tell anyone about this I will kill you.

Silence is a weapon. I didn't know, of course, how much Pappanauer knew about what had happened on the previous evening. And I was determined not to say anything to him about the fact that, last night, Peter Taylor was convinced he had seen the face of my attacker out in the street. It was possible that Peter had told him that he had taken me to my mother's. But I didn't, for some reason, think it likely that he would have told him why he had done so. Pappanauer wasn't smiling or winking or leering – which, for Pappanauer, is most unusual. He had the sort of artificial seriousness children assume in the presence of death and, as I came down the stairs towards him, I had to stifle a sudden, irrational urge to giggle.

The girl I had been the week before hadn't liked him. Now, as he stood in the hall in his leather jacket, his hands clasped over his navel (which only increased his resemblance to a professional mourner) I found myself wondering whether I had ever really looked beyond all that laddishness that he likes to display in the office. If I was going to be able to understand which of them was telling the truth I was going to have to learn to ask and listen and suspend judgement. I think, now, that this was the moment when I started to grow up, looking down at a man I neither knew nor liked and realising that, if

I was going to understand the world and what had happened to me, I was going to have to do it by myself. It was the awful, helpless *naïveté* of my diary that had done it. Shame is the only teacher.

"I just wanted to see you," said Pappanauer, "and make sure you were all right!" I smiled at him, very sweetly.

"That's kind of you." I said.

That was obviously not the reason he was here. My Mum was staring at him. Before she started to wink or toss her head or do any of the things she does when any man under the age of sixty is in the vicinity I said, "I'm very busy with something at the moment . . ."

Mum took that as her cue to leave and Pappanauer and I stood in silence in the hall. He looked, now, even more like a little boy. Although I knew I had to get back to those papers upstairs I also knew that it was important not to waste a single moment while he was here.

"Tell me, John," I said, with great casualness, "your parents . . ." His jaw dropped. This was the last thing he had expected me to say. Once he had got over the surprise his face took on a look of intense suspicion.

"What about them?" he said.

"I don't know . . ." I let my voice trail away to nothing.

"You never mention them," I said, eventually. Pappanauer tucked his chin into his neck. He had clearly come here to say something. The last thing he expected was to be asked personal questions. Perhaps that was the only reason he started to rock from foot to foot, and, without even trying to answer me, said, "Could we talk in the front room?"

"Sure!" I said. "But you will have to wait some time. I'm in the middle of something rather important."

"As long as it takes," said Pappanauer.

I showed him into the small room that looks on to the street. Then I went back up the stairs. I was starting to feel, you see, that somewhere in the parcel that Paul had sent me there was a clue that only I could understand. I felt like a lawyer, who needs to be briefed before each conversation, and as he sat looking out at the rain I went into the small room off the landing and, once more, started to read, greedily, my own indecipherable scrawl. Immediately I had begun to read I was back with myself, seven days ago, scribbling, alone in the office, on the morning after HE first attacked me. I forgot about my mother, rattling dishes in the kitchen, about the rain on the roof and about the strangely subdued and serious figure of Pappanauer, crouched awkwardly, in the gloom, behind the net curtains, on one of our drab sofas.

TUESDAY APRIL 6TH. 12 NOON. (F)

Paul Jackson, Peter Taylor, John Pappanauer. Those are the men in my life at the moment. I don't see any others. There have been times, since Dave and I finished, when I've felt so lonely that I've seriously thought about going back to Mum's. I'm waiting for someone, you see. I see myself with him in some bar in town. I'm looking into his eyes, of course, and laughing. I have no idea what his face is like. All I know is that when people come up to our table they stop, and look, and smile and move on. All I can see are his eyes. If I try to build a face around the eyes, it always ends up with bits of Peter's face or Paul's face or even (God help us!) John's face.

I couldn't see *his* eyes. I don't think I could have borne that. I lay on my bed for nearly an hour afterwards. I didn't put on my clothes. I just lay there. When I did get up – to have a bath – I moved very quietly. I didn't want anyone to hear me, you see. I didn't want to see anyone. The thing I was most afraid of was that somebody – Mum or maybe Dave or someone from the office – would walk through that door and expect me to behave normally. When I went to bed I fell asleep almost immediately. The funny thing was I wasn't scared at all. I knew he would not come back. I'd known from the first moments after he ran out of the flat that I wouldn't call the police.

So here I am in the office, that safest of safe places. It's as cool and grey and neutral as I could wish. Pappanauer has gone out to see a client. Peter has been in a meeting upstairs with Mr Forrester. And Paul is sitting at his . . . Oh no. He's getting up. *Embarrassing.* He's coming in this direction. Not exactly in this direction. He's trying to look as if he's just pacing around the place but he quite clearly wants to speak to me. Perhaps I should stop writing. I don't want anyone to read this.

He's got a rather solemn expression on his face. Have I done something wrong? In order to stop him coming closer – because, for a reason I can't quite explain, I very much don't want him to come any closer – I am writing faster and faster but even the thought that I might be absorbed in my work doesn't look as if it is going to stop him. He has stopped by Pappanauer's desk and is pretending to look at some papers. He isn't really looking at them. He's looking at me. He has turned away from Pappanauer's desk and he is walking across the blue carpet. He is getting closer and closer and closer. And now he is going to speak to me and, though I still don't know why I should feel like this, I am very frightened about what he might say. I don't want him to speak but I am afraid he will speak and that, when he does, I will have to answer.

3.30. P.M.

Hey guys! Surprise surprise!

He asked me to lunch! Hey! Things are looking up!

This has never happened in the recorded history of the office. It is not *supposed* to happen, if you know what I mean. Usually Peter wanders off to some posh restaurant. John trots off to the canteen, while trying to give the impression he is actually *en route* for some fashionable eating place. Paul disappears out of the main gate – probably to do yoga in some nearby park. Miss Macmillan goes to the tea bar and buys a soggy sandwich and a cup of tea, which she eats at her workstation.

But today, *today* I went to the pizza place with Paul.

It's a big, airy restaurant and there's a view out across the shopping mall. We were at a table on an upper level. When I sat down, Paul pulled out my chair for me – something I've only previously seen men do in black and white films – and, leaning his elbows on the table, asked me if I would have a glass of wine. I said I would. I could feel myself getting really flushed as I said this. It felt as if I was doing something shocking. Then Paul got out the menu and studied it really carefully – the way he studies his columns of figures when he's in the office. It was as if, having got me there, he had suddenly run out of steam. As if the only point of the exercise was to find out whether he dared ask me. He didn't speak at all. "It's a lovely place!" I said. I could hear my voice, sounding about two octaves too low. Sometimes when I was listening to Mum have a go at Dad I knew where I had got it from. Most of the time I don't worry about it, but sitting opposite Paul I was acutely aware of everything about myself. My hands seemed even bigger than usual and were never in the right place. If I put them in my lap, every time I dropped my eyes they looked fishily up at me as if to say "What are you going to do with us now, Fiona?" And when I tried steepling them up beneath my chin I felt as if I was a woman from an agency interviewing him for a job.

My hair wasn't much help either. It bounces around shaggily, like a dog's. Its only usefulness is that sometimes it falls so far forward that it temporarily obscures my nose. The nose is *bad*, guys. I caught sight of it in the mirror behind the bar and thought, not for the first time, how amazingly like Richard the Third I look. I've sometimes thought I should just go with the concept and rush out and buy a suit of armour and a horse.

I couldn't think of any way of breaking the silence. It just seemed to go on and on and on. So I looked at my menu, chose the cheapest thing I could find and waited for him to say something. But he didn't. I started to count under my breath. I was almost up to three hundred by the time the waiter arrived.

After we'd ordered, Paul set about trying to look at me. First, he rearranged the cutlery on the table in front of him. Then he fiddled with his fingers. Then he looked over his shoulder. Then he started to look over my shoulder. Then, as far as I could make out, he started to look *at* my shoulder. Then he allowed his eyes to travel slowly across to my neck. I was wearing a rather low-cut dress so I was rather intrigued as to which direction his eyes would take next. They did a lightning dip towards my tits and then, in panic, bolted upwards to my throat. They seemed to come to rest horribly close to the bruise under my scarf. After that, there was a pause, and after the pause a mad dash past my chin, an inevitable, but mercifully brief encounter with my nose and he was looking into my eyes. I'd been looking straight at him all the time. I can't stop looking at people. It used to drive Dave mad.

"There's something I want to tell you." He said this in a way that made it sound really important and serious. As if he was going to tell me he loved me or something. I didn't know quite how to react. So, like a stupid little girl, I laughed. I've noticed that quite a lot of girls laugh all the time. Not because we're amused. Because we're afraid.

"Oh," I said, when I'd stopped laughing, "what is it?" He kept his eyes on my face.

"It's very, very important." he said.

At that moment, the waiter came up, carrying one of those huge, wooden pepper mills. He waved it at us menacingly. "You like some black peppair?" We pointed out to him that we hadn't got anything to put it on. A look of panic came over him as he saw our empty table and he said he was vair vair sorry. Then another man in a red shirt arrived and offered us more wine and Paul and I started talking about completely different things.

I was trying to find out where he was born and what his parents did – which is always the first thing I ask people. But he didn't seem to want to talk about any of that. First of all he told me about economics, which I have never understood at all, and then he talked for a long time about cash flow, which I thought I understood until he started talking about it. I asked intelligent questions. I nodded and smiled and when they brought my salad I tried to fork it into my mouth without looking too much like a shark. After he'd talked about cash flow he started talking about the Newsom Project. I perked up a bit then. I've always been partial to a bit of crime. He seemed to think it was fairly certain that somebody had been up to a most *enormous* fiddle but he also seemed to think it was very unlikely that anyone would ever find out who it was. He just kept saying, "It's adrift. That's all we know. It is very seriously adrift." I was adrift myself. I was waiting for him to come back to the very serious and important thing he had been going to tell me. But he didn't.

Although he was a bit boring, I was starting to like him. I liked the way that, once his eyes had decided to meet mine, they didn't seem to want to let go. He hung on my every look, the way a dog does when it wants food. That's the sort of thing that usually irritates me. It didn't with him. He did something most men aren't very good at. He listened. And, as I talked, I found that I wasn't shy, bolshie Fiona. I was telling stories about the pompous woman in the organiser's office. Once or twice I managed to make him laugh. When he opened his small, regular mouth I could see all of his *efficient*-looking teeth.

It's funny how some men can make you feel at ease. It's nothing to do with whether they are good or bad people. It certainly has nothing to do with whether they are interested in *you*. It is a process as mysterious to me as my father's absences or returns. It is something I crave more than anything else in the world but not something I can engineer. I sit waiting for it like some religious fanatic awaiting the arrival of the Messiah.

It all went *really* well. Before I knew where I was it was after two and I was drinking black coffee and a sticky liqueur that he insisted on buying. There weren't any more silences – just me rattling on about my Mum and Dad and how I didn't want to be a secretary all the days of my life. And he'd got the bill and he was drinking *his* coffee and saying the only thing he said about himself the whole lunchtime.

"Sometimes, " he said, "I get really lonely. And I really want . . . you know . . ." He let this sentence hang in the air. He looked, suddenly, like he had at the beginning of the meal.

"Someone else?" I said. He didn't answer. "Have you . . . I mean . . ." I went on, "Are you sort of . . .?" I was fishing. He didn't like that. His mouth snapped shut and his face got a kind of closed look. For a moment I felt the way I had when he came up to me in the office that time. There was something about his expression that I didn't quite like.

"People judge people," he said, "but they don't understand. You might find out things about me that really put you off. But that might not be the *real* me. Do you understand?" He looked straight at me as he said this.

My God, where have all the normal males gone? Whatever happened to the decent men – beaming away in their corners, puffing their pipes and doing their roses? Is every last one of them a pervert now? With that thought an image of the attack in the flat the night before came back to me and for a moment I felt as if I couldn't breathe. I felt shame too – as if I had done something wicked and wrong and as if it was showing in my face. I bit my lower lip, hard and stared at the table in front of me. Only when I was absolutely sure I was in control did I raise my eyes to Paul's face.

"What were you trying to tell me earlier that was so serious?" I said.

He started to blink, very rapidly. Then he looked away. Whatever it was he was not going to tell me. Not now anyway. The lunch, that had started so slowly and then gone so well, was now awkward and uncomfortable again. We got up and went out into the mall. It was still raining. The flats that rise above the shops like prison guards almost disappeared into the grey day that was now half-mist half-water, a mood that made me long again for promised spring. When we got to the main gate and were struggling for our identity cards, once again his eyes met mine.

"I'm very sorry," he said, "I didn't mean to say what I just said. I'm very sorry. I'm not good with people." He looked up at our building. He strained his eyes as if he might see our desks and papers, six floors up. "You see . . ." he went on, "You see . . ."

"What were you trying to tell me?" I said.

"I was brought up in an orphanage . . ." Paul began. But that was all he said. The two of us went into the building and we didn't talk at all after that.

I'm writing this on my own in the office. All three of them have gone out to a meeting somewhere. I think it's the same meeting. But it might be different meetings. But, whether they are together or miles apart, you can bet that they will be sitting in the same kind of windowless room, nodding in the same way to men who have the same kind of cuffs and jackets and opinions. I'm writing because the day is getting darker outside and I can't help thinking about how I will have to go back to the flat. I don't want to go back to the flat. But I have nowhere else to go.

When we got back to our desks John Pappanauer started to be

rather offensive. I don't usually mind his jokes but this time they got on my nerves. As I sat down I noticed he was actually *winking* at me. I ask you. I sat over my computer and ignored him for a while, but, when I looked again, he was still winking away, like a Belisha beacon.

"Yes?" I said.

"Good lunch?" said Pappanauer.

"Very nice . . ." I said. Paul was deep into his figures.

"I once took a Mrs to a pizza place. I was giving her one as a matter of fact and very nice it was too . . ."

"I'm sure," I said acidly, "that the other diners enjoyed it!"

"But you know something," John went on, completely unabashed, "when she started cramming this pizza into her face I suddenly felt really revolted. Just like that. And packed it in the next day."

Normally this sort of stuff doesn't bother me too much. But, although I had managed to put it out of my mind nearly the whole time I was with Paul, something about Pappanauer's smooth face and slicked-down hair, made me think of *that*. I felt suddenly, violently sick. He wasn't just the office joker. He was somebody who might quite easily have done *that*. I found myself using a voice I don't think I've ever used in the office before. It was my voice, suddenly – sharp, unafraid of its intelligence.

"What is the matter with you, John?" I said, "Did some girl say she'd had enough of your horrible manners?"

His face changed colour. It went all dark red. For a minute I was quite frightened. I thought he was going to walk across the office and slap me across the face. Then the look went away. He laughed. But it wasn't his usual laugh. It sounded false.

"All I was wondering," went on John, in an ingratiating voice, "was whether you and the Professor were an Item!"

That's the sort of thing he is always saying – like "tough *hombre*" – it always sends me reaching for the sick bag. And he always calls Paul the Professor. I suppose because Paul is cleverer than he is and he resents it.

I was waiting for Paul to say something but he didn't. He flushed a bit but he didn't speak. At first I was annoyed with him. Then, when I looked at him, hunched miserably over his computer, I felt suddenly sorry for him. People like Pappanauer had probably been teasing him all his life. I tried to imagine what an orphanage must be like. It made me think of some building with high walls and no windows. I could see a long drive and, at the old-fashioned front door, a stern woman in a black dress, with a heavy bunch of keys at her waist.

"Well," I said, "being an Item with Paul would be a lot more fun than being an Item with you!"

Paul looked up then. A quick glance that he did not intend me to see. There was something about the way he did it that scared me. But not half as much as something I have only just seen over by the door. Something that stops my breath and freezes my hand over the pen. I can't believe that what I have seen is what I think it is and . . .

And now they've all come in. Through the door. All three of them. They've just come back, talking loudly and laughing and I can't compose my face because of what I have seen over by the door but I must compose it because if it *is* what I think it is then I must learn to keep my face absolutely still and not let anyone know what I am thinking or that my heart is knocking at my ribs like a hangman at a prison door. And I must stop writing. No one must see this. I must stop writing.

I'm so scared.

•

As I read these words I heard a cough behind me. When I looked up John Pappanauer was standing at the door. I had, I realised, completely forgotten that he was in the house. He looked different.

"Look," he said, "if you don't want to see me that's fine. But don't leave me here to die I beg of you."

I looked between him and the pages of my diary. I was simply unable to respond. My eyes went down to the page again. There was a gap after that terrifying moment in the office. I had started writing it again at eleven on the night after I was first attacked. I looked from my handwriting to Pappanauer's face. He still looked uncomfortably serious. I found I was concentrating on his Adam's apple. He had shaved this morning – he's one of those men who has to shave his neck as well as his face – and all the colours of his skin seemed to be milk white or blood red.

"I wanted to talk to you," he said, "about Paul."

I looked back, almost furtively, at my diary. "I'm sorry, John," I said, "I'll come down. I'll come down now."

He didn't make any move. In the end I picked up the papers – for some reason I didn't want to leave them where anyone else might see them – and followed him down the narrow stairs.

8

"Well then," I said, taking up a seat on the other side of the room, "what was it you wanted to say about Paul?"

Pappanauer started to twine his fingers into each other. He gave an oddly formal little cough. Then he said, "Actually I really like Paul!"

"But . . ." I said.

"But nothing," said Pappanauer, "may the best man win. I mean . . . you know I always fancied you!"

Men have such strange ways of showing they like you. Leering at you, making blue jokes, not listening to anything you say. It had simply never occurred to me that Pappanauer might approve of me in any way at all. The news made me more, not less, frightened of him. I found I was sitting up very straight and listening for the noise of my mother in the kitchen. But Pappanauer, staring at the carpet, was quite unaware of me. He looked, suddenly, listless. "But," he went on, "and there is a but . . . there are things you should know about him."

I chose the words of my next sentence very carefully. "Peter Taylor," I said, "is convinced that Paul is the man who attacked me."

Pappanauer nodded. This was obviously not news to him. "Peter Taylor," he said, " is a devious bastard . ."

"Unlike you!" I said brightly.

Pappanauer did some more finger twining. When he spoke again it reminded me how difficult he was to place, how his voice shifted between received and officially unwelcome pronunciation. But then, we are all becoming more difficult to place.

"In actual fact," he said, "I'm quite a lonely person."

"I'm not really surprised!" I said.

Pappanauer got up and went to the window. He looked out at the rainy street and, for a long time, didn't say anything. I let my eyes travel down to my diary and found myself reading the passage I had written when I had got home to the flat on the evening of that first day after HE attacked me.

TUESDAY APRIL 6TH. 11 P.M. (F)

I don't know how to start writing this. I watch my letters form like a kid watching raindrops cannon into each other on the windowpane. They don't seem to belong to me at all. I have double locked the door and I have taken a kitchen knife out of the cupboard. If he comes again I'll be ready for him. I'd like to push this knife in between his ribs and watch his stupid expression – like a stuck pig. And, you see, I think maybe he will come. I think he was looking for me. I don't think it was an accident.

All three of the men in my office have exactly the same briefcases. I used to joke about it. But it isn't a laughing matter any more.

I couldn't write it down as I saw it. I didn't dare. But, as they came back from their meeting this afternoon, and as Peter went straight to his telephone and started talking about "serious implications" I looked over towards the double doors to where their briefcases are always stacked, like shoes outside a hotel bedroom. What I saw, protruding out of the corner of one of them, was a fragment of yellow rubber material. I knew it at once – the tip of a finger of a pair of kitchen gloves. I assumed, at first, that whoever had closed the briefcase simply hadn't noticed that it was sticking out, although, even from where I was sitting, it was clearly visible. I couldn't see how they could have missed it. I couldn't see, either, why someone else in the office hadn't noticed it and commented on it. Maybe it was just because of what it was. Maybe it seemed horribly public to me because of that.

I knew what it was with the same kind of certainty that I knew my Dad was going to die the last time he came to the flat – his skin as white as paper and his voice shaking as he tried to get me to stay with Dave.

"Got to have some continuity, girly! I never managed to stick at anything! Try and stick at it, girly!"

I looked around the office, carefully. Peter was still on the phone. Pappanauer was staring out at the rain. Paul was busy with his computer. There was absolutely no way of telling, from the way the briefcases were arranged, which case belonged to which accountant. And the briefcase containing the gloves — there was still no doubt in my mind that that is what it was — was in the middle of the other two. I just couldn't bear to be there. In the same room as *that*. In the same room as HIM.

•

I looked up from my diary. Pappanauer was still there, standing looking out at the street. If I didn't speak, it occurred to me, he would just go on standing there, in silence.

"I'm just sitting here reading. Isn't that boring for you?"

Pappanauer looked back at me.

"I'm fine," he said, "Take as long as you need."

I got up. I walked towards the double doors. I didn't look at any of them. I didn't dare look at the briefcases. I didn't want him to know that I had seen the fragment of the gloves. I didn't want him to suspect for a moment that I knew he was in the room with me. And, most of all, I didn't want him to see that I was frightened.

I was frightened. I was very, very frightened.

I suppose, now I think about it, it is possible that he meant me to see it. That he was playing a game with me. That he was watching me, closely, all the time. That thought, even now, with the door locked and a wicked knife close to hand, makes me frightened again. I can see myself go to the double doors. I push them open really casually, as if I was going to the loo or something. I can sense his eyes on me, now, watching me.

I couldn't see his eyes through the mask. I don't know what colour they were. All I could see was . . .

I am not, repeat not, going to describe *that*.

Once I was in the corridor I ran. I ran away from the lifts until I got to the passageway that leads from our building into the Contracts Block. It's a weird place. The offices are all small and old-fashioned, often with just one desk in them, and the whitewood furniture has dated in the way of modern things. Sometimes there is a crusty old member of the Contract Department actually sitting on the furniture. They never seem to be working. They are always staring at the wall as if they were trying to remember what they were doing the night President Kennedy died. Once I saw a very, very old woman holding up an old-fashioned telephone and giving it the sort of suspicious look people usually reserve for new inventions.

I find it spooky sometimes. Today it felt like the only safe place on the planet. I went right to the end of the corridor and looked down the stairwell to the side lobby of our building. Hundreds of feet below were two men in suits, talking about somebody called Derek Slater. Their voices, amplified as in a whispering gallery, drifted up to me, quiet but distinct. "Derek Slater," one of them was saying in a braying voice, "Derek Slater said he liked it!"

Derek Slater's opinion was obviously important. But the other suit had an expert of his own. He came back with, "Julie *Waite* felt . . ." even from six floors up I could see that this suit had a bald head, "Julie *Waite* felt that there were problems . . ."

I stood there, leaning against the blue steel rail that snakes down the innumerable steps and wondered why people use other people's names to impress each other and why they don't say what they think or feel about anything, and what we all think we're *doing* in these gigantic offices, shifting bits of paper about and pretending to be grown up when inside we're all almost as frightened as I was then. I thought, too, about why it was that I hadn't told anyone about *that* and whether I was ever going to tell anyone. Then the two men went away.

Suddenly I didn't feel afraid any more. One of them might

be . . . HIM but that didn't mean the other two wouldn't be prepared to . . . Prepared to do what? How would I tell them, now? I tried to picture myself walking back in there, picking up the briefcase in the middle and then holding it up to the three of them. "Which of you owns this?" I'd say. One of them would have to answer. I would make him get out the gloves and hold them up and I'd say "What is *this*?" And I would tell them all that had happened to me and . . .

Would they believe me? I didn't care if they believed me. I simply knew that I had to go back in there and face out my fear. I had to find out whose briefcase it was. I turned back and marched towards the Building Department, swinging my arms. I could hear my Dad's voice, slightly slurred after a few drinks, as his pale eyes met mine and raised his glass to toast his own return from some long, mysterious trip.

"Watch out for Fiona Macmillan! She is a *killer!*"

I held the image of my Dad up before me. I tried to think of myself being as courageously careless as he had always been, as I strode back to the office to . . .

To what? It couldn't be Peter, Paul or John. It just couldn't. I was seeing things. That was all I was doing. I had had a terrible experience. I hadn't told anyone. I was in shock. I looked up at a clock on the wall and saw it was going home time. You're tired, Fiona, that's all. It was then I realised that if I didn't get back to the office I would never know whether I really had seen that strip of yellow rubber. They were going to some meeting at half-past five – I had heard one of them mention it earlier. It was almost exactly half-past five. I started to run.

I know I look stupid running. I don't usually do it. I keep my elbows into my sides and, while trying to look ladylike, usually only succeed in resembling a duck. My head sort of wobbles about too, and always feels as if it is about to fall off at any moment. But I ran hard. As the floor beneath my feet changed from grey carpet (Contracts) to polished wood (No Man's Land) to blue lino tiles (Accounts and Building Auditing i.e. us) I felt as if I was moving through a forest and that the walls, the ceilings and the floor were changing the way vegetation changes. As I got closer and closer to the office it seemed as if I was leaving the edge of the forest and climbing, so that soon I would be able to stop and look down on my life. I now had the very strong conviction that I hadn't seen anything – that, in a minute, everything about what had happened last night would become clear.

But when I rounded the corner just before our office I saw the three Apostles were already almost at the lifts. Each was carrying his briefcase. It was impossible, at this distance, to tell which, if any of them was carrying the one with a corner of yellow rubber poking out of the lid. I was going to call something but I couldn't think of the words. Then the mouth of the lift had opened and they were gone. I didn't stop running. I ran to the lift and jabbed at the button but it was too late. Peter, Paul and John had gone out into the rainy April evening and I was alone in the huge building. Further along the corridor came the echoes of strangers' conversations. Another lift rose to the doors. It opened its awkward steel on emptiness. I walked away back towards my coat and scarf.

•

I looked up from the page as I realised that Pappanauer was speaking to me. He might well have been talking for some time. He still had his back to me. I found it almost impossible to concentrate on what he was saying. I heard his words all right. I saw sentences, paragraphs, inverted commas – just as if I was looking at a page of print, but I was unable to shape them into any kind of meaning.

". . . he must have had it for ages and when I saw it there were some pretty strange, you know, well . . ."

Who had had what for ages? And what was strange?

". . . and if Peter Taylor says that, well, I know he's a bit you know what but he's a serious person and although I'm a bit of a . . . well you know . . ."

People don't really talk to each other at all. They don't think of something to say, choose the words to express it and then carefully pronounce those words. They use language to disguise meaning as much as to convey it. But other things tell us what they have in mind – and sometimes we have no idea of what they are. I heard myself say, although I could not have said quite how I had acquired this information, "You're saying Paul has a kind of . . . secret hideout? Is that what you're saying?"

My voice must have expressed anger or disbelief because, when at last he turned from the window, Pappanauer had assumed his serious undertaker's face again.

"I'm saying he has a room he uses. And I'm saying he might be there. Now. And that if he isn't there . . ."

"What?"

"We might find something that . . . you know . . . tells us what . . . you know . . . he . . ."

They were all telling me it was Paul. The idea that he had some secret room made him sound horribly like the author of A:/AIR. It was possible that Pappanauer was lying to me. That he wanted me to come with him somewhere where he would become HE, where that newly shaved, executive's face would suddenly develop a snarl and the eyes flicker into life like a wolf's and HIS hands would reach for me because, for some reason only HE knows I was no longer playing to HIS rules so it was time to take me by the neck and shake me until I was as lifeless as a broken doll. I looked down at the pages of my diary and thought, again, about the girl I had been last week.

I am alone now, in my flat. It is dark. There is the noise of traffic from the main road. Somewhere, two or three doors down, someone has started to play reggae, very loudly. It pushes against the wood and brickwork of these apartments, pulsing into me as I sit at this rented table, writing on and on into the night.

I don't know, you see. I only suspect I know. But now, with the dark and the rain outside, my suspicion has become worse than certain knowledge. It is a doubt that is also a demonstration. It's a fear that is also a hope. It resolves itself into a single, short sentence, like something you might read on the front cover of the paperback thriller that still lies, face down, on my shabby sofa.

There are three men in my office and one of them is trying to kill me.

•

Then I looked up at Pappanauer. "We'd better go there!" I said, in a voice that surprised me by its steadiness, "I just need to change." I picked up my papers and went to the door. Pappanauer was, once more, talking about Paul. He seemed to be trying to tell me how much he liked him. I didn't listen to him. As I climbed back up the stairs I started to flick through what Peter Taylor had written. If I assumed that Paul was innocent – and, for the moment I was going to have to assume that – then the man most concerned to denounce him was probably the most likely to be guilty. I spread the papers out on the bed as I changed into jeans and white polo-necked sweater. As far as I could make out Peter had been keeping a diary too, and the pages I had been sent seemed to start the day after my diary began. Strange? Or not?

Confidential

Notes on the Investigation into the Newsom
Project.
Wednesday April 7th. 9 p.m. (PT)

I think it is time I started to record my progress on tracking the money. Not only to clarify things for myself, but also to make sure that, if anything should happen to me, there is some record of my investigations so far. I haven't communicated them to anyone for the very good reason that there isn't really anyone I can trust with this information. Until I have proof of my suspicions, revealing them to anyone will not only put me at risk but also frighten Jimmy into covering his tracks. I call him Jimmy. Well. I have to call him something. I could just write HIM I suppose but there's something a little too sinister about that. And I have, already, the sneaking feeling that Jimmy might just be a little bit more than someone with his hand in the till. I don't know why I should feel that – but I do.

It's strange to be taking time off away from the family, to do something I haven't done since university – addressing the blank page.

I feel curiously self-conscious about it. I find myself with the urge to come on like the narrator of a Victorian novel and to start by characterising myself. *My name is Peter Taylor and I am the head of the Building Audit Unit of a large British-based company. I have two children and I live in the suburbs of London . . .*

But of course I am going to do nothing of the kind. Like any executive in early middle age I am going to start by sounding off about the car park. Why are there three grades of car park in the company? Senior Management are red. Middle Management are blue. If, like me, you are a company man who has been there a little too long (nearly twenty years) you get to go in the green car park – which is a kind of muddy patch of waste ground about three hundred yards from the main buildings. I took Epstein, one of the project directors, back to my car the other day (I think his chauffeur was sick) and he went white when he saw the distance I had to walk.

"You mean," he said, in a low voice as we trudged over the broken tarmac, "that people actually *park* here?"

"Some people," I said, "go by bus."

I pass them every day as I go into work. Young and old, they stand, craning their necks at the empty road ahead, with worn or hopeful faces, and whenever I pass them, I think to myself – they're waiting for more than just a *bus*. They're waiting for life to start while people like me drive past in big, expensive cars. I suppose this country was built on greed. Greed built the towns and the cathedrals and the roads. Greed built the art galleries and got the art painted and sent ships out to every corner of the globe to bring back gold and crops and slaves to these shores. And greed shouldered aside the ones who wait in the bus queues.

It was greed that led to the business I'm investigating. The business of the conference centre. It was greed that siphoned off millions out of the company and into the pockets of the people on the project. It was greed that, I think, led some of those people to pay themselves handsomely for work that hasn't actually been done. I know, of course, that I will probably not be thanked by the company for uncovering whoever is responsible. When I've found out who it is I will have to actually tell them how much has gone missing and – in this company – it's common practice to shoot the messenger.

The costs for the conference centre started to go through the roof about six months ago. At first, there seemed to be a very good explanation for the inaccuracy of the estimates. The material they were using on the whole of the west side of the building – a kind of toughened glass – turned out not to be suitable. A number of load-bearing walls had to be re-sited. And, at the last minute, all the quotes from one of our suppliers were found to be almost complete fantasy. But even so, I found it very hard to believe the figures. Someone is up to something. It's simply a question of finding out what it is. Anyway – I wasn't going to go back over stuff. I was going to start by putting down what happened today as clearly and simply as possible. I don't want to draw conclusions until I have evidence.

I always drive in by the same route across the river and through the park, to company headquarters. I try not to think about my work until the moment when I actually start doing it. I was an English student, not a mathematician or an economist and, to me, tracking figures and grasping the patterns of expenditure is a human science. As I follow the trail of the money on the Newsom Project it seems more and more to me like a map or like a picture that emerges from apparently random patterns in sand or water blown about by the wind. You see, the suppliers . . .

Don't jump the gun, Peter. Stick to the facts, as father would have said. My father was the headmaster of a small public school in the country. He was a devoutly religious man. One of my earliest memories is of going with him to the school chapel and creaking uneasily to my knees while he flung himself forward on to the pew in front, crossing himself and murmuring curious snatches of prayer. After a few years of it I found a certain comfort in the ritual. I never thought I believed any of it. Even when I told him I had "lost my faith" at the age of sixteen I thought I was expressing nothing more than embarrassment at having to kneel next to him week after week. But what happened in that chapel left me with more than a habit of bowing and mumbling certain Latin words. I have always, to this very day, had a vague dread of something following me, tempting me, that I can only describe by the word my father would have used – wickedness.

People at work don't see that side of me. Which is why, when I saw Fiona this morning, shambling down the road that leads from the railway station to our building, I was almost tempted to drive past her. She didn't belong with the thoughts that occupy me on these occasions. But the sight of her – white-faced, robed like a nun in her long brown coat, with her lank hair muffled under a scarf, reminded me of one of those curious, grandiloquent sentences of which my father was so fond. "Take pity on the lonely traveller, boy! For the way should be equal to all of us poor mortals!"

Poor mortals was a favourite phrase of his. Things that sounded as if they had come out of a dimly remembered sermon. I always suspected that they might be off-cuts from the enormous novel he was supposed to be writing. "We are born like seeds on the wind, boy! And our pleasures are as vain as the brief day!" That was a favourite one. When I was very small I was sure these were all probably quotations from some great poet. Until I asked him, one day, as he swept across the quadrangle, his gown billowing out behind him, whether what he had just said was by William Wordsworth. He rounded on me. "My scraps of Wisdom are my Own, dear boy! Since your Mother's Death my Solace has been Thought!" He had the kind of grand manner that can only be evolved after years of performing for undiscerning schoolboys.

I was thinking of my father as I slowed the car, wound down the window and said, "You look half-dead, Fiona!" She jumped when she saw me. Literally. At the time I thought I had surprised her in some daydream. Why did she do that?

"It's all right, Peter," she said. I grinned. She's very like my wife when she's like that. She is determined not to accept favours from anyone. Although she is reserved to the point of secretiveness, there is clearly an intelligence at work, even though she is determined not to let any of us be too aware of the fact.

"Look," I said, "I'll only take you to the main gate. And then I'll flog out to the green car park . . ."

She couldn't resist the thought of the boss suffering. It amused her. But, although she laughed I caught that shadow in her face again. As if she was frightened of something.

•

I wasn't reading Peter Taylor's journal with the same greedy desperation that had been provoked in me by A:/AIR or by Paul's letter. I block read it, in paragraphs, not really taking in its style. Although in one sense, I suppose, I responded to it as if to its author – I was looking, quite coldly and dispassionately, for information.

He was talking about the Wednesday, the day after Paul and I went to lunch. I couldn't remember feeling the way he'd described me here. I recalled, quite vividly, the sound of his engine slowing behind me, but for some reason it didn't disturb me in any way. I was thinking, you see, about Paul.

I looked back through the pages Peter had written. He sounded, as he seems, so dammed reasonable. Almost as if this document had been written for someone else's benefit.

Listening out for Pappanauer downstairs, I flicked on through the pages, wondering why, as I did so, that a document apparently dedicated to describing some financial scandal, should spend so much time on little old me.

I opened the door. She got into the car, drawing her pretty legs over to her side and, as we moved off, seemed to relax. We hadn't gone more than a few yards when she said, "Peter – I hope this isn't awkward. But I just need to take a couple of days off. Maybe go this afternoon or tomorrow and get away somewhere . . ."

She's never ever asked for anything like that. As long as I've known her. Something in the office wasn't right. I think that was the moment when I first had the idea that Jimmy might be up to even more than I suspected. And I think that was the moment when I started seriously to consider the idea that Jimmy might be John Pappanauer.

"Well," I said, "it's quite busy at the moment. But . . ."

"Please," she said, "please!" She said this so piteously that, suddenly, I saw her as a child, a fatherless child.

Actually my first thought was that she had been through some crisis at home that she was unable to talk about. As I think I said, she hardly ever talks about her private life, although I did once see her sitting in Reception with a gangly youth she introduced, with some embarrassment, as Dave. I didn't, however, have a way of moving the conversation on to those things. We don't talk to each other like that in our office – and I suppose that is my fault.

"Are you sure you're OK?" I said, as I dropped her by the main gate. An Indian commissionaire was standing, staring straight ahead of him at the already darkening day. He looked, I thought, almost entirely decorative.

"I'm fine," she said, in that funny, low, cracked voice of hers. I drove off towards the green car park.

I was pretty sure that if there was anyone causing her difficulties at work, it was liable to be John Pappanauer. And, by the time I had got back to the main gate I had almost worked myself up to having an argument with the man. Even though I knew that I would not do so. I should never have hired him, of course.

Everything about Pappanauer's interview was, now I come to think of it, a masterly piece of deception. Particularly the suit. I don't think I ever saw him wear the suit again. It was a solid, tweedy affair. He had bought some smart brown shoes to go with it. And a curriculum vitae that, I suspect, was chosen to go with the shoes rather than for any relation it might have had to reality. But, just as people don't bother to authenticate your guilt or innocence these days, so they seem to display an alarming lack of interest in the authenticity of your qualifications. Maybe we are living through the Age of Credulity. I believed in the degree from a business studies course. I didn't bother to check it. Neither did I bother to check whether he really did come from a small town in Wales or was raised by his uncle. I do remember him saying he was rather shy but I am now almost positive that he had acquired the stammer for the purposes of the interview.

Certainly the person to whom I had given the job bore no relation to the shambling slob who turned up to do it. He seemed, as far as I can recall, to have had a hair transplant and what looked like the reverse of a nose-job. And, from day one, he seemed to be a fountain of off-colour stories, crude sexual innuendo and the kind of rudeness that stops just short of the punishable. His accent had changed as radically as his appearance. "Mornin' all!" is his usual opening line. I

119

think he had only been with us two days when he came out with, "Don't look such a miserable bastard, Petey, willyer?"

He was, also – this was the unforgivable thing – very good at his job and positively servile to the people immediately above me. As time has gone on he has been more and more careful to let me know he lied his way into the company.

As I went up in the lift towards our floor I decided that, not only had he been bothering Fiona but, if any of us in the office was auditioning for the role of Jimmy – and it has to be someone in our office – it was almost certain to be John Pappanauer.

•

There was a cough out on the landing. When I looked up from Peter Taylor's journal I saw Pappanauer standing there. He tried a smile. I noticed, not for the first time, how oddly prissy his mouth looked. He speaks from way back in his throat, too. If he were trying to disguise his voice, I thought, how would it sound? Are those weird shifts in accent something more than someone trying to conceal their origins?

"Look, I can wait all day," he said, "But what is it you're reading?" I didn't answer him. I was too absorbed in trying to make sense of what I had been reading. The financial scandal that Paul had talked about when we had lunch the day after the first attack must, I realised, have been more serious than I had thought. Money going missing. I had never really paid much attention to what Peter Taylor always calls "high corporate politics". One of the things I like about having a rather lowly job is that you can be invisible. You are not required to have opinions about things. But the money business was disturbing. If it was true that someone in the office had their hand in the till, it was also possible that that person was the one who had attacked me. Or was it? It would make my attacker a very peculiar kind of mental case. People who commit fraud are driven by rational emotions. Greed, after all, is something now almost entirely approved of by society. And yet, the thought that the financial criminal and the man who had attacked me might be the same person, in a strange way, made some kind of sense of a tone I had caught in that horrible document.

"Give me a minute," I said, "Wait downstairs!"

He nodded and then clattered off, dutifully, down to the hall. I picked up the computer disk and the rest of the papers and slipped them into a plastic carrier bag next to the bed. Then, with almost guilty swiftness, I picked up the black-handled claw hammer that was on the floor by the window – I think my mother had been using it to hang pictures – and, on top of it I put my night-dress, the one I had been wearing last week. The one that still carried the stains from the first attack – the one that I had not, yet, spoken of to anyone. Then, squaring my shoulders, swinging the bag slightly, aware of the weight of the hammer inside it, I went out on to the landing.

Why was I going out, alone, with the man who might well be the one who – if I was right about him – was only waiting for the right time to kill me? Was it because I wanted him to try? Because, this time, I was determined to deal with him myself? Would that explain why I didn't even tell my mother where I was going? Well, you could say I went with Pappanauer because he was going to lead me to a secret place Paul used. You could also say I went with Pappanauer because I needed to see and confront the man everyone seemed to think was the one who raped me. You could say I went with Pappanauer because I was, in spite of everything, still hopelessly, desperately in love with Paul, and even if his were the eyes that had watched me from behind that hideous yellow mask, his was the face I needed to see more than any other in the world. But these are all rational reasons for an irrational act.

I didn't care how dangerous it might be. I went with him because, only then, nearly half-way through a rainy day, seven days after I was first attacked, was I starting to be moved by the emotion that drove me through the rest of that long afternoon. Now, recalled at a distance, it still makes me stop and draw my breath as I see how much it has transformed the landscape of my life. It is with me still as I write these lines and see another of my old selves follow Pappanauer out into the street.

I was, at long last, starting to be angry.

9

My Mum didn't ask why I had decided suddenly to go out. She didn't even mention the fact that I was supposed to be ill. I think she had decided that this was something to do with my emotional life and that one or other or both of these men who had suddenly showed up at her house were probably having an affair with me. My Mum's life is almost entirely dominated by an unquenchable urge to marry off her daughter.

Pappanauer had brought his bright red company car. He didn't have an umbrella but he steered me towards it, through the unending rain, as if placing his hand in the small of my back (something I hate men doing) was going to keep me dry. I found Pappanauer the Chivalrous almost more disconcerting than Pappanauer the Yob. If he was able to slip into both roles so easily, it suggested a chameleon-like character. Wasn't that how the author of A:/AIR must be? Someone who took pleasure in disappearing into roles, like an actor?

When we got to the car he was going to show me into the front seat. I told him I would prefer to sit in the back. As he opened the door for me I tightened my grip on the bag I was carrying. When I got into the seat I moved over to the driver's side, so that I was sitting immediately behind him. If Pappanauer realised what the implications of all these manoeuvres were, he didn't show it. In fact, he didn't say anything at all. I was glad of that.

"Where is this place?" I said, as we pulled away from the kerb.

"It's in South London," said Pappanauer. He didn't tell me any more than that. I didn't ask any more questions. As we drove out towards the main road, where cars and lorries queued in the enclosing rain, I fished into my bag and took out Peter Taylor's journal.

No one else, apart from him and the author of A:/AIR had ever clearly stated that the missing money on the Newsom Project was, in part anyway, due to corruption as well as inefficiency. I suppose the two are often closely related. I wasn't sure, yet, what all this meant as far as I was concerned. I was more interested in *how* he wrote than in what he wrote. Although there were flashes of the kind of sharpness that the author of the document sometimes showed, for the most part, Peter came over much as he does in life – a serious operator with a passionate interest in systems rather than people.

Wednesday April 7th. 9.50 p.m. (PT)

Ours is an old-fashioned organisation. Every department – we're in Building Finance – is divided into sections. The head of each section is responsible to a departmental head who is, in his or her turn, responsible to a head of group. No wonder we managed to lose three million pounds. It's amazing we manage to find each other in the corridors.

My head of department is called Rosy, a small, very fat person in her late fifties, with a strong west country accent. At first sight she might seem to be an unlikely person to be in charge of a corporate budget that runs into millions. But, on reflection, she is perfect. She chain smokes, laughs a lot, and when things get tough, says things like "How much are we down, darling?"

As I trudged through the company piazza towards the company lifts, I wondered, not for the first time, whether the invoices on the Newsom Conference Centre might not merit my close attention. The number of firms we were dealing with seemed to have multiplied by a factor of ten in the last few months. And if we were looking at someone forging a signature on an invoice, say, then that was precisely the kind of thing I could imagine John Pappanauer doing. I tried not to think about things like this as I went round the edge of the main building and through a walkway to the Building and Operations Area. We are, of course, located in the most run-down and shabby corner of what is known to company wags as BO. "If you can live in this shit," our bosses seem to be saying, "then you can reduce others to accepting it!" The carpets are the kind of blue you see in cinemas. The view, on all sides, has been selected for its menacing qualities. The double doors that lead out to the corridor creak like the gates of a dungeon in a fairy story.

And, of course the head of Building Finance Auditing (if that's what they're calling me this week) does not have a separate office. We live, like a Neapolitan family, in one apartment, and have done for five years. We spy on each other's phone calls and read each other's mail. When I find myself cooing at Jimmy or Jonny or being playfully affectionate with my wife down the phone I sometimes look up to find Fiona watching me. When Pappanauer is trying to impress one of his women (if they are women – I sometimes think he is probably bragging to his own answering machine) then I often catch Paul Jackson looking at him, bug-eyed with what seems to be admiration.

"Romance is blossoming!" Pappanauer was saying, as I came in, "Miss Macmillan and Mr Jackson are definitely going to make passionate love on their desks by the end of the morning. Watch this space!"

I didn't respond. I looked across at Fiona. She wasn't even blushing. She was sitting at her desk, her elbows perched either side of the telephone, staring out across at the station. She looked terribly lost and terribly alone. Clouds had massed above the railway, and from the west I could see already dark rain clouds were queuing to take their place across the city. Fiona didn't seem to have heard anything of what Pappanauer said. Then, as I watched her, she gave him a brief glance. There was such hatred in that look! Paul didn't say anything. But then he never does. Fiona was still looking at Pappanauer. Once again, as I had in the car, I found myself wondering what could be the matter with her. I went over to her desk. I kept my voice low. "Look. You don't have to tell me," I said, "but I can see something's upset you. Is it to do with work? Is it a personal matter?"

She looked from me to Paul and then, for a long time, at Pappanauer. "Not now, Peter," she said, "please . . ."

I glanced over at Pappanauer who was sitting with the kind of primness that usually follows one of his bouts of offensive behaviour.

"I'm not asking you to tell me," I said. "I'll get a temp. Take tomorrow off. And the next day. OK? And the day after that if you want."

She looked up at me. She seemed almost pathetically grateful. "Thanks," she said, "thanks so much . . ."

I turned to both John and Paul and assumed the formal voice that I use on these occasions.

"Fiona's going to take a few days off. For a rest." I looked back at her. "You should go to the sea or something."

Why did I say that? I think because I wanted Fiona to see Dartsea. I think of her as a member of my family rather than someone I work with. And I thought that sending her there might give her some of the happiness that has always seemed natural to me. But my suggestion didn't seem to make her feel any easier or calmer. "She should go to that great hotel, boss!" I looked quickly at Paul. Before I had the chance to say anything else, Pappanauer went on, "The one you took us to. Executive stress!" Paul started to chew his lower lip. Pappanauer was taking pleasure in his discomfort. "Dartsea," he said, the Cliff Hotel!"

I knew why Paul was chewing his lower lip. I didn't regret anything about the weekend the three of us had spent down there. And I refused to acknowledge that there had been anything unusual about that weekend. One of the important things to remember about being a boss is the attempt to preserve one's emotional neutrality. I kept my face deliberately free of expression as I said, "That might be a nice idea." And then I heard myself say, "Look – why don't you all go? It's been really hard just lately and I can spare you. Why don't you all go to Dartsea?"

Fiona was looking white and scared again. I couldn't understand why the thought of going away to the country with two accountants should suddenly empty her face of colour. It was as if I had offered to send her into a combat zone or to Dracula's castle.

Dartsea is on the North Devon coast. It's a small fishing village, set between green cliffs. The houses are piled up on each other along a narrow street that winds back up the hill from the sea and, a few hundred yards clear of the village, right on the edge of the cliff, is the hotel. It's a huge, sprawling building, put up before the First World War, that suggests the England that painted the map red and saluted the flag at sundown. Even when I was young there were still red-faced colonels sitting outside on the lawn in bath chairs, who looked as if they remembered the Indian Mutiny and, indeed, still called it that. They came, of course, for the view, and that hasn't changed in centuries. There has always been a level field, strewn with grey rocks and, beyond that, the rugged acres of the unchanging sea.

Beside the hotel is a comparatively recent addition to the landscape – a Norman church, complete with lych-gate, pebbled wall and quaint tombstones. On Sunday mornings, the bell nods and claps out a call to prayer past the grave of Anna James, wife to Henry and mother to Sarah (1702–53) and "God have mercie on her soule". It's an England that seems further away than a mere few hundred years, from the obscenity and corruption and decay that rule this island now.

The rooms at the front of the hotel, with views across the bay, are fronted by a common balcony. At either end of the building, a wide wooden staircase leads down from the balcony to a huge lawn that in spring is studded with clumps of daffodils. Sometimes, when the wind is high, you can hear the sea on the rocks below, hurling itself up into the caves hollowed out by thousands of tides and storms, but I always think of it as calm and quiet. The sun is always shining there – it's a land of white linen under blue and gold skies.

●

I put Peter Tayor's journal to one side and looked out of the window. The London sky was grey. In the doorway of a shop a young man of about twenty was lying in a sleeping bag. Around his neck was a placard that said HOMELESS. He wasn't stretching out his hand to anybody, and as far as I could see nobody was interested in him. An elderly lady, on her way into the shop, stepped over him carefully. He didn't look at her.

Pappanauer peered out through the rain on the windscreen to the rain beyond it. He seemed irritated about something.

"How far is it?" I said.

"Not far," said Pappanauer. "I'm right behind you, Fi! You know?" I didn't respond.

"I mean," he went on, "we're the same kind of people you and I, are we not?"

I couldn't think what he might mean by this. I looked down at Peter Taylor's journal. Peter hadn't quite got him right. Perhaps, as so often in England, it was a question of class. Once he started to drop that relentlessly laddish manner you began to see a completely different person. I heard myself say, once again, "Tell me about your parents, John."

He flicked his eyes up to the driving mirror. Just for a moment he had that intense, concentrated look he sometimes gets when he's bent over a pile of figures. Like an animal intent on food. "They died," he said, "a long, long time ago."

The traffic started to move again and he fell silent. I was hoping he would say more but he didn't. And, partly because I was suddenly frightened again, I didn't want to ask him any more direct questions. He hadn't been very happy about the last one. There was nowhere else for my eyes to go but back to the journal.

Wednesday April 7th 10.30 p.m. (PT)

Anna has just come in. "What are you writing?" she asks me. I don't tell her. I won't tell anyone any of this until I have found out what I think and, in my experience, you only find out what you think by trying to write it down. I suppose I am frightened by the anger the whole case awakens in me – the anger and need for vengeance that is the heart and stomach of the law. I don't want to make a mistake. I always think of the company's money as mine. That's absurd I know. But this business of the conference centre gets to me. I imagine myself getting hold of the bastard behind it, grabbing hold of him and shaking his head against the wall until he confesses.

Anna says I'm a violent man. A typical repressed Englishman, full of anger and unsatisfied rage. A middle management casualty. "A novel!" I said. And she laughed. She knows I have no imagination. She *is* a little like Fiona. Sometimes I literally do not understand the sudden passions that seem to overwhelm her.

What was bothering Fiona? Just after we had started to talk

about Dartsea, she did something I had been waiting for her to do all morning. She burst into tears. I went to her and put my arm around her again. This time she didn't rear up as if I had been trying to assault her.

"I'm sorry, Fi!" I said, "I was only trying to help! I mean if you want . . ."

I looked at Paul. Then I looked at Pappanauer. "If you just want to go with Paul . . ."

She got to her feet. "What do you mean?" she said, "what do any of you mean? What do any of you know, come to that? None of you have the faintest idea of what I might be thinking or feeling, do you? How could any of you know what I might be feeling? I'm just the damn secretary, aren't I? Who cares a damn about me?" And, moving with awkwardness of a bird on land, she ran from the room and clattered off down the corridor.

I still don't know why she ran out like that. But now, I can see something in her outburst that I did not perceive at the time. I thought this was hysterical behaviour. It wasn't. It was very, very serious. She was angry. It seemed to be a moment when she found the courage to resolve some horrific struggle within her. There was a great strength about what she said. At the time I found her as bewildering as I sometimes find my wife, but if I was asked what I felt about Fiona now I think I would probably say that I admired her.

Paul went after her first. He didn't speak. He just glared at Pappanauer and then ran out through the double doors. Pappanauer leered at me. "Can't let Jackson get all of this one, can we?" he said. I looked at him blankly. He really is the master of the inappropriate remark. Before I had a chance to tell him he was one of the most loathsome people ever to add up figures for a living he followed Paul out.

I stood looking out of the window and the skyline. The rain was back. The clouds were low again over the railway bridge and down below, in the forecourt, umbrellas, lowered like charging rhinoceri, fought their way through the drizzle. So. Pappanauer was interested in her. Seriously attracted. Not just office jokes. I don't know why I hadn't seen it before. I had other things to think about.

Immediately they were gone I started on the Newsom

Conference Centre material. There were several very good reasons why I hadn't wanted them there when I went into my files. The computers in the office are logged into a network and although we all have a completely secret password that only we can use to gain access to our confidential files, I hardly ever use mine. My own hard disk is so badly organised that I quite often have to ramble through ten or twenty documents before I come across the one I want to use. I am afraid that one day, when I am staring at the screen, Pappanauer or Jackson will steal up behind me, peer over my shoulder and find out things they should not know.

If some of the losses on the Newsom Project are attributable to false invoicing, then, whoever is involved has very probably got the help of someone in this office. Because all the stuff that goes out through Howlett's is looked at by either Paul or Pappanauer. I like to deal with what I call the "bigger picture" – in other words, have lunch with people. I went into my file on Newsom. Our files are, on the whole, common property. And I think it was Pappanauer who started the habit of naming them with the elements. I usually call mine by quite arbitrary names like BUGGER or OH DAMN or LOST IT. A particularly long costing report was once named TITS because it was getting on mine so badly. But it was Pappanauer who called an assessment he was asked to perform FIRE and, a few days later, Paul countered by naming a draft budget on a new warehouse WATER.

Maybe that was why I chose EARTH as the title of my document that deals with what promises to be one of the biggest financial scandals ever to hit the company. One of the main companies discussed in the document is a firm called Ainscombe Ltd, who made most of their money out of earth removal. Earth is my element. I am solid, a little dull, but, as my father always used to say – "As reliable as the Clay to Whence We shall Return!" When I am going through the thousands of invoices and reports that go to make up the picture of how that ill-fated place was built I think about myself shifting huge quantities of mud and slime. "I'm dishing the dirt!" I say to myself.

Ainscombe are, now, not only builders themselves but agents for other builders. They put together packages involving specialist trades and companies from all over the world; this part of their business is run by a wholly owned subsidiary of theirs called Howlett and Partners. Howlett's usually farm out the work to a select group of people, most of whom are close to Ainscombe's, the parent company. This is, in my experience, the normal way that business works, i.e. corrupt; there is something reassuringly predictable about it. What worried me about the Newsom Project was the huge number of companies that Howlett's seemed to have involved. Where names were available – and some of the amounts were quite considerable – they were often not familiar to me.

A great number of these invoices had been handled by two people, not from Howlett's, but from the Ainscombe head office. It was quite difficult to work out who was responsible for contracting this maze of small companies, but two names came up enough times for me to think that they were heavily involved. One of them – a fairly junior figure called Al Hunter – was unknown to me. The other one – a florid character called Harold Porter – was known to me (and to John and Paul) very well. I know Harold's plump red face, his beef and claret voice and his almost entirely invented posh accent. I also know that he is as corrupt as hell.

I looked through the figures. Their network of suppliers seemed to have grown by fission. Inventing companies is a fraud so simple and so easy to detect that I couldn't believe anyone in my office was liable even to contemplate it. But I did become determined to get some more information about, say, Pratt and Lewis or The Wright Company or a firm calling itself Schoenbaum International that seemed to have billed for services upward of four hundred thousand pounds. I knew I wasn't going to find an explanation straight away. But I decided to pick up the phone to someone. I paced up and down for a while, looked at my file for one last time and called the Ainscombe office.

It was at that moment that Fiona came back into the room. She looked as if she had been running. She didn't look at me. Instead she went straight to her desk and started to type up the minutes of a meeting that I was fairly sure was a week old and not very important. At least I think that was what she was typing. She was followed, a minute or two later, by Paul. I thought, for a moment, that he was going to say something to her, but, when he saw that I was on the phone, he decided against it. Finally Pappanauer pushed his way in through the double doors.

The two men gave each other a look of extreme hostility and then settled themselves at their desks. I swung around in my seat until my back was facing the rest of the office. I found myself looking out of the window once again. The wind had risen and was driving the rain against the huge panel of glass at the far end of the room. I tried to keep my voice as low as I could as I said "Could I speak to Al Hunter please?" I wasn't going to tackle Harold Porter until I had more information. I'm not sure about anything where Harold Porter is concerned – least of all whether that really was his name.

Al Hunter was only a name to me. Simply a person who might be involved, in a lowly capacity, in something rather nasty. I think I was very concerned to keep my initial exchanges with him very simple and unthreatening. A routine enquiry about one of the subcontractors with whom he had been dealing. And I was also anxious that neither Paul nor Pappanauer should have any idea of who I was calling or why I was calling them.

Outside, the rain slackened a little. A pale light filtered down from somewhere between the massed banks of cloud. The silence in the room had become oppressive. I think we were all, suddenly, uncomfortably aware of each other. I certainly felt that the office, once a neutral place in which people came together, each day, to operate under an agreed set of rules, was subtly changing into something else. I didn't know what kind of place it had become but there was something lurid about the growing squares of light on the wall next to me.

And there was a feeling I didn't like. Like an odour of decay you can't quite locate, until you open a door in the kitchen on to something rotting, there was a whiff of staleness. It was like a noise, dimly heard, too, like the low growl of a dog that is angry or the noise of thunder a long way away. As I talked my way through to Mr Hunter its presence grew sharper and stronger until I was no longer sure whether the dark April day, the tense faces around me or the silence at the other end of the phone weren't all saying – *something wicked, Peter, something not quite nice.*

"I'm afraid," said a small voice at the other end of the line, "that you can't speak to Mr Hunter."

"Is he in a meeting?"

There was a nervous laugh from the other end. "No, he's not in a meeting." The laugh died away. In fact it was hard to believe it had ever been there at all.

"Where is he?" I said.

"Actually," said the voice, "he's dead."

I started to say how sorry I was. I found it remarkably easy to feel genuine remorse about the fact that someone I had never really known was no longer there. In many ways it was easier than summoning up emotions about friends or acquaintances, since my conventional pieties were no more than an acknowledgement of my own mortality. They made the person at the end of the line considerably chattier.

"In fact," said the voice, that at first I had thought to be that of a young woman and only now realised was that of a young man, "Al Hunter was murdered. He was murdered extremely brutally, in fact!"

He started to give me details. Had I ever seen anyone beaten to death? I said I hadn't. Had I ever seen anyone beaten to death with a *frying pan?* I said I was afraid I had never come across that either. I had seen pictures of an earthquake, would that do him? The young man wouldn't stop though. He had read the local newspaper reports, he said. There was blood everywhere, he said. There were bits of bone buried deep in the carpet, he said. Someone somewhere, he said, had heard terrible screams and had assumed it was a party. I held the phone away from my face. He still didn't stop. Wasn't life frightening these days? he said. Wasn't I terrified? Wasn't Britain finished and narrow and hopeless and frightening and without morals? I didn't say anything. I just put the phone back, very carefully and quietly, on to the receiver as he was still talking and looked across at John and Paul. Their heads were bowed over their desks. They didn't see me. But I whispered to myself, so loud that I was almost sure they could have heard if they had wanted to listen. "It's one of you bastards. Isn't it?"

I think I now know why I am writing this, alone in my study late at night, as the rain comes in across the fields beyond my quiet house. I think I should not have suggested they go. I think something terrible may happen down at Dartsea. And if it does I think it will be my fault.

●

How right you were Peter, I thought, as Pappanauer slowed the car to a halt outside a modern block of flats. I had no idea of where we were. I had seen bits of London pass in the rain – Brixton, Streatham, Croydon . . . but now, although I thought I recognised details in the landscape – a house here, or a tobacconists' shop there – I realised I was in fact recognising memories of other places. It was as if we had travelled in a huge circle and had arrived at some unknown corner of a place I had known since childhood.

"His flat's in there!" said Pappanauer. I didn't answer. Through the front doors of the place I could see a uniformed commissionaire pacing up and down an expensive-looking lobby. Pappanauer turned around in his seat. He screwed up his eyes and looked into my face.

"I've got a key to it," he said, "do you want to go in?"

I dropped my hand into the bag and closed it around the reassuring shape of that black-handled claw hammer. Why should Pappanauer have a key to Paul's second flat? Were relations between these two men rather more cordial than I had thought? Was there even, I wondered, something corrupt or sinister about both of them? Did they both use it for orgies? Were the two of them up to some crooked deal?

"Just lead the way, Mr Pappanauer!" I said, "Just lead the way."

Part
2

10

My first thought as Pappanauer and I climbed the stairs together was "How does Paul afford anything like this?" I could have lived quite comfortably in the lobby or on the stairs of his apartment block. As Pappanauer opened the door of his flat I asked the question out loud.

"He has money from somewhere," said Pappanauer, "but God knows where it is. I was always hoping he might bung me some."

As if answering my unspoken question he went on, "He lets me use it sometimes. When I'm . . . you know . . . well, he doesn't live here." His voice trailed away. When you're what, Pappanauer? Picking your nose? Indulging in a more than usually lengthy session of self-abuse? An auto-erotic dirty weekend?

But Pappanauer seemed to have lost the nerve for *doubles entendres*. He looked, I thought, rather hopeless and sad, as if he was about to start apologising for the person he was. I kept behind him. I gripped the handle of the carrier bag as we went inside.

If Paul had a secret store of money somewhere, he certainly hadn't spent it on the décor. As far as I could tell the pale green wallpaper was the same as the one round the lifts. The prints on the walls looked as if they had been sold as a job lot with the rest of the building. For some reason, behind the kitchen door was a large black and white photograph of an orange.

I looked around for clothes or books or for anything that might tell me that this was Paul's place. There was nothing. In the sitting room, overlooking the rainy main street, was a small dining table and a computer. Pappanauer and I sat on the anonymous armchairs under a picture window that didn't seem to open. We could have been sitting in an airport lounge.

"He keeps all the stuff," said Pappanauer, "in the spare room." Here he gave me a flash of unreconstructed Pappanauer, a sort of leer and a sideways movement of the head. Then he suddenly remembered that this wasn't the way you were supposed to behave to rape victims.

"What stuff?" I said.

"Paul," said Pappanauer, "is a bit of a lad!"

I thought this was a quite sensationally inaccurate way of describing him. I was no longer sure, really, why either of us were there. But, although home is supposed to be safe, I knew I was very glad to be away from my mother's house. Pappanauer stretched out his legs, folded his arms and sighed heavily.

"You think he'll just . . . show up here, do you?" I said.

Pappanauer pursed his lips. I was starting to get irritated with him again. I reached down into the carrier bag by my side and pulled out a sheaf of papers.

"What is it you're reading all the time?" said Pappanauer.

"Papers," I said.

"What papers?" said Pappanauer.

I let my hand slide down to the carrier bag once again. "Stay right where you are, John!" I said. Then I smiled, showing all of my teeth. "Or I'll kill you!"

THURSDAY APRIL 8TH 11.45 A.M. (F)

I'm writing this, in my convent-school hand, as the train sways out of the station. And, I presume, he's somewhere on the train, and, pretty soon, he'll come up and smile and sit next to me. I do trust him. Honestly. I do trust him. Although I do notice that I have taken a seat in an open compartment and that there are people all around me.

Houses and roads and factories are unreeling past the window. The rain seems to have given up at last, and soon we will be looking at that familiar bit of England called the country – all poised and green and gone before you know it. The cows will be there, and the rivers and the odd, isolated white house, all waiting for someone (me probably) to think they're cute, before the next redbrick town chugs its way in from the right of the square of glass next to me. Maybe it's just that the rain has gone. Maybe it's the light coming in from the west. But, for the first time since this business started, I am beginning to feel happy. It is stupid to be happy of course but I am stupidly happy.

I'm allowing myself to be happy because, when the two of them followed me out of the office after Peter Taylor's offer of this trip to Dartsea, I noticed something about Pappanauer as he followed me and Paul into the corridor. When I got to the lifts and saw that both of them had come out after me, my tears evaporated. I felt the need to study them both, coldly, objectively, as if I were a detective, or a lawyer. That was when I saw this thing about Mr Pappanauer, the half-hearted office lecher. It wasn't his face. It was his hands. He was looking down at them. He turned the left one backwards and for-wards, stroking its fingers as if it didn't belong to him. I looked at the fingers' ends. They're square-ended and the backs are as hairy as a spider's. Which doesn't quite fit with the neatness of the rest of him. What's curious about them, though, is how strong they look. He caught me looking at them. His eyes clouded suddenly. *That's why you wore gloves*, I thought to myself.

Once I had decided it was him – and, of course I had no evi-dence – I felt strangely relieved. It wasn't that I was sure it was him. It was that I had decided to behave as if I was. Which gave me – at last – a clue as to how to behave. Firstly, it was very important not to let him know that I suspected. Because I still believed that that one sentence he had spoken to me, in that weird, untraceable voice, was true. Secondly, I knew I had to start to watch for evidence because intuitions and feelings are not really welcome in a court of law.

I walked back down the corridor towards the two of them. Pappanauer let his mouth dangle open like a fish's. The way he does when he thinks he is being sexy. He moved his eyes from me to Paul. "Why don't we all go?" he said. I wanted to laugh out loud suddenly. He was playing into my hands. Keeping my eyes on Pappanauer's face I took hold of Paul's arm. And then, when I was sure Paul had hold of me, I slowly reached out and took hold of Pappanauer's right hand. It was very, very difficult to do. I grasped him, not in a hand-shake, but over the knuckles, as if I wanted to dispense with ceremony and simply let him know that I cared about him. As my fingers closed over his fist I felt, once again, absolutely certain that it was him. But I still had that sense of exaltation. I knew that, although at any moment I would be back to fear and ignorance and loneliness, I had for the present that *operating certainty*. I think it was a phrase of my father's. Sometimes it was a horse, sometimes it was a woman he'd met and most often it was a business venture, but it was always "an operating certainty, girly . . ."

I moved my hand on to Pappanauer's arm and grabbed him by the elbow. I was now walking between the two of them, arm in arm in arm. I noticed that Mr Pappanauer was wheezing quite badly. Asthma or something I supposed.

I think that was when I remembered that *he* had made a noise. At least I was almost sure he had. I couldn't have said – so confused were my impressions – what kind of noise it was. But there had been something. Pappanauer stopped and started to cough. *You're the one*, I said, once again, to myself. *It's you . . .*

•

When I looked up again I saw that Pappanauer was watching me.

"It's my diary I'm reading. From last Thursday. When Paul and I went down on the train to Dartsea," I said. Pappanauer coughed.

"I know," he said.

I didn't ask him how he knew. I squinted down at my carrier bag and saw the handle of the hammer pointing up at me. Its silver claw head was face down in my night-dress.

"I've got hold of a lot of stuff", I went on, "about what's been happening. Especially down at Dartsea."

"I thought", said Pappanauer, "that you weren't really telling us all of what happened. I mean – about who attacked you."

I let that sentence hang in the air for a while. Then I said, "No." Pappanauer didn't move. "No," I went on, "I wasn't." Then I went back to my diary.

FRIDAY APRIL 9TH. DARTSEA. 1 A.M. (F)

I can't sleep, I'm writing things down again.

My Dad loved the sea. I first went to the seaside when I was five or six. I can still remember my Dad saying, as we drove up the hill above the town where we were staying – "In a minute, my girl, you'll see it!" My heart was in my mouth, honestly. I remember, first of all, a silver space beyond the house tops and a breathless wonder at the idea that land could ever end. It seemed to make sense of everything. It wasn't the gulls' cacophony or the unusual breeze – it was that I had found a place where I felt I could stand and look back at myself A feeling that I was, for the first time in my life, both really travelling and really coming home.

It was funny. When the branch line train pulled into Dartsea – a tiny station with one platform and only a white wooden fence to mark where the seacliffs ended and the railway began, I had exactly the feeling I had had with my Dad that time. The clouds and the rain had cleared. Out over the sea, cumulus clouds were stuck in a gigantic sky. It was the kind of pale blue that looked as if it had been dreamed up by a really clever interior designer. There was a small wind ruffling the flowers by the station office, and, next to the office, a small red-cheeked man in black baggy trousers, a peaked hat and a white shirt.

"Is he real?" I said to Paul, as we got out of the train. Paul grinned. The two of us walked up the narrow road that led from the station to the hotel. I could smell the air, spiced with salt and I shook my hair out in the breeze. The road ran through a wide swathe of brilliant grass; the grey rocks that broke its surface gave it a cosmetic look. As we turned our backs on the sea and came up to the steps that led to the front porch of Cliff View, I saw John Pappanauer through the open door. He was lounging by the front desk. He was wearing shades, which seemed to be impressing the receptionist. When he saw us he took them off and waved them in our direction. "What's up, kids?" he shouted.

Paul looked away from him, back towards the silver distance of the bay. He hadn't talked much on the way down and he didn't look as if he was about to start now. He had spent most of the time peering over his left shoulder, as if he expected someone to leap out at him from behind one of the seats. But now it seemed worse. Was he, I wondered, frightened of Pappanauer? I had the uncomfortable feeling that he was although I couldn't think why this should be the case.

"Nothing's up, Mr Pappanauer," I said, as we went in through the door, "apart from you trying to look like a rock star."

At which Pappanauer put his glasses back on his hawk-like nose. Paul went over to the desk and started to check us in. "Here we all are!" Pappanauer was saying, "back in our old stomping grounds, Paul! Place of many confidences!"

Paul didn't say anything but he gave him another look. I would not have liked to have been on the receiving end of it. But Pappanauer paid no attention. "Now we are here," he went on, "and you two haven't hurried away somewhere we must all buy buckets and spades. And sit on the sand and dig a hole into which we can put the lovely Fiona!"

He's always calling me the lovely Fiona. I can't stand it. It's as if he's trying to distinguish me from the ugly Fiona he's got chained to the wall at home. I sort of tossed my head and shook my hair about, which is what I do when I want people to remember that I am not a pushover. My Dad used to call it "horse-acting". I said, "We'll dig a huge pit and we'll upend Mr Pappanauer into it, shall we, Paul?"

The two of them gave each other a look of pure dislike. But, I told myself, *you are not here for pleasure*, Fiona. You have to watch him and provoke him and see if he does something stupid. And you have to stay close to Paul.

Then we took the cases up and the three of us went to the bar, which looks out on a putting green, with the sea spread out beyond it and below it. There were yachts out in the bay – like red and white butterflies on the neat expanse of blue. It was blue now, the water, like something in a box of child's paints. As we sat waiting for our drinks and Pappanauer talked I listened to his voice. He stretches out his vowels in the way that he stretches, sometimes, at his desk at work. As if he was trying to get you to admire him. I tried to listen to what was behind the voice. Could it have said – *that*?

I tried to remember exactly what HE had said and how HE had said each word. I deliberately didn't think about the whole sentence. I couldn't bear to do that. I started by concentrating on the first word. "If" – I waited for Pappanauer to use it. It's a common enough word. But for some reason he seemed nervous of the conditional. I even went so far as to try and devise questions that would make it difficult for him to avoid it. "You" was easier. "I" is the word Pappanauer uses most of the time, but he occasionally deigns to tell "you" what "I" thinks "you" ought to think or do. I couldn't match it to that hideous voice in the flat though. In fact it was hard to connect this frightening game I was playing with any of the things going on around me. The sun winked back at me off the glasses on the heavy wooden table. Out on the putting green a family prepared to play golf. The dad was clowning around, pretending to miss. I heard his voice, carried by the breeze – "Oh no-oo Jackie! Oh no-oo!" Up at the bar a man in white jacket, who didn't look at all glad to be in Dartsea, was polishing a glass as if it was the last glass in the Cliff View Hotel and he wanted to get it right.

Pappanauer went up to the bar and ordered us another round of drinks. "If you tell anyone . . ." Had he said the word "anyone"? I couldn't remember. "If you tell anyone about . . ." A glass of half-full vodka and tonic was slipped into my hand by his hand. His hands on my hands. The way he forced my face into the pillow. That first sight of him, like some space monster or a horrific, living scarecrow sent out at Hallowe'en to terrify the children suddenly swam in front of my eyes, as unbidden as nausea and I heard the whole sentence.

If you tell anyone about this I will kill you.

That was it. And that was the first time I'd allowed myself to hear and see and remember what had happened to me. But although the voice was as clear as the day outside I still couldn't understand whether any of the words were Pappanauer's. I wasn't really thinking about that any more. I was trying to fight down the picture of HIM swarming out of my bathroom in that hideous mask and those lurid gloves. "If you tell anyone about this I'll kill you."

"I was reading a thriller the other day!" I heard myself say in a tinny voice. They both looked at me. I wasn't sure what to say next. I think I had some mad idea that I was going to introduce that sentence as if it was something I had read in a book, and provoke Pappanauer into declaring himself. There are times, you see, when I think that whoever did that thing to me got the idea from some book. Who says books can't corrupt you or give you horrible ideas? "If you tell anyone about this I will . . ."

"If you tell anyone about this I will kill you!" said a voice.

I thought at first that the voice must be mine. Or that I had heard it in my head. But I realised, almost immediately, that it belonged to Paul. I froze. Paul's voice had a hesitant quality as if he was trying out the words for the first time. As if, I thought wildly, he was auditioning. Pappanauer had leaned across the table and, in that sneering voice he uses for the most innocent words, he too was saying, "If – you – tell anyone about this – I will kill you!"

I looked down. I'd been doodling with a pencil on the blank spaces of a beer mat. I hadn't even been aware that I was doing it. But I had carved out, deep into the damp cardboard, in capital letters, the legend IF YOU TELL ANYONE ABOUT THIS I WILL KILL YOU! I didn't dare look at either of them. I couldn't begin to tell if the way in which either of them had spoken gave any clue as to whether their voices were the same voice as the man who did *that*. There was no one, I realised, to whom I could confide these thoughts.

I thought of Dad in the side room of that hospital – his mouth horribly ajar – his teeth, yellow stumps fixed in the immovable yawn of death. I thought about how I wanted to close his eyes but did not dare to do so. I thought about how I wanted the blood to come back to his face and for his voice to be telling me I was his little girl and no one else would ever be his little girl. Stupid, comforting things, whose only comfort, really, was that I was once stupid enough to believe them. And then I thought about how it was all too late for me. I would never find anyone to trust and love. But by then I had run out of the bar, up the wide stairs and I was crying, alone in my room, as if the tears would never, never stop.

•

I looked up from the pages of my diary. There had been a noise. A doorbell. Why hadn't I heard it? As I listened – it came again. Three short rings, well spaced. Then a long silence. Like a pre-arranged signal. Pappanauer was peering down the front of the building. He turned back to me. "That's Paul!" he said.

I had to do something to calm myself. I got up, holding the papers and the carrier bag and walked over to the window. I was about to pretend to look out of it when I remembered that I should not turn my back on any of them. I leaned against the glass, looked back into the room and listened to the beating of my heart.

11

As usual, he came into the room without my noticing he had arrived. There was a great deal of fuss around his arrival. It was simply that Paul chose not to be part of it. Pappanauer went to let him in and I heard him out in the hall. I even heard my name mentioned once or twice. But I could not have, quite, said precisely when the door to the living room opened and, somehow or other, Paul was standing shyly by the wall, his hands up to the lapels of his neat, black jacket, like a child on a school trip, waiting to be told where to go. And then, of course, he smiled. He went from schoolboy to dazzling gentleman in a fraction of a second. I noticed, for the first time, that he had tucked that smart red handkerchief of his into the breast pocket of his jacket. In some people this might have seemed an affectation. In Paul's case it seemed to grant him a sudden clarity and elegance. "Hullo, Fiona!" he said.

I realised that I was smiling. Was he smiling because I was smiling? Or was it the other way around? I had lost all consciousness of what this smile of his might mean. It was simply a hypnotic arrangement of teeth and eyes and glitter that, for all I could tell, had been blown into the hall by the wind and the rain and plastered across his face as a kind of disguise. "It's great to see you!"

No. He was smiling because I made him happy. That was it. And that was why I was smiling. We stood together, pooling these ridiculous smiles of ours, oblivious to Pappanauer, who was moving from one foot to the other, and coughing like a nervous chaperone.

"You got my letter?" said Paul.

"Yes," I said, and then heard myself tell him that I hadn't really read it. That made him laugh for some reason. He said something about not being a letter writer. Then I said, "The police are after you!" That made everybody laugh. Pappanauer practically doubled up. I didn't say anything else after that. And although there were things I knew I had to ask him – it seemed, from something that Pappanauer was saying – as if now was not the time. They had something urgent to discuss. Would I mind if they went into the next room? They promised not to be long. "I'll be fine," I said to them. They went like a couple of schoolboys to the door. I let them almost get out of the room before I added "I have something to say to you two. To both of you. But it'll wait until you have finished. "

Pappanauer nodded seriously. Then I said to Paul, "Peter Taylor is sure that you're the man who attacked me. I don't know who attacked me." Paul nodded briefly. "But," I went on, "I am determined to find out. I am going to find out."

"Yes!" said Paul.

I looked around at the sitting room. "Where did you get the money for this place?" I said, "what do you use it for?"

Paul chewed his lip and looked up at Pappanauer. He seemed to me to be trying to work out what, if anything, Pappanauer might have told me about all of this. "If I get out of this," said Paul, "I am not going to be using it ever again. For anything."

Then they went next door. As soon as they had gone I sat down with the pile of papers and the carrier bag and, once more, started to read the diary I had scribbled while I was in that hotel room in Dartsea.

DARTSEA. FRIDAY APRIL 9TH. 4.00 A.M. (F)

It's four in the morning. I've only had three hours sleep. I am writing this in bed. The same pen, the same childish letters. I started to write when I woke, suddenly, several hours ago. I'm writing the way I have been writing since this business began. The pen moves across the paper as if I was taking dictation. I do not know why I find it so easy. In a way, what I am trying to describe is as hard to explain as *that*. In a way it's harder.

I'm writing on hotel notepaper. I want to record that fact too. I want to tell it all, as it was, right up to the moment when I opened the door to him. If I don't leave out things like hotel notepaper or how the sea or the sun or moon looked perhaps whoever reads this will understand what we did. I want *you*, whoever you are, to understand it, because I want to wipe out the memory of *that*.

In the early evening, the three of us went on to the beach. There was a path that led out from the hotel towards the cliff edge, and, as we came out of the building, John started down it as if he knew where he was going. At first this surprised me, until I remembered that the two of them had been here with Peter. The sun was going down over the sea – lowering itself over the rim of the sky, slowly and gracefully. A decorous English sunset. As the light shrank from the sky and piled up like a bonfire in the west, the green cliffs blackened with shadows and the wind, that up to now had felt like a promise of something, started to claw at my face like a warning.

We were some way behind John. I turned to Paul. "Shall we just stay in and get pissed?"

But John turned back to us. "Come on! It's a great view!"

Paul stepped out in front of me. "I can't remember taking this path down to the beach with Peter . . ."

Pappanauer grinned. "Have you wiped the memory of our little stay from your brain?"

There was something really nasty about the way he said this. Paul looked at the ground. He started to chew his lip. I found I was looking at his hands. He has thin, wiry fingers. He was lacing them together and twisting them, now this way, now that. I thought he was going to speak but he didn't. He pushed his way on towards the cliff edge. The wind had conjured a dark red out of his cheeks. He gave Pappanauer a look of pure hatred.

Now, if I say that the way he made me feel was to do with his shoulders or his eyes or his voice you'll think that that is because I am the sort of girl who is impressed by shoulders or eyes or voices. "Oh!" I hear you say, "If we had known this was a *love story*!" It wasn't that. All I could think about, as I followed Paul and Pappanauer down the cliff path, was keeping close to Paul. "Is it worth seeing?" I was saying to him. But Pappanauer intercepted my remark, like someone fielding a ball in the cricket field. He smirked. "It's ama-azing!" he

148

said. As he said this, I decided that I had probably dreamed seeing those glove fingers peeping out of one of the briefcases. I don't know why I thought that then, except that, down here, above the darkening sea with the Edwardian hotel behind us, it was difficult to believe in the horrible or the frightening. Everything about this place was so familiar. Everything about it seemed so safe.

Paul had moved in front of me. "It's quite steep for the first part," he said, "I'd better go first!" Then he grinned. "You can watch me slide to my death. It's all I deserve."

"I don't think you deserve that, Paul," I said. "There's nothing wrong with you that a bit of *strict discipline* won't cure!"

Suddenly we were both grinning at each other like idiots. We couldn't stop. The grins became giggles. The giggles became helpless hysteria. We were now at the edge of the cliff, and, some way down, I saw Pappanauer looking back up at us. "When you two have quite finished!" he said.

He didn't sound angry about this. In fact, out here, on a cliff, above the sea, just before sunset, he seemed a different person from the leering buffoon back at company headquarters. Perhaps Peter was right. Perhaps these few days were going to change us.

We were taking a route downwards now, picking our way through red soil, on a path cut deep into the springy turf. Above, gulls beat their way up into the strengthening wind, circled, swooped and then were carried out across the now lead-coloured waves towards the miles and miles of drifting clouds, burning their way into the west where the sun was going down like a Viking funeral.

"Watch your footing!" Paul called.

"When were you here?" I called back to him. I saw his back grow tense. What had happened down here between him and Pappanauer and Peter Taylor? He stopped and looked back up at me. He looked wistful, like a little boy. "A long time ago," he said, "when I was a different person."

It was when we got down to the beach that it happened. John had gone into a cave at the far end of the shoreline, where some steep rocks cut off the beach from the next cove. Paul and I were throwing pebbles into the sea. Not skimming them. We lobbed them up past the white fringes of the tide and watched the waves, now grey, now slate, now black, close over them with an awful kind of finality. "What were you going to tell me that day at lunch?" I said to him.

Paul put his arm on my shoulders.

It was such an unexpected gesture that it shocked me into more moods than are usually contained in a moment. I felt, briefly, the way I did when my Dad was going to tell me something Really Important – like What Boys Will Try to Do to You in the Back of Cars. And then I felt the way I had in our local cinema on the night Victor Parsons put his arms over my shoulders and, after the long journey from his lips to mine, and the negotiation of the difficult passage of both our noses, managed to land on target so precisely and sweetly, that I can still remember the dry, yet soft touch of his mouth and the way my arm reached for him in the darkness. And then I felt as if something was rushing out from me, from the centre of me, up towards my fingers' ends, my lips, my hair, my shoulders, my breasts and, looking for a way out finally found it through my eyes which lit up with something that felt like my soul made visible. The thing that was making it visible was his eyes. I seemed to be looking into them without knowing why I was doing this at all.

"It doesn't matter," he said, "it's something that isn't really to do with me. It's like it happened to another person. You see . . ."

He didn't get a chance to finish the sentence. Because, somehow, my arms seemed to have got around his body without my elbows making a public spectacle of themselves, and I was glueing my lips to his. Other bits of me were colliding with other bits of him. My knee seemed to have got rather close to his crotch and my right hand, for some embarrassing reason, was in the area of his bum. But it felt as if we were only really joined at the mouth because whatever was passing from him to me was the very same thing that had risen in my eyes only a moment ago. It fed the centre of me and started again back to every nerve ending I had until all of me was sparking and glowing and coming alive for the first time. I don't know how long we kissed or where any of our hands had got to by the time our lips came unstuck and he released me – I felt as if I was falling towards the beach – but his arms found me again and somehow we were hanging on to each other, once more, as if without each other we might both rise or sink or fly apart wildly like iron filings trapped in contrary magnetic fields.

I felt as if I had just run an enormous distance or landed after a transatlantic flight.

Pappanauer was coming towards us along the beach. "Separate bedrooms!" he said, "We promised the boss!" He gave Paul an angry glance. Then he looked straight at me. "I hope he's told you all about what kind of person he is!" he said. I thought Paul was going to hit him. But he didn't. Pappanauer turned and walked back up the cliff.

Peter Taylor, I thought, as Paul and I followed him, still keeping a safe distance apart, is a bit like a father and we're naughty kids, enjoying ourselves, literally, at his expense. There was a sort of hysteria about our behaviour that is typical of people who have been leading dull lives for years and years and then are suddenly told they can do anything they like.

•

Something next door had disturbed me. With a shock, I realised Paul and Pappanauer were shouting at each other. I put the pages of my diary down (I think I remember being struck by how much more like me she was than the dim little thing who had started writing it the morning after she had been raped.) Although both their voices were loud, I found it hard to make out individual words. I went to the wall and glued my ear to it. Wasn't there some trick you could do with a glass that would amplify sounds in a neighbouring room?

Now I was closer to them, I could make out one or two words. They were the most common ones in the argument. First they surfaced in Paul's conversation (he sounded quite different – angry, harsh) and then Pappanauer was practically screaming them. "Prostitute" – that was one word. Usually with "bloody" in front of it. "Bloody prostitute". The other word, of course, was my name. They kept taking that in vain. "Fiona" was or wasn't something. Sometimes she too was "bloody Fiona" and then, once or twice, she was given the reverential treatment by both of them. "Fiona is a person who . . ." I heard from Paul, I think. And from Pappanauer, "Fiona is a good . . ." A good what? Secretary? Daughter? Screw? I went back to my diary.

As we climbed the cliff, Paul and I started to talk. It was as if we had planned to say all this to each other for years but had only just found the way to say it. It wasn't just that what he said surprised me. What I said surprised myself. I found myself talking in whole paragraphs that reminded me of the kind of things really clever people said.

He was talking too. Not as he usually talked, with long silences between each sentence, but rapidly, as if he was frightened he wouldn't get the time to tell me everything he needed to say. His pale regular face was flushed and, as he talked, he used his hands for emphasis, or, sometimes, when he couldn't find a word, grabbed at the empty air as if it might supply it.

"You see," he was saying, "the thing about the orphanage –" I hadn't even *mentioned* it – "was that the name was almost the worst thing about it. I *enjoyed* being an orphan!"

I don't know why but I thought that this was the funniest thing I had ever heard in my life. I could hardly stand. I stood, just under the rim of the cliff, pulsating with laughter, and Paul, who was trying to tell me something serious about a weird Reverend who used to come and lecture to them, started to laugh hysterically too.

I didn't care any more. I didn't care what happened. All I cared about was that I was here, with an enormous sunset behind me, above a bay in a quiet corner of England, with a man I suddenly realised I wanted very much indeed.

We went on over the brow of the cliff and saw Pappanauer. The wind had scraped his hair off his face. He was as pale as ever, but now the dying sun illuminated his features like the embers of a used camp fire. He seemed once more like the man I knew from the city – sneering, empty-headed, and trying to conceal some weakness that no one had yet discovered. "I'll leave you two lovebirds together!" he said.

That was when I knew I wanted Paul to come to my room. I didn't know whether that was what he wanted. But I hugged the thought to myself. And, as the two of us walked up the steps of the hotel towards the bar, arm in arm, I decided it was rather more than an operating certainty.

I don't know what happened to John in the evening. Or what happened to my plan to get Paul to watch him. If I'd ever had a plan I certainly didn't have one now. We couldn't stop talking. We had gone beyond telling each other bits of our lives. We were having discussions now, arguments. But, like the stories we had exchanged, they were more an amazed recognition of our differences than anything else. "How can you possibly like *that* when I like you so much?" That kind of thing. After the discussion we went back to stories again. Is it that your whole life sleeps in your mind, waiting to be woken up by a stranger?

Paul seemed to make me remember happiness. We'd eaten a huge meringue with chocolate sauce and I had two glasses of sweet wine the colour of buttercups, and the memory that I didn't want to be a memory was no longer standing at my shoulder, like Hamlet, all in black at the wedding of his murderous uncle.

There was a candle burning on the table. It flickered in his eyes as I picked up my wine glass. I didn't want to hear about any other life apart from the life that lay in front of us. I didn't want to think about him doing anything apart from putting his arms around me, as he had done on the beach. Folding me into him until both of us were earthed, like live current, through his arms and chest and lips and hands and his legs, braced against the slipping pebbles on the shore. "Let's go upstairs!" I said.

I love sex when it's funny. It is funny sometimes. And it should be funny. I hate it when people approach it as if it was a cross between press-ups and morning prayers. I'm also very particular about the words you use to describe it, and, even more so, about the words you use, if you feel compelled to use words, when you're actually in the middle of it.

Dave was very much the holy gymnast kind of lover. And, although it could be nice with him, I could never quite believe that the person in bed with him was me. I'm not a crude person but I like to *be* crude occasionally. I think, sometimes, people mistake the crude for the obvious.

When we got to my room I put my hand inside his shirt, and, as we kissed, I felt out the hard line of his chest. He was holding on to me really tightly. But this wasn't, any more, a grip to maintain his balance.

He was holding me because he wanted me to stay here and to do what he wanted. I remember the smell of him. He smelt of the beach – the salt and the sea – of the wine and of the meat and spices and polish of the dining room, but he also smelt of soap and clean clothes shot through with a scent I could only conjure by name. Not that I knew it was musk or amber or verdigris but those were the names it suggested.

The mechanics of sex are awful. How to get to the bed. Where to leave your clothes *en route*. How you lie when you're on the bed. Does he want you flat on your back or with your arse in the air? Or does he want you to tell him how he wants you? And, while we're on this subject, what do *you* want? Do you know what you want any more? The mechanics of sex . . . But this wasn't mechanical.

I thought for a minute he was going to fumble at me, amateurishly, the way Dave used to do sometimes, but, as the two of us moved, like clumsy ballroom dancers or deep-sea divers, towards the big, clean, hotel bed, the rhythm of his hands slowed and the two of us started shedding clothes. There didn't seem to be any time at all, though, between his fierce tugs at the blouse at my waist or the shelling of each breast out into the still lit room and the swarming and feeding at each other's mouths. And, if you'll excuse Fiona for being vulgar for a moment, I was as wet as a weekend in Ireland or a sponge in the bath like the one Dad had when he bathed me. Oh, it started as small and dry as a ration of pemmican or army tack, but as the water engorged it, it swelled and he knelt over the edge of the bath and washed me all over Fiona on the *neck* Fiona Fiona on the *back* Fiona Fiona on the *legs* Fiona Fiona and then down and into your little *cleft* Fiona Fiona no more than a quick flick of it but make no mistake about it I knew and he knew and I was wet two times over because I wasn't on the bed or in the bath or back in the city or out over the sea or up in the air. I wasn't burning or smouldering or thawing or freezing or as big as a big girl should be or really small like the person I think I am sometimes like a miniature doll, the smallest one of all in a nest of Russian dolls. I was just becoming all of these things – as if that small doll was being massaged and was growing under his fingers and was forcing its way out through the eight or nine or ten pairs of shoulders and thighs and breasts and lips and was turning into this great big Russian Fiona. She was taking hold of him and clamping one hand on the small of his back and guiding his *protuberance* (this honestly was the word that occurred to me as we were doing it and it made me want to burst out laughing) right into me with no questions about protection because I didn't care you see I just didn't care. I wanted it or him and it and him were the same thing and *that* thing (as unlike *that* as any thing could be) was stirring and shaking me like a cocktail until I was swooning over his shoulder in a horizontal dance that took me right up over the bed, out of the window, across the wide green lawns and over the cliff edge until I was going up, up, up like a glider or a night gull through the moonlight over the wrinkled sea.

You know, don't you? You know when it's right. Don't you? Or do you? *Do you?*

It was afterwards, you see, that I started to get frightened. Frightened of everything. Frightened of disease. Frightened of him. Frightened of myself. Frightened of what I'd become. Frightened, most of all, of what *we* had done. Because I wasn't sure that it meant what I thought it had meant.

Everything he did, that, an hour or so ago, had seemed so natural and safe, now had changed. So that, even when he lay next to me, his arm draped across my naked body, I was waiting for him to go. But when, as he did after a while, he got up and kissed me and said he would go to his own room, I wanted him to stay but I didn't dare to ask him in case I asked him and his mood changed. I was frightened his face might cloud over, his eyes darken and his lips press together. I'm frightened of these moods you see in men's faces. I'm frightened of the way their desires and feelings don't lay them open. I'm frightened of the way they close up afterwards and the light goes out of their eyes and it's like looking into the windows of an empty house – blank, threatening, mysterious.

"Can't you stay?" I said.

"If you want me to . . ." he said. But he was dressing as he said this. He didn't look as if *he* wanted to. I was frightened then. But it was too late to start talking to him about any of that.

"Of course I don't want you to stay!" I said. "Whatever gave you that idea?"

He was dressed now. He looked, I thought, ridiculous. A bit like a waiter who had suddenly arrived to bring me champagne and smoked salmon sandwiches.

"And," I said, "when you go you can't come back. Because I shall lock the door."

I should have told him about *that*. I was starting to look nervously across at the door. You could lock it from the inside with the room key but there was no bolt. He leaned over me. "I shall get a key from reception," he was saying, in a jokey voice. I just looked back at him. I couldn't think how to start to say all the things I needed to say to him. He grinned again. "And I shall ravish you!" he said.

I could feel my face closing up. My eyes got as narrow as my Mum's. "Just go, OK!" I said. "Just go!"

He went, looking like a dog that's been kicked. I was rather drunk. I got up, locked the door after him, staggered back to the bed and fell asleep almost immediately. But about an hour or so ago, not long before the dawn, and, sitting up in bed, I started to scribble these pages What was it that woke me? Why exactly did I wake?

As I have been writing, a horrible and frightening thought has been forming in my brain. I didn't wake by accident. I have tried to put the thought aside but I cannot do so any more. I am writing it down and the act of writing it makes it more, not less, frightening. I think, you see, that HE may be in the room. I can't think how HE got in but I can't rid myself of the idea that HE is here. HE's been here the whole time I have been writing. HE's in that cupboard. HE's under that bed. HE is waiting for me the way HE was waiting for me that night when HE came for me in that horrible mask and that hideous, distorted voice that, now, I keep thinking I recognise from somewhere.

I'm going to get up and go to the door. I'm going to pick up the phone. I'm going to move. I'm going to escape. I'm not going to let that happen to me again.

This time he is going to kill me.

12

Next door the two of them were still arguing. I heard my name again, once or twice. Sometimes I thought I heard them mention Peter Taylor. But, now, I was thinking about only one thing. Ever since I had caught sight of the computer on the dining table I had been determined to take another look at the disk. I wasn't absolutely sure that there was anything else on it. But I knew that I had to see if there was.

I suppose I wasn't necessarily expecting the computer to be running the same format as was on the disk. And I wasn't particularly pleased to find that it was. All of these things made it just that much more likely that Paul could be the person who had written it. What I wasn't prepared for, however, was to find that the next passage of text – some twenty or thirty blank pages beyond the opening section – should pick up, with such horrible neatness, from the passage in my diary I had just finished reading.

It was as if HE had the power to conjure himself next to my elbow whenever he chose, as if HE knew that now would be the moment when I would find myself back in that hotel room, suddenly frozen with terror at a tiny, half-audible noise under my bed. As if HE wanted to make me go back over what had happened again and again and again.

```
>A:/AIR
I had started waiting in the bathroom, just like before.
Actually, when I first got into the room, I just stood
for a little while, watching her, sprawled across the
sheets with her legs open, smelling of sex. I suppose
she was pissed.
        They say women are the gentler gender. I don't
think that's true. They're every bit as crude and cruel
```

as we are. They abuse children, they murder, they torture, they seek power, they plan campaigns and run wars . . . and also, sometimes, when they've shoved a few glasses of wine down them they want to get fucked the same as us. The only difference between them and us is that, these days, they are the only ones who care about their reputations. My reputation is shot to hell, isn't it? I mean — how could anyone trust a guy who gets a yellow mask over his face, slips on a pair of yellow kitchen gloves (how sweet it was getting those on my fingers!) and hangs around ladies' bathrooms?

I was really angry, I think, that I hadn't fucked her last time and, by now, it was pretty obvious that she was dying for it. All that come on to me, all that pretence of *modesty*, all that tossing of the head and demure lowering of the eyes in innocence (surely the most beautiful word in the English language) concealed a scrubber whose cunt is so hot it's amazing she can sit on it for any time at all. She obviously swivels backwards and forwards on that stupid chair of hers in order to rub herself off. We should charge her for dripping on to the upholstery. I really hate her now. I really hate her.

It would be hard, I decided, to fuck her properly if she was making a noise. A certain level of *joie de vivre* is, if you'll excuse the expression, *de rigeur* in love-making these days, and, with the women I go to in London, I quite often feel inspired to shout things like "Oh fuck me harder, Slave Mistress!" which in my view keeps things bubbling along nicely. Between you and me, even being buggered by an eight-inch dildo strapped to the waist of a woman wearing nothing but a Nazi officer's cap and a pair of Wellingtons, can be as boring as going round the supermarket. There are days when I feel like saying to them "Look! Let's call this off! Let's have a nice cup of tea!"

Fiona had started to snore. I tiptoed over to the

bathroom, went in and closed the door carefully behind me. What should I do to her? She'd left half her underclothes on the floor, on her way to the nuptial couch, but I found her things in the bathroom much more erotic. There was a half-empty jar of face cream. I got it open, dipped in my finger and smeared a little on my cheek. Then, watching myself in the mirror, I lowered my pants and smeared some more on my cock. It started to get hard. "I love being a girl . . . da da. I love being a girl . . ."

The safe thing to do would be to kill her and then fuck her. That way she wouldn't make so much noise. But I am a little bit too much of a gentleman for that kind of thing. As far as I can tell she hasn't told anybody yet and until she does I will honour my side of the bargain. There are limits. I could never, for example, dream of having sex with an animal. It just wouldn't be right. Anyway, I *like* animals.

Catching sight of myself — in the mask *of course* — in the mirror, I decided I looked like an animal liberationist. Those wonderful men and women who blow up people who are cruel to bunny rabbits. A terrific bunch. The idea of slaughtering a fellow human for crimes against, say, the bank vole, struck me as so humorous that I had to stuff my fist in my face to stop myself from laughing.

It ought to be possible to shut her up. I could tie a towel round her face. Or shove a lavatory roll in that wide, cunning mouth of hers. Yack yack yack. She thinks she's clever. Don't let the common voice and the common turns of speech fool you. Miss Fiona is a Clever Girl. It's funny how much doing it to her has made me think the less of her. When we were in the office, the morning after, when she walked in as cool as a cucumber it was all I could do to stop myself from walking over to her desk and slapping her in the face. Women won't lie down these days even when you rape them. They just keep coming back like ducks in a fucking shooting gallery.

To amuse myself – I still hadn't decided what to do with her – I slipped off the mask and looked at myself in the mirror. Raping a woman – no, not rape, I didn't rape her I *assaulted* her – assaulting a woman, has done wonders for my self-esteem. I know who I am now. It explains so much about me. I could not, before, understand why my reflection was so anxious not to meet my eyes. Well – obviously – he was ashamed of the master of his image. Even now there was a sense that mirror me still hadn't made the grade. I'd come all over her sheets. Not inside her, where it counts. I looked at myself. "That's no way to treat a lady!" I said. I put on the mask once more.

Look. You don't have to read this. You can skip it if you haven't got the stomach for it. Because I can keep it up for longer than you could imagine. But I think you should read it. It's out there this stuff. You can't ignore it. *Nihil humanum alienum a me puto*, old bean! All criminal behaviour is human, what? The human animal is an animal that, as Goethe pointed out, does everything which it is capable of imagining.

There is a danger that someone has read it. I like that danger. Because there is nothing in it that can *really* be traced back to me. It's just a voice coming out of the air – the same AIR into which a document vanishes when you press the DELETE key. After I had finished the opening pages I copied it on to a disk, and, on the day after I had had that pleasurable evening with Fiona I took the disk into work with me. There was quite a lot of satisfaction in knowing that, while she was sitting only yards away from me I had the definitive account of her experiences in my top pocket. It was the same sort of illicit pleasure I get out of saying "Good morning!" to the man on the main gate or smiling at our head of department and saying "How are things?" when I know that only a few hours earlier I have paid a woman

to urinate on the floor while I thrashed her with a
leather belt.
    The pleasure of flirting with the idea of being
discovered is about the only thing that makes what I do
seem real. I didn't only take the disk into work. I laid
A:/AIR on the carpet, next to the filing cabinets,
after everyone had gone home. Just to see if anyone
would find it. They didn't. Or, if they did, they put it
back exactly where they found it. Oh, what I really want
is for a heavy hand to fall on my shoulder and for a
heavier voice to say, "You stole from the company! You
raped an employee! Exactly the sort of person we should
be employing!">

Everything had gone quiet next door. Well, yes, the men in the company are hired to be aggressive and are expected to be unpleasant. I
could hear that bantering, male tone in all of their voices from time to
time. I could even read it into Paul and Pappanauer's silence, in the
next room.

    As I listened I heard the door open. First, one of them (were
they Paul's footsteps?) came out into the hall. Then they started to talk
again. This time it was in low tones, as if they were frightened someone might hear. But once again there was one word to which they
kept returning. The trouble was, I simply couldn't make it out.
"Enough"? "The stuff?" After a while I gave up. I was half expecting
to hear them go back into the room next door or, at least, to tap on
mine. But they didn't. They just stayed out there, muttering. What
was that word? "Too rough?" "In the buff?" I went back to the screen,
still dimly aware of their voices. Only very gradually did they fade
down until all I could hear was HIM, mocking, preening and horribly
distinct.

>A:/AIR
As I think I said I was damned certain that I was going
to fuck her but I needed to wait until everyone else in
the hotel was asleep. Never mind, by the way, how I got
there. Let's just say I can walk through walls. I wanted

no doors slamming in the distance, no footsteps creaking along the corridor outside. I wanted the time — very pale and still — just before the dawn, when everyone is asleep apart from wicked little me.

When Bill killed the Carter kid, he did it in the toilets, watched by me and three other boys. He dragged him into the cubicle, pushed his face down into the bowl, and though the Carter kid kept gagging every time he came up, Bill just kept on pushing him down. The Carter kid was gasping for air. The noise he made when he surfaced was like someone tearing strips off the atmosphere. The last time he came up he was blue and he made a noise I can't forget. It wasn't human — it was all air and tissue.

I put the mask back on. I was wearing the jersey and the jeans and the trainers I had been wearing last Monday night. I wanted her to see me just as I was. As if there had been no time at all between that first time and the consummation of our love. As if I was reaching out across all those miles of steel rail, from the heart of the city to the heart of the country — to strike terror into her heart.

Should I turn her round and fuck her from behind? Or take her just as she lay in wine-soaked sleep? She'd be asleep and she'd wake up with me inside her. But I didn't like the idea of getting too close. Something about me — my smell or some small tell-tale gesture might give me away. Since I left the gloves in my briefcase I have seen her, from time to time, look nervously between the three of us. I was definitely going to have to kill her.

Over in the corner of the bathroom there was a plastic lavatory brush. It didn't look heavy enough to do any serious damage. Otherwise — it was a question of pelting her to death with soap or choking her on the wide selection of shampoos and body lotions available for the use of guests. Or perhaps I could strangle her with the shower cap. This, too, struck me as funny.

I went to the door and opened it a fraction. During the time I'd been in the bathroom she'd managed to roll herself under the duvet — although whether she'd woken during this manoeuvre was unclear. I found the idea that she had woken, and perhaps even walked about the room, stark naked, while I was in the bathroom, extremely erotic.

You could still see her arms. I tiptoed across the carpet and looked down at her. She doesn't shave under her arms. There were tufts of brown hair, as rank and coarse as the earth by the canal over behind the orphanage — but I found them exciting. They were like a physical expression of the smell of her — sweaty, acrid. When you looked at her closely — the beaky nose, the thick brown tresses — she was much less pretty than when she tries to compose her face for her varied audience of men. But, this time, I liked that crudeness. There was a suspicion of hair, too, on her upper lip — a light down that I had never noticed before. As I watched, she stirred in her sleep and one breast flopped away from the duvet. I held out one yellow, rubber glove — closer, closer, closer. One more inch and she would wake and scream.

I didn't touch her though. All this was too interesting. I wanted it to last a long time. I wouldn't wait in the bathroom. It was too obvious. I'd done bathrooms. Presumably, after a while, rape or assault or whatever you like to call it, can get as tedious as sex. As I wondered where I should hide, I thought about all those dull, dull, dull serial killers and rapists who *have* to go through the same routine over and over again. Always shooting couples in the head or drearily compelled to strangle gay men while they are sucking someone's cock or *having* to torture women of over sixty. I thought to myself — my friend, you are such a perfectionist that unless conditions are absolutely right you may end up walking away from this one!

I thought that might be rather sweet. To stay there, in the room, moving around it, possessing it, watching her — and then, as dawn came up, stealing out quickly by the way I came, replacing the room key behind the desk at reception and then on out to the cliff, perhaps to rip off the mask and hurl it down towards the grey sea.

He just likes to watch women with a rug over his head. Is there anything wrong with that, officer?

Then she stirred again. It was the way her arm draped over the side of the bed that made me decide. Her hand was splayed out, only a few feet above the carpet. I couldn't stop thinking about how it would look if I were lying *under* the bed, watching her shape distort the mattress. I liked the idea of going down on my hands and knees and crawling, very, very carefully under her fingers as if they were an alarm that the slightest touch might wake into life. I would go on my belly, like a snake, and wriggle along the carpet, on into the blank space between the bottom of the mattress and the floor. I would be underneath Fiona.>

"I would be underneath Fiona!" said a voice over my shoulder. I stopped. It was some time before I realised that someone who wasn't me had actually spoken these words. And, at first, I couldn't have said whether it was a man's voice or a woman's. There was something obscene about that. When I had been reading what he had to say I gave him, at least in part, my own tones and accents.

Now that those five words had been spoken aloud I would have to start the complicated business of putting a name or a face to them. For a moment I thought that it might have been Peter Taylor's voice. Then — because I wanted that to be the case — I was almost sure it was John Pappanauer who had read them aloud over my shoulder. It was only when I had exhausted these two possibilities that I realised that Paul was in the room with me. And I was afraid again — as I had been in the room, when I heard that tiny noise somewhere below me under the bed.

"You're reading it," said Paul.

"Yes," I said.

Pappanauer had come into the room as well. "What is she reading?" he said.

"A story!" said Paul.

Pappanauer came over to the computer and leaned over the screen. He started to read, aloud. "I inched my way into position. And I was only just there, when, above me, there was cough and I felt her body move with sudden, conscious urgency. She leaned over to the bedside table over to the right and I heard her take something off it."

He stopped and looked between me and Paul. "What is this?" he said.

"Don't you know?" I asked Pappanauer.

"No!"

Paul coughed and let his eyes wander back to the screen. Nobody spoke. Then I said, "It's something the man who attacked me wrote."

"You what?"

"Read it!"

The three of us crowded up to the computer screen. I started to scroll down. Once or twice, when I moved too fast, Pappanauer leaned forward and put his hand on my arm, indicating that I should go more slowly. It was only when he did this that I remembered that, for the first time since he had called on me that morning I was not facing him. I was also about five yards from the carrier bag and the black-handled claw hammer. That didn't worry me of course. Paul was in the room. That was the only thing I cared about. That was the only reason I had allowed such a thing to happen. Paul was in the room. I was all right.

>A:/AIR
Then there was a lot of thumping and a ridiculous, arse-shaped sag and she sat up in bed and started to do something. I thought at first that she was doing her

nails. But such was the silence in the room that, after a minute or two, I could make out, quite clearly, the scritch-scratch of a pen across paper — like a busy insect tracing and retracing its steps. Oh Fiona! She's writing her fucking diary! "Dear Diary, today I got fucked by a gorilla!" Oh Fiona!

I think what I hate about her is the way she carries herself. There's an arrogance about the sulky way she tosses her head. She's only a fucking *secretary* for Christ's sake! Even if she did get someone to fill her hole in the Cliff View Hotel, Dartsea. Was that what she was writing about?

Dear Diary,
I am sitting up in bed thinking about the power of HIS love and hotting up my quim for next bout of SHAGGING! One day I dream of becoming a famous authoress. But not yet. First I must encourage the new man in my life to shag me more and more so that we can have kiddy widdies like normal people!

Ah, the kiddie widdies! Ah, the expression on the Carter kiddy as he went down for the last time, and then, as Bill held his body, it wilted in the water. Ah, the teeny tinies! They die just like anyone else.

I read somewhere that in the Nazi death camps, when they were hanging a child, they would hang a stone to its legs to make the drop quicker. I think about that when I think about my childhood — or the lack of it — and I bless it. Because my childhood — or the lack of it — freed me from the tyranny of conscience. And what is conscience? Just another human invention — another feather in the cap of those wonderful people who gave you Auschwitz and the Hundred Years War.

Miss Fiona, Authoress, was writing furiously now. The pen was flying across the paper. Cliché after cliché I presume. Schoolgirl crap. But, however bad it was, it was certainly giving her the illusion of usefulness. I have never heard anyone write so fast for so long. It would take a bit of grievous bodily harm to get her to slow up let alone stop. I lay, quite still, on the pile carpet, listening to her pen scratch, the way I hear my own fingers patter over the keyboard of my computer like mice in tap-shoes.

I like, sometimes, to imagine I am writing this for someone. I imagine this someone very distinctly. It's a woman, I think, and she is reading this alone, by the light of a bedside lamp. She doesn't like it. She wants to put it away but it nags at her, like all the thoughts she has never dared express. Are you looking for clues as to who I am in how I write? In the patterns of my prose? You won't find anything there. The patterns we see in words are arbitrary. And, anyway, I might be fooling you. Who said you could look over my shoulder anyway?

She must have written for nearly an hour. Maybe longer. There were a few token pauses, in which, presumably, she pretended to think, but, for most of the time she kept up her relentless scrawl — as fast as if she was trying to transcribe the patter of a cattle auctioneer. And then, suddenly, I moved. Just a slight shifting of the right leg but it came in one of her pauses, and the pause lengthened into a dangerous silence. She had stopped writing. *She knows*, I thought, *she knows I'm here. If she's clever, she'll call out.*

But then, it's four in the morning. The walls are thick. No one bothers to respond to people screaming these days. They find all sorts of ways to re-interpret a cry for help as something that has absolutely nothing to do with them.

She didn't call. For what seemed an age she did not move at all. And then, with immense care, trying to keep as quiet as possible, she rolled towards the right-hand side of the bed. The side nearest the window. Perhaps she's doing that, I thought to myself, because the light is there and the light makes her feel safer. I watched her movements across the bed. I was fairly sure that she had no idea of where I was in the room. She just knew there was somebody in there.

I matched her movements, so that they masked the sound of mine. As she made her way right I made my left, so that, as one naked leg (she was still naked!) hit the floor, I was right at the edge of the bed on the side that lay between her and the door. I watched as her other naked foot came down and poised itself, with a ballerina's care, on the pale green carpet. Then, keeping close to the side of the nuptial couch — presumably to give herself some feeling of security — she started down towards the bathroom. *She'll head for the door*, I thought, *but I will cut her off*.

I didn't move out from under the bed until she had passed my side and was walking, still naked, towards the bedroom door. Even then I didn't suddenly spring to my feet like a pantomime villain. I lay, motionless, like a child playing grandmother's footsteps, as Fiona, too frightened to look behind her, froze, aware of a slight rustling noise on the carpet. But when she ran — which she did soon after I had crawled out like some gigantic insect on to her floor — I jackknifed up and out after her and was on her before she had time to compose herself into a scream. It's the costume as does it.

She had made the mistake, you see, of turning and seeing this *thing* coming towards her up from the carpet, with its yellow hands in front of it. And by the time she had thought all the things that decent citizens think in such situations I was on her. My yellow mitts were stopping her mouth and I had forced her to the floor. I was determined to have her on the floor.>

I looked over my shoulder.

Paul and Pappanauer were both staring at the screen. They were both doing a good impression of men in shock. Even though Paul was supposed to have seen all this stuff before, he wore the look of a man prepared to be horrified by it all over again. And Pappanauer was now solemn to the point of idiocy.

"This is him," he said, "this is the geezer who . . ."

"Yes," I said, "this is his authentic voice. This is his account of what happened to me."

Neither of them spoke. I said, almost brightly – "I think he enjoyed writing it. Shall I scroll down the page for you two gentlemen?"

Paul said, "Fiona . . ."

And I replied, in a harsher voice than I had intended, "That's my name!"

Then we all fell to our reading once again, like good pupils in a classroom.

>A:/AIR
She fought quite hard. She was a credit to the Women's Movement. But I am afraid – *sister* – we are bigger and stronger than you are – *sister*. And by this time I was a graduate student. I knew where my hands should go and just how I should use my knees to force her thighs apart. Oh and how I should drive my elbow into her neck until she made a noise like slate being dragged backwards across a blackboard. There was only one thing on her mind, I thought, and that was how to get some AIR into her EARTH.

It was clever of me, I thought, to have come at her with my prick hanging out of my trousers. It improved the look of the thing I thought. It signalled my intentions in a manly and straightforward manner. And, assuming I was going to let her live at the end of it all, not particularly incriminating. One prick looks very like another. An angry stub of veins capped like a mushroom. Anyway, on our previous trysts I had noticed a distinct reluctance to cast her peepers in the direction my chopper. It is, after all, a lethal instrument. So, when I forced myself up her – and I made damn sure

I didn't come too quickly this time — it was curiously easy. The pressure on her neck made it harder and harder for her to struggle. She was concentrating on staying alive. In fact, as I rammed myself into her, the horrible thought occurred to me that she might actually be *enjoying* this. Which was not the point of the exercise at all. It is a point of pride with me that no woman can look on me without a certain twinge of revulsion and that when I rape I rape. I know what I'm doing. I think she said "please" or something. Pretty please. It was much too late for pretty please and thank you.

When I had come she lay very very still. Her face was blue. I'm not an expert on dead people. I've seen a few besides the Carter kid. The boy at Ainscombe's was not a pretty sight after I did him. I hit Al Hunter on the side of the head with the edge of a heavy frying pan. I must have hit him four or five or six times. Maybe more — after I got started I just couldn't stop. He was making this noise that really annoyed me. He fell after the first blow and he was lying crouched on the floor but, I remember, I couldn't get his hands out of the way. He held them over his scalp as if that was going to save him. I had to prise one of them off, because, again I don't know why, it was really important to me to get a clear, uninterrupted shot at the side of his cracked skull, matted with hair and blood.

I didn't really look at her to be honest. The one thing I wanted to do was to get out of there. To my surprise I felt no urge to take off the mask. I felt OK in the mask. I wanted to walk out on to the cliff, just as I was. I went to the window, levered it up and stepped out on to the balcony that runs along the frontage of the hotel. I felt like someone leaving a lover asleep, just before dawn, as I crept out towards the wooden steps and off down the lawn to where the sea lay, quiet under the spring moon.

I looked back at her, once, before I crept out of

the room. She stirred slightly. That, I will have to admit, relieved me. There is no point in killing them if they do what they're told, and, as far as I can tell she did do what she was told. I'd warned her that if she did say anything about what had happened the other time I would kill her. But she hadn't. She might have come into the office shaking like a leaf and looking the colour of self-raising flour but she hadn't said anything to any-one, had she? I could, I suppose, have warned her again — which might have spared all of us a great deal of trouble — but I did not do so. She knows what our secret is and until she breaks that confidence she can live in peace. I don't want her to be unhappy. All she has to be is a good girl. That's all she has to be. And next time I will tell her precisely and clearly what she has to do to be that. For me. Eh Fiona?>

The next few pages seemed to be blank. I took my hands off the keyboard and looked up at the two of them. There was a long silence in the room.

"He wants to kill me," I said, "but he hasn't got the nerve." Paul coughed. "This was written by someone in the office," I went on, "one of you three. Whoever it is."

I switched off the machine, pulled out the disk and put it in the pocket of my jeans. Then I went back to my seat by the carrier bag. Still neither of them had spoken. I sat there for a moment, then I said, "But I think, you see, I am starting to understand him." I found I was looking at Paul as I said this. "I mean I think I know the rules by which he plays. I thought at first that I would be able to track him down by the way he writes. The sort of crazy idea that would only occur to someone who has spent too much of her time studying English literature."

Neither of them spoke. I don't think either of them had ever heard me talk like this before. "That isn't how I'm going to do it," I went on, "but I am going to do it. There's one thing he's forgotten, you see. Or rather, there's a thing he thinks I won't dare mention. But I will. And when I do he won't be able to stop himself."

Paul looked as if he was about to say something but I held up my hand. There's no such thing, of course, as character. Thinking about how he was, reading letters from him or my account of him in my diary – none of this had made him any clearer. It came down, I decided, to his smile. Why should a man who could at one minute look like an officious hamster be able to turn on a smile that had set me giggling and twisting in the air like something on a Christmas tree? And why should the same man, by a downwards flick of his eyes, suddenly convince me that he was protecting the sort of horrible secret life nursed by the author of A:/AIR? Because – whether it was the anonymous flat or the rain or the fact that, now I was seeing him armed with everything I had read and seen since we were at Dartsea – I was no longer sure that it wasn't Paul.

"Pappanauer," I said, "I want you to ring Peter Taylor! I want the three of you together. Him and Paul and you. OK? I don't care where. But that's what I want."

"Look," said Pappanauer, "I have no idea of what any of this is about. No one has said anything to me about anything. Perhaps I am too unimportant to be told anything but I . . ."

Paul made a very slight movement. Pappanauer's voice died away. I held up my hand again.

"And no police," I went on. "Tell him I don't want any police. Afterwards he can have all the police he wants. But not now."

Paul started to try and say something again. "And Paul," I said, "I want you to tell me about this place. What you use it for. Why you keep it."

Paul didn't try to answer that. But Pappanauer took a key from the pocket of his jacket and tossed it over to me. "It's all in the spare room. The locked door off the hall. Look in there."

"Listen –" Paul began. But I was already on my feet. I had the carrier bag in my right hand and I swung it to and fro, feeling, once again, the comforting weight of the hammer inside it. I went out into the hall, leaving the two of them behind me. I stopped once I was outside the room and listened. But neither of them said a thing. I put the key into the lock of the spare room door and pushed it open.

13

I had more or less expected to find what was in the spare room. But I hadn't anticipated there would be quite so much of it. Over the years I seem to have seen quite a bit of pornography but have never found any of it as stimulating as, say, my man of the moment undoing the top button of his shirt. I think it's the expressions on the participants' faces I find so wearing. If they try to look cheerful they end up looking obviously silly. If they try to look ecstatic they look even worse. If, as they often do, they try and look committed and/or attractive they end up looking like people on the verge of a nervous breakdown. There are some occasions when I have a great deal of sympathy with Barbara Cartland. One of them is when I find myself looking at full colour reproductions of people having sexual intercourse. Paul seemed to have enough of this sort of image to have kept a small town in continuous employment for about the last ten years.

Quite a lot of the pictures were of people in chains or manacles. These people – they were mainly men – looked, I thought, even sillier than the people actually screwing. One guy seemed to be chained to what looked like a wooden chopping block, and, just to make it absolutely clear that he wasn't going anywhere, had been equipped with what looked like a large black plastic bag. A woman in black bra and suspenders (they all seemed to be wearing black bras and suspenders) was in the process of dropping this thing over his head. The chap was stark naked apart from what looked like a pair of jump leads, affixed to his nipples.

There was also, scattered about the place, the occasional item that looked as if it was intended for livening up the dreary business of taking off one's clothes and having sexual intercourse. There was something that – although I didn't look too closely – might well have been a whip, on the far wall. After I had looked in a couple of the books, I took up a chair by the door and, without really scanning the print, took out my sheaf of papers again. I realised that my hands were shaking.

I hadn't been bluffing out there. I thought I had begun to understand what it was about HIM. The idea had started when I remembered a news item about the guy who had been attacking those women down by the river. It had been as guarded as such news reports must inevitably be, but it had hinted, strongly, that the man in most of the attacks had stopped short of ultimate physical violence. And they had quoted one woman who said that he had "said something to her". She didn't say what it was but the report said that this woman was now living in hiding because of it.

If you tell anyone about this I will kill you.

Suppose that is what he had said to her. Suppose I was wasting my time trying to understand anything about him from what he wrote. Action is character. Suppose the first attack was, as that remark implied, a horrific kind of approach, a moment when HE thought he was doing something perfectly legitimate. The barrier was crossed when the victim fought back.

I have often noticed that people such as President Hastings Banda, or Klaus Barbie, are particularly keen on being well represented legally. It is also true that sadistic perverts have a very well developed sense of their own rights and privileges. I had done the right thing — although I couldn't have known that this was the case — by coming into work and looking, as far as possible, as if nothing had happened.

If you tell anyone about this I will kill you.

I hadn't told anyone. Not yet.

The other thought that had occurred to me was that there might, possibly, be two completely different sets of crimes here. Somebody was taking money from the company and was prepared to kill to conceal the fact. And somebody else — who, perhaps, knew about what this person was doing — was stalking me, playing some complicated game

174

of obedience and dominance and, perhaps, using this second person as a shield.

I was looking at the next section of Peter Taylor's journal. It seemed to refer, retrospectively, to the investigation he had started while we were down at Dartsea.

Saturday April 10th. 3 p.m. (PT)

In printing out chunks of that document – *that* I like to call it, not wishing, any more than poor darling Fiona – to put a name to the obscene emptiness it reveals – I sometimes feel like editing it. Indeed I have left out some passages. I am certainly not one of those people who think texts have no power to corrupt. Look at the Bible, for God's sake.

But evidence is evidence. And there are things in the document that point very specifically to one person. At the moment, I cannot believe that the person could do even half the things mentioned in A:/AIR. That is neither here nor there. What I need is evidence.

Although the internal evidence of the document points with almost worrying crudeness to the fact that its author is the very same person who has been involved in the Newsom Project business, I persist in thinking that things aren't quite as simple as that. Let's put it simply. If it *is* Pappanauer – as I think it is – and if he is trying to incriminate Paul, he may well have decided to heap anything he can think of on to his chosen victim. Al Hunter could quite easily have been disposed of by someone with whom he was in partnership. Harold Porter is, in my view, quite capable of murder. It's impossible, at the moment, to stand back from this and understand how the various unpleasantnesses with which I seem to be surrounded, may or may not be related.

The afternoon they left on the train I got the home address of Al Hunter, and, in my capacity as a concerned business colleague, went to see his widow. She sounded, on the phone, as if she was being positively chirpy about the fact that an unknown assailant had broken into her modest suburban home and bludgeoned the poor man to death while she was out at the cinema. "I keep thinking," she said, "that it could have been me!" Which seemed, when I met her, to be the full extent of her concern for the late Alan Hunter.

I only remembered him when I got to the house. He was working in Porter's outer office and I suppose I must have met him several times. But, until she answered the door, I can honestly say I had no recollection of him whatsoever. Mrs Hunter, however, looked uncannily like her late husband. She had the same receding chin, the same puffy cheeks and, like him, she looked as if she was in the early stages of going bald. There was a feudal quality to her. "Mr Taylor," she said, wiping her hands on her apron, "come in. You were always so good to Alan!"

I had no recollection of doing anything to Alan apart from walking past him on my way in to see Harold Porter. But I assumed she meant I wasn't actively hostile to him, as I remember some of his colleagues being. She showed me into a mean little back room, looking out on to a sunless garden. There was no sign of children. There was a shabby dining room table with six newish-looking chairs. I couldn't imagine Mr and Mrs Hunter *knowing* four other people, let alone having them all in the house at the same time. Perhaps, I thought, as I sat reverently on one of them, they were a bargain.

My life has been so simple. I met a woman I loved ten years ago and have not stopped loving her since we married. I love my children and enjoy my work. I am, I'm afraid, and this is perhaps what Fiona has picked up, a happy man. One of the reasons I stay away from philosophy is that, in my view, too much thought can do a person permanent damage. I thought all this as Mrs Hunter brought me a drink and pushed what was left of her greying hair away from her forehead. She was younger than she looked. Isn't that the saddest thing you can say about a woman?

"They broke in through the back," she said. "Just broke down the door. It was . . ."

"Go on . . ."

"Like they *wanted* to do it. Like they just wanted to kill someone and he was in the way."

Cities, now, in England, I wanted to say to her, are full to bursting with people who want to kill someone. And most of them aren't really particular about who it is. But that wasn't what I had come to discuss. I was looking for something special.

"They took stuff. Money . . ."

She nodded. "They broke into Alan's desk. And took some papers. But not important papers."

I coughed. "How do you mean not important?"

She put her head to one side. "I mean, only to do with the company. And they can't have been important, can they? Otherwise they would never have let him take them home, would they?"

She looked suddenly anxious, as if she suspected that her husband might have done something wrong. I told her that I was sure they weren't important and that Alan had been a conscientious and worthwhile employee who was greatly missed. This seemed to cheer her up.

I took quite a long time to persuade her to let me in to what Hunter called "his office" although it was really no more than a cupboard, between the front room and the dining room. The desk was a cheap, wooden affair. It looked to me as if the police had left it just as they found it. He had kept bills in a closed compartment and whoever had broken into the desk had ripped open the compartment's lid. It was still hanging, drunkenly, by its hinges.

"That was where he kept the stuff from the company . . ." said Mrs Hunter. She was looking at me nervously. I tried to keep my face as expressionless as possible. I had no idea, you see, how much she knew, or how much this worried little woman stuff was an act. "He hasn't done anything wrong, has he?" she said.

I didn't answer her. What was worrying was that, whoever had broken in hadn't even bothered to touch the rest of the stuff in the desk. They had known what they were looking for. That was what sent me back to the office and led me to the computer disk. I drove straight back, ran into the building and started to go through both their desks. I've always made sure that I know where their keys are, even though they don't know that I know. I have always made it my business to be fully informed about my employees.

In Pappanauer's drawer were a couple of motoring magazines and a paperback novel about a serial killer. I read a couple of pages, or at least enough to realise that almost any incident in the book was capable of inspiring Pappanauer to do something even more disgusting. There was also – I thought this rather odd – a crumpled dress shirt. The rest of the stuff was mainly letters. There was one from a woman called Julia, who seemed rather upset about something that had happened last Saturday night. I thought I knew how she felt.

Curiously enough, in Paul's desk, there was nothing personal at all. There were rulers and Post It notes and calculators. At the back of the top drawer there were about twenty paper clips. But, mixed in with all this stuff, were things that looked at first like office equipment but weren't. There was a bundle of things next to the calculators that at first I took for fancy rubbers. They turned out to be toy soldiers. There were two or three street maps of London, tied up neatly together and, in the middle of them, a volume of medieval love poetry. Nothing else. It was getting late now. After seven. Outside it was getting dark. There were no lights on in any of the buildings on our side of the complex. Outside, in the corridor, I could hear a cleaner thumping and banging her way towards me. I felt a rush of the kind of anger that had swept over me just after I first heard of Hunter's death. A feeling that something terrible was going to happen and that I, or someone like me, was the only person who could stop it.

I found the computer disk on the floor over by the stationery cupboard. I wasn't looking for it. Usually disks are kept at the back of the cupboard itself. This one was blue – not of the type we usually use in the company – and looked as if someone had dropped it. I picked it up, went back to my computer and slipped it in. The system listed only one file. Not a very long one either. The name caught my eye. It was in drive A and it was called AIR. A:/AIR. It had been written in Word Perfect 5.1 – the word-processing package we use in the office. I ran the document. It was the opening section of the narrative I am now putting together – the description of the rape at the flat.

I went through both their desks again but found nothing. I even threw some of Pappanauer's magazines across the office. When I had recovered myself, I replaced all their things exactly as I had found them and even put the computer disk back in the same place on the carpet. As I worked I went over the document in my mind. There was something about the way it was written . . .

When the office was as it had been I rang Anna and told her I had been called to a business meeting out of town. I would see her tomorrow, I said. As usual, she asked me no questions about where I was going or why. All she said – all she ever says on these occasions – was "drive safely". Then I called Michael. Michael is the son of the man who ran Cliff View when I went there with my father, all those years ago. Yes, he had three guests. Yes, they were all, as far as he knew, well. I tried to find a way of telling him what I suspected and, for the first time, understood a little of what Fiona had been suffering. There were simply not the words to express it. I had no evidence, apart from the horrible authenticity of that document, that Fiona had ever been attacked. Michael said he would keep a room for me and wait up until I arrived. He said he still thought about my father a lot. I said I did too. Then I went down to the car and drove out towards the motorway.

I kept thinking about my father as I drove. The Dartsea where he grew up – that was why we always went there on holiday – was part of a country that still smelt faintly of greatness. The sedate families who ranged themselves along the beach every summer and faced the lurching sea in the secure knowledge that they were superior to anything on the other side of it, have all gone now. "It's all gone," I hear him say, echoing the words of his favourite poet, "There's nothing left but the slum of Europe, with a cast of crooks and tarts!"

Out of the blackness of the motorway, lights came on towards me, eating out a passage through the chilly April night. It was nearly one in the morning. On the radio they were playing an old country song, "Your cheating heart, will make you blue . . . You'll cry and cry the whole night through" and, as the gaps between towns lengthened, I beat on the wheel in time to the music. *It's all gone*, I kept repeating to myself, *it's all long gone*.

I must have got to the hotel around three. As he had promised, Michael was there to meet me. He was alone in the bar, and, when I first saw him I had a violent shock of recognition. He has the same stooped shoulders and careworn face as his father had. Looking at him, I suddenly remembered that we had first met when we were both about eight. It was, briefly, like looking at myself accurately for the first time. It was as if I had never before faced the reality of what

I was – a middle-aged man. I went towards him, looking for some gesture of greeting but all I could find was a limp wave of the hand and a few remarks that seemed to belong to some actor playing the part of a so-called serious person. As we exchanged the kind of opening remarks that the middle-aged exchange on these occasions – cautious, heavily neutral – I wanted, for a moment, to rediscover the way in which we would have greeted each other all those years ago. But, like anyone looking again for their own childhood, I was lost, suddenly, in the silly solemnities of advancing age.

He didn't ask me why I was there or why I should have suddenly decided to descend upon him. He didn't have to explain that the room keys were ranged, as usual, on hooks behind the desk in the hall, that the barometer was out of order, that there were sticks and hats and maps by the mirror in the hall and that everything in here was, still, thank God, in the 1950s. "I've put you in one of the sea-rooms. At the far end," he said, and went off, leaving me alone, a whisky glass in my hand.

I wasn't ready for sleep. The journey, and the fear that had inspired it, had wound me up to such a pitch, that I found I was listening, through the silence, for a scream or a struggle somewhere from the rooms above me. I had no indication that HE, whoever HE was, would try anything. But neither could I go to my room and settle down for a few hours' sleep without worrying whether Paul or Pappanauer were assaulting Fiona.

I went out, down the steps and on to the lawn. I looked back at the hotel. I was opening the front door of the place, getting ready to go to my room, when I heard the noise. At first I thought it was coming from the landing above me. I went to the foot of the hall stairs and listened. It was only then that I realised that it hadn't come from the inside at all. There was someone out on the stairs that lead down from the balcony to the hotel lawn. I went, as quietly as before, to the front entrance of the hotel, and then I saw him.

He was wearing the yellow mask he described in the document I had read. And on his hands were the yellow kitchen gloves, so lovingly described in the same narrative. His appearance was oddly familiar. And yet it was quite impossible to tell, from looking at him, whether this was Paul or Pappanauer or neither of them. He was moving very slowly down the stairs, and, as I watched, he stopped suddenly, and started to sniff the air, like a dog.

I should have shouted out. I should have woken the whole hotel. I should have dashed inside and found Fiona in her room. I should have done a lot of things. But I did none of them. I just stood there, transfixed by this apparition, wondering whether *it* would move over the smooth lawn towards the waiting sea and whether, if it did, I would be bound to follow it.

When life started again – slowly, as it does after such moments – it seemed a crude and noisy affair. I was running out through the door calling something. HE had turned round and had seen me. He, too, was running. Away from me and towards the steep path that zig-zags down the cliff to the cove below. Even when he was on the track he did not slow his pace. I was thirty or forty yards behind him when he got to the beach. I thought I was safe then. I thought I had him. I know, have known since I was nine, that there is no obvious route out of Dartsea Cove. I certainly couldn't remember telling either Paul or Pappanauer about it when we were down here. I was still trying to work out, you see, what the passage of events during those few days, *meant*.

There is a path that leads out through the caves at the far western end of the beach, but no one who didn't know the area well would be aware of that. To be honest, I was more than a little frightened of the fact that, when we got to the end of the shore, where granite rocks rise up steeply from the pebbles, our friend in the yellow mask might turn on me. He was about my height and weight – we all are in the office, which is one of the reasons why I still had absolutely no clue as to which one it might be – and I couldn't connect his movements with anyone I knew. For a moment I wondered whether I might be wrong. Whether the computer disk was all part of a plan to misinform me and send me off down here while something happened back at head office. All I had proof of was that someone, somewhere, had lifted a lot of money on the Newsom Project, and that a person or persons unknown had brutally murdered Al Hunter. I had no evidence whatsoever that these things were connected with the rape of a girl in my office.

•

I put down Peter Taylor's journal and listened hard. I could hear nothing from next door. A moment ago I had thought I had heard John Pappanauer on the telephone. Now I wasn't so sure. Then I heard steps in the hall. I got up and opened the door. There, standing a little way back from me, his face ghostly pale in the dim, rain sodden light, was Paul. I found myself, without expecting to be so, near to tears.

"What's all this about?" I said.

Paul bit his lip. "Didn't you read my letter?"

"Some of it!" I said.

I realised why I hadn't finished it. I didn't want to discover anything to make it possible that Paul was the man who had attacked me. And, although I could see Peter Taylor in every confident phrase of what he had written, I simply did not recognise Paul in the style of his letter. I looked at him very closely. Conscious of the fact that I must be very careful about every word I chose I heard myself say, "Do you think you ever know people?"

"Not really . . ." said Paul. "I mean, you think you do but you don't."

I didn't want to stay in that room any more. Nor did I wish to discuss its contents with Paul. "How did Peter Taylor know?" I said. "Or, at any rate, what was it made him think he knows?"

Paul shrugged. "I think somebody told him something," he said, "and he believed it!" Then he went on, "Shall I tell you about me then?"

I closed the door of the room behind me. "I don't", I said carefully, "really know anything about you."

"Read the rest of what's there first," said Paul. "You might as well know it all."

I didn't want to go back into the other room. It had Pappanauer in it. I let myself slide down the wall and, watched by Paul, aware of, but not touching, the carrier bag next to me, I read on through what Peter Taylor had to say.

14

Standing there on the beach, watching the figure ahead of me, I found myself starting to question the reality of what I was seeing. There was something so horrible about the oddly contrasting colours he was wearing – the bluish grey of his jersey and anorak, the bold brightness of his weird headgear and the buttercup yellow of his gloved fingers – a colour chosen to suggest optimism and cleanliness and all the things he transparently was not. Was it, I wondered, necessarily, even a "he". The bulky shape, the movements, the way it held itself could have suggested male or female. But, of course, being a man, I couldn't resist the male pronoun. I couldn't resist the muttered "right, you bastard" under my breath as I moved towards *him* along the tide-soaked beach.

To my surprise, when he got to the end of the cove, still running at a good pace, I was breathing heavily, and, at one point on the shoreline, had to clamp my hands on to my knees and bend double over the wet pebbles in order to recover myself. He turned smartly left towards the cave as if he knew where he was going. "Stop!" It was a ridiculous thing to shout. Down here on the deserted beach, it was curiously intimate; the cliffs rose above us like a wall, on three sides, and, to our right, the sea stretched away to the horizon, as quietly expectant as an empty auditorium. "You there! Stop!" He turned, just at the mouth of the caves. He put his head to one side. Then, in a gesture that I found oddly disturbing – he put both his hands on his hips. The light of the moon was on him and I remember thinking – "Surely at this distance I'd know which of them it was. *It isn't either of them!*" And then, briefly, I was absolutely positive it was Pappanauer.

But, a moment later, I wasn't sure of that either. And he – she –

183

it seemed to be teasing me with this thought, deliberately challenging me with a crude, home-grown disguise. For what must have been a full minute we stood, confronting each other, about twenty yards apart across the pebbles, rustling with the sound of the ever-present sea. Then he turned and legged it into the cave. I followed.

As soon as I got inside I realised he knew where he was going. For a start, it was too dark to see clearly, but he was picking his way across the huge boulders that lie near the entrance with absolute confidence and certainty. Why? When we had been down together – who had spent more time down at the beach? Pappanauer or Jackson?

I don't think I had time to understand, then, how the stranger must have known where to go or why it was, as he went deeper into the cave, striking away up to the left where the stones give way to the same dark-red soil that you find on the cliff, that he still seemed sure of his ground. I certainly wasn't. He seemed to be leading the way. If the light of the moon had not been so strong, we would not have been able to make out the exit to the cliff path. As it was, the shaft leaked a ghostly, silver light into the underground chamber, like the filtered illumination of a great cathedral, marking our passage upwards. The last section of the path that leads out on to the cliffs is very steep. It gutters out into loose shale and the only way to get up is to use your hands to haul yourself up by the grey rocks that jut out of the surface of the earth.

He was finding this section difficult. Once or twice he stopped and craned his head upwards, trying to see the way to go. And so, by the time he had pulled himself up to the entrance to the cave, I was only a few feet below him. I saw him stoop down. When he was standing he had in his right hand a fistful of loose stones. He hurled these at my head. There was something almost petulant about the gesture. They didn't deflect me. They simply rained past my ears and skittered down the slope. I had gained a few feet. I was almost on him. I had expected him to turn and run, but, instead, he stooped to the earth again. When he rose he was carrying a huge boulder, about three feet across. He raised the thing above his head like some Neanderthal man about to crush the skull of a rival. I saw his jersey ride up and caught, on the instant, a white crescent of flesh. Paul or

John? Put one man next to another what's the difference? That was when he brought the thing down.

I threw myself over to the left, as it bounced off the rock next to me. It made a noise like a neutered gong – deep, percussive, leaden, and the earth shook around me. But, before I could take any comfort from the fact that I could hear it cartwheeling its way down towards the beach, I had missed my own foothold on the loose stones and was sliding back down the way I had come. I could feel earth and pebbles dashing and striking at my face. For a second I thought I was going to slide right back down the hillside but then there was a violent pain in my right leg and I had come to rest against a jagged stone, only yards away from a steep drop down to the stream which runs down the cliff face on the west side of the cave. By the time I had recovered myself and gone back up to the entrance there was no sign of the man in the mask.

It was only then that I thought of Fiona. The apparition had made me forget that it was for her that he had come. And, while I had been acting out some boyhood fantasy of pursuit and capture, she had probably been lying on the floor of her room, battered, abused, maybe even . . . I started to run back up to the hotel. My lungs ached with every breath. My hands and face were stained with blood. The hotel, like a toy model, set in the smooth lawns at the head of the cliff, obstinately refused to come any closer with each painful step. She mustn't be – I thought to myself – *say she isn't* . . .

•

I looked up. Paul was watching me.

"You still don't want to read my letter," he said.

"Writing something down doesn't make it true!" I said.

Paul nodded slowly. I shifted through the pile of papers until I found his handwriting. The sight of it was curiously reassuring.

"It's funny," Paul said, "I can't believe I only wrote it this morning. It seems like ages ago. It seems like I was a different person when I wrote it . . ."

I looked up at him and looked down at the letter. Outside the rain was still coming down. I didn't know what the time was. We were lost, somewhere in the grey afternoon. All I knew was that soon it was going to be dark.

"It's been a long day," I said in a cold, level voice, looking straight at him, "and it isn't finished yet." And, with those words, I lowered my eyes to the rest of his letter.

8.45 a.m. Tuesday April 13th

Have you broken off to read all this stuff I've sent you? Do you understand? Can you imagine how I felt when I read it? I can live with the fact that you think I'm a murderer. In a funny way that isn't half as bad as the thought that you showed him all that stuff about us at Dartsea. Perhaps you only did that *because* you think I'm the one who attacked you. You wanted to hurt me and that was as good a way to do it as any. I think being in love with someone creates a very precious form of privacy; I felt I could have said almost anything to you. But, then, I didn't think it was going to be written down and broadcast to the Metropolitan Police.

There is one possibility. That you're sure I *didn't* do it but you can see how bad the evidence against me is and that you thought by showing him what happened between us, just as it was, as beautiful and straightforward and *necessary* as it seemed, you might convince him that he could not be dealing with someone capable of rape, theft and double murder. That's the way you wrote it. That was me on those pages.

You're playing some kind of game with me. What is it? I suppose I'll never know now. Nothing that happens between us, it seems, is secret any more. So I suppose I owe you a proper account of myself and you owe me a careful reading of it. I've kept things back from you because I wanted you so much that I did not want you to think of me the way I think of myself – a hopeless sort of person. Worse than that.

What tell-tale sound do I make, what giveaway smell do I give off that should suddenly make you think, as late in this horrible business as *last night*, that I am a fiend in human form? I never said that to you. Why did you say I did? If I said "No peace for the wicked" to anyone, does it prove I'm the sick bastard who wrote A:/AIR? Of course it doesn't. Anyone could have written that. It's just some sick fantasy that's drifted in out of the ether – like so much of what passes for culture these days. Somebody, Fiona, is setting me up. I swear it.

I wasn't *anywhere near* your flat last night. If Peter Taylor saw someone it wasn't me. I know he may have wanted it to be me. If Pappanauer is doing these things it could have been him. If it is Peter Taylor who's doing this to me maybe he deliberately pretended to have glimpsed my face out there in the darkness. Well then, this is me. You have a right to know it all.

Both of my parents died when I was young – four or five years old – and until I was twelve I was brought up by my uncle. David Jackson is my father's brother. He's a bookseller, but he is, as all his friends and neighbours kept telling me when I was growing up, "much more than a bookseller". I don't know whether it's a profession that is usually a byword for inadequacy. He's a big, goodlooking man with a violent shock of red hair – a bit like Peter Taylor's – and he looks more like a rugby player than a bookseller. He's very kind. His wife left him long before I was born. I can't think why. He still kept a picture of her in the hall but I don't think I ever heard him talk about her. He was very kind to me. I think my first clear memory is of him picking me up and carrying me to the window of his house in the country. When he held me it was like I was flying. His hands were cupped around me like the God who figured in the hymns we sang every Sunday (David was an extremely religious man). Of course it wasn't really his hands that made me feel so safe. It was his decency. If I think of him now it is in the words to one his favourite religious tunes, that I can still see him belting out in a cracked bass voice across a flower-laden church.

> Blest are the pure in heart
> For they shall see our God
> The secrets of the Lord are theirs
> Their soul is Christ's abode . . .

I remember when I first went to school, I said, as we were getting into the car, "Will I like it, Daddy?" He leaned down to me. He smelt, as he always did, of soap and tobacco and aftershave. "You mustn't call me Daddy, OK?"

He said it very, very gently. But I still remember the remark as an affront. Even now, twenty odd years later, it still strikes me as shockingly as cold water in the face. *Why couldn't I call him Daddy?* I didn't ask of course, because I could tell he didn't want to talk about it. But, as I watched him move crates of books about the house, or sit at his desk over his papers, flooded with yellow light from the Anglepoise lamp at his side, I can remember thinking that there must be some secret, special reason for what he had said. The last thought that occurred to me was that he was not my real father.

When he did tell me – I think I was eight or nine – what he had to say seemed an odd mixture of the banal and the incredible. They had been killed in a climbing accident. I can remember wondering, as he told me about it, why they should ever have thought of doing something as stupid as climbing up a sheer rock face. For years, the only picture I had of my parents was of two tiny figures in shorts and yellow helmets, falling away from a huge slab of grey stone. This isn't, actually, how the accident happened. It was something to do with the Alps and the wrong kind of snow, but that was always how I saw it. I think I was confusing it with some film I'd seen on the television.

•

I put the letter down and looked across at Paul. "In the earlier bit," I said, "you use inverted commas all the time. Here you don't."

"Don't I?" said Paul.

But I was beginning to understand why he couldn't say any of this stuff to my face. Looking across at him in the dim hall, I tried, and failed, to imagine what his childhood must have been like.

"When you and Pappanauer were down at Dartsea before," I began, but before I could finish my sentence Pappanauer interrupted by shouting from the hall.

"Peter will meet us at the office," he said, "we're to go there straightaway!"

I didn't wait for either of them to say anything else. I got up, jammed the papers back in the carrier bag and started towards the front door. When I realised that no one was following me, I stopped and turned.

"Well, come on!" I said, "what are you frightened of?" I looked straight at Paul. "I'm the one who is supposed to be frightened. Aren't I?"

Then I stood back against the wall to let them pass. I wanted to get out of that place more than anything else in the world. But I also wanted to make sure that I was behind both of them as we went down the narrow stairs out into the rainy afternoon.

Part
3

15

Once again I sat in the back of the car. Although I wanted to ask Paul about his letter – curiously enough, now I had started to read it, the words on the page weren't enough – it was impossible to do so with Pappanauer in the car. The two of them didn't speak. Once or twice Paul said something about the route we were taking but otherwise they completely ignored each other.

I looked at the back of Paul's head and tried to connect it with what was in the letter he had written to me. The connection wasn't apparent at first, but, as I read on, I thought I had started to understand it. Funnily enough that also helped to explain why it was I found him so attractive.

There is a theory of human attraction that maintains we are all looking for some lost part of our childhood – a lost brother or sister, a lost or incompletely realised father or mother. In Paul's case, I suddenly realised, I was looking at a younger brother. Something about the angle of his neck, the nervous, slightly scholarly way he moved his shoulders and the aching tentativeness with which, from time to time, he tried to look back at me without my noticing, brought back the misery of his growing up so vividly that it felt like my childhood, not his. Was this what he had been trying to tell me that day we had had lunch? And, when I had finished reading it, would I finally understand what it was about him, and not question his every inflection or gesture and match it against HIS.

I was twelve when he started to act strangely. I came home from school one day and found him in the front garden, bending over his plants. Gardening was the only thing about which David was unbalanced. You could not stop him. Sometimes I would have to go out in the darkness, find him, somewhere at the end of the long lawn, in among the shrubs and flowers and have to drag him into the house before he would make my tea. He looked up at me and said, "Whose little boy are you?" It's the sort of thing one might say to a little boy – gentle, teasing, affectionately unsettling – the sort of thing that David was always saying. But I knew from the slightly anxious expression on his face that this was a more serious kind of question. One he was asking himself.

"I'm your little boy!" I said, "I'm Paul!"

"Oh," he said.

And he went on looking at me. In his right hand was a dismembered weed, stained with black peat. I can't remember what he said next or how I replied, but I do remember that, after that, he went on to forget other things. Whether he had come out or gone in, whether we had just eaten or were waiting to eat, whether I was a friend or a stranger, and, finally, who he was or what he was doing there in that big, rambling house, at the edge of a wood, deep in the country.

The only thing that kept him straight were his flowers and shrubs. Right up until they came to take him away to the hospital he would hold them up to his face and murmur the names that seemed, to me, so easy to forget – laburnum, cyanothus, large-leaved gunnera, towering over bluish hosta sieboldaria, and, waving up between the woodshaded greens, candelabra primulas, pink and mauve, their flowers like newly alighted seeds.

They took him away and on the same day they came for me as well. I hadn't told anyone you see. I suppose I looked after him, in secret, for months. Sometimes he would not forget and that was even worse because he would cry and hold me and say he was frightened and they were going to come for him. I had to do the shopping and answer the phone and say he wasn't well and lie for him, but in the end I didn't lie well enough.

After that there were a lot of inquisitive people who talked to me and took notes while they talked. There were (although I didn't know that was what they were) assessment centres and reference reports and counselling meetings and, in the end, there was the orphanage. We called it the orphanage as a kind of joke. Actually it was a children's home, run by a woman who had the most extraordinary natural talent for motherhood. You could have filled the Albert Hall with orphans and it still wouldn't have been enough for Mother Mamie. I think she was actually called Mary but for some reason we all addressed her as Mamie. She was almost perverted in her enthusiasm for people who had lost parents. She would line us up – there were only about fifteen of us – and cluck gently to herself, "You poor babies! You poor, poor babies!"

She really liked clearing up after people and cooking for them and listening to them and admiring them. She was brilliant at settling disputes, and at putting troubles into perspective. She treated boys and girls as equals – there were five girls in the home – and she was tolerant to the point of blatant moral laziness. All Mother Mamie's energies went into love. Even the pompous vicar, the Reverend, who came round most Sundays, or the even more poisonous rat-faced woman from the social services, reeled back from Mother Mamie's love like a fireman who has opened a door in a blazing house and caught a furnace full in the face as it leaps towards the street.

Isn't it funny how the imagination can betray you? Looking back at what I've written I can see how easy it would be to picture Mother Mamie as a big, bosomy lady but in fact she was tiny. She was almost painfully thin, had bright, peroxide hair, wore thick make-up, including a quite savage red lipstick and an enormous pair of horn-rimmed glasses. She also had, as well as her orphans, three lurchers, a parrot, four cats and five children of her own – mainly men of about forty whom she treated as if they had just left primary school. It was funny. I loved her. We all loved her. But from the very first I hated being touched by her.

Maybe it was that I had never really had anything to do with women. Occasionally David's cleaning lady would make half-hearted attempts to mother me, but I was never able to take them very seriously. To me, concern and love and physical affection were hopelessly intertwined with a big, gentle man in tweed trousers who wasn't there any more. And, though I pretended to like Mother Mamie's kisses and hugs and pets, in fact they grated on my nerves from my very first day. "Good night darling!" she'd say. "Good night!" And then the kiss. Meant so well. But, to me, like the dry touch of a dead leaf, like an unwelcome memory of something.

•

I looked up. Paul had slewed round in his seat and was watching me read. We were on an arterial road somewhere and, ahead of us, a huge truck scored wheels of spray out of the puddles at the side of the road. The window on my right was starting to mist up. I wiped my hand against it and stared out at the cars in the oncoming lane. There was a startling confidence about the way Paul was writing. Did this mean that he was now telling the truth? Or was the sudden elegance – like that red pocket handkerchief lolling out of his breast pocket – the sign of the dangerous facility of the liar? I was almost beginning to miss those quotation marks, or else to suspect that they, not these easy sentences, might not be the affectation, the deliberate disguise.

Paul didn't say anything but I saw his eyes move to the papers I was holding in front of me. I held his gaze for a moment and then went back to my reading, as we ground on through the rain.

8.45 a.m. Tuesday April 13th

The person who got me through those first days at the orphanage was Bill.

Bill was a thin, wiry kid about four years older than me. He always referred to his parents as "the bastards". I don't think they were particularly poor or particularly distressed. As far as I could make out they were simply into neglect. I think his father was an architect, although Bill's description of him would change from week to week. Sometimes he was a lawyer, sometimes in medicine and once, I seem to recall, an actor. But the *heart* of Bill's story was true. How do I know that? How do you know how I am telling the truth? By a tone of voice and a leap of faith – an alchemy of narrative.

"The bastards once left me in a supermarket," Bill would say, "and found they enjoyed the experience. So they started leaving me in other places. They left me in a park – only somebody saw them and brought me back. They left me in a church, on a boat and even on the top deck of a bus but someone *always* spotted them at it and chased after 'em waving me round their 'eads!"

It was somebody else who told me that in fact Bill had been abused. These people – whoever they were they were quite prosperous – had tied him to his bed, beaten him savagely on his arms and legs and made him go without food for days. If it hadn't been for a neighbour I don't think he would have got much past his tenth birthday.

Bill was unbroken by all of this. "The way I look at it," he used to say, "you've got to get used to three things in this life. Number One – nobody gives a fuck about anybody else. Number Two – nobody gives a fuck about anybody else. And Number Three – come to think of it why should I tell you Number Three you bastard . . ."

Somewhere along the way Bill had acquired a Cockney accent – and I don't think it was the voice he was born with. But his attitude – hardness, mistrust, defiance – was all his own and it was something I admired beyond belief. It suggested to me a way of dealing with the world – something no religion or morality has ever managed to do.

Bill was suspicious of all adults but particularly suspicious of women. I don't know what his mother had done to him – nor did I care to ask. Although he was passionately fond of Mother Mamie (he once headbutted a lad in the village who said something offensive about her) on the whole he thought females were not to be trusted. "Shag 'em an' leave 'em!" was his advice to me. Although how he had come to the astonishing conclusion that this was the way to deal with the opposite sex remains a mystery. He was, after all, only fourteen. "Wiv' birds . . ." he used to say, "you 'ave to do it to them really hard. Then they like it!" By his account – though I never once saw him with a woman – he had done it almost as many locations as there are grid references on the map.

"Iss good in the snow," was another of his lines, "because 'er bum gets all tangy. And iss great in the rain. On a mountain. Caves are good too."

I think that was why I grew up not exactly frightened of women but wholly and completely ignorant of them. Because – from the age of ten until the age of eighteen – Bill was my family and my every experience of the female sex was negotiated through him. I went to a local comprehensive, but, for some reason I never fathomed, no one at the school ever talked to what they called "Mamies' boys". Bill was more than my family. He was my world. And I completely believed every single thing he told me. "During their time a' the month," I remember him saying, "you 'ave to do it on the side. They can be vicious then . . ."

Bill wasn't clever like me. He wasn't even particularly good with his hands. Unless he was in a fight. One night a few of the local kids were picking on us by the gravel pits. Bill went in like a Kung Fu fighter, kicking and screaming, and in a couple of minutes he had laid out four lads, two of whom were twice the size of him. Bill looked after me, the way my uncle had looked after me.

I carry his attitudes, or rather my understanding of his attitudes, with me to this day. When I went to university to study mathematics, a subject which, from the first day I looked into Euclid's Elements, has been for me the most truthful and beautiful thing imaginable, I used to look at the women in the bar as if they were an exotic species of wild animal. I couldn't think how to talk to one, let alone how to put my arms around her. Since I was very young, since as far back as I can remember, I have not been able to bear being touched. Until you that is.

I started going to prostitutes in my second year at university. At first I went to men. Well, I assumed, you see, that I was gay. But I found the experience too weirdly remote to suggest that I was anything else but depressingly heterosexual. I remember one guy rolling my cock between his palms like a Boy Scout trying to set light to a wooden stick, only breaking off from his routine to ask me, in tones of puzzled surprise, "Why did you come here?"

The women, I am sorry to say, were not much better. And, on the whole, rather more expensive. But, over the years, I have been to hundreds of them. I have stood, night after night, in telephone kiosks, calling the numbers of girls who have only been identified by a name and a sexual service. Every time I did it I felt ashamed and ugly and pathetic. But that didn't stop me doing it. It was something, I felt, that put me apart from everyone else on the planet. The other people who have sunk so low as to have to pay for it – and I did meet them on the stairs or in the hallways of countless flats in this huge impersonal city – only confirmed my fear that I had joined a cavalcade of freaks. Once, I remember, I was told to wait in a cupboard with a plump man who told me he was a quantity surveyor. It was a bit like being in the queue at the casualty department of a London teaching hospital.

I thought that no normal, decent woman – like Mother Mamie for example – would ever look at me. I lift my head, now, from the crowded desk in Peter Taylor's study, and I see my reflection in the rain-studded window. Who would want this? I say to myself. You see, Fiona, everyone whom I have ever loved has died on me. They just die like flies when I start to like them. Bill died, although that's another story. Mother Mamie died. And the Carter kid died – although that's a story that since I read that obscene document I feel is no longer mine. What I haven't been able to tell you since that first day we had lunch (and, yes, I had been planning that for months) is that I am completely and utterly alone in the world.

•

I put down Paul's letter. Ahead of us I recognised the main road that runs past the front of the company's offices. Pappanauer was slowing to drive into the car park. When Paul turned round to me I saw his eyes flick down to see where I had got to in the letter. I looked away from him.

I simply couldn't bear to read it any more. The trouble was – I wasn't even sure I believed it. It had become so intermingled with the text of that document – and, indeed with all the other voices in my head – that I had ceased to be able to trust it. All these voices – that I thought I had known and been able to distinguish – were now merging.

In a curious way my reading of A:/AIR has enabled me to say things to you that a few weeks ago I could never have dreamed of saying. What that man wrote in that document was what I've been doing for nearly ten years. But that man wasn't me. He seemed almost to glory in it, didn't he? I don't glory in it. I never have. I'm ashamed of all of it. The only sexual act that ever meant anything to me was what happened between us in that hotel in Dartsea. And look where that wound up. In the pages of the case against me.

I started to think about you about a year ago. It all started because of your name. Have you noticed how people with the same names quite often have other things in common? Georges are always a little stolid. Alisons often a touch pretentious. Alans are frequently tolerant of other's eccentricities. Susans are, I am afraid, a little worthy and sometimes frankly dull, whereas Suzannes are never less than exciting.

I was in a telephone booth near the office. There was a line drawing of a woman – bare-arsed, with a leather top and a pair of high-heeled shoes. She was showing her bottom off and looking back cheekily at the punters. Out of her mouth was a balloon in which were the words, I'M FIONA. I BEND OVER.

I don't know what it was . . . At first I thought it was funny. Prostitution is quite a competitive business and the girls need a slogan or an angle quite as much as a new brand of lager. But, as I looked at it, as it stopped being funny, as it stopped being erotic or silly or anything apart from terribly, terribly sad, the only thing that stayed with me was the name. I thought of all the things that go with being Fiona – Scottish pride I suppose, a particular kind of decency, a variety of head-tossing independence – and I suddenly had the very clear impression that whoever had pinned this card up was *really* called Fiona. It wasn't just a marketing strategy. Some Mum and Dad had bent over her cot and decided to call her that. They wanted the name for her because of all the things a name means and now it had become no more than the label on a piece of meat.

Then I thought about you. I couldn't stop thinking about you. But my thoughts about you were inextricably linked to that girl in the picture. And, of course, to my shame about what I am and how I've lived my life. Which is why I couldn't tell you any of this to your face. The more I couldn't tell you the more I loved you. I couldn't even begin to think how I might talk to you. It's because we love the idea of people and not how they are – that's how the trouble starts. We never act on how we feel but on how we think we ought to feel. We beat about looking for the truth and trample it into the ground. Our imaginations twist the world out of shape which is what's happened here.

I told all this stuff to Peter Taylor at Dartsea. John Pappanauer was in the bar with us. I didn't want him to hear but he did. One of them – Pappanauer or Peter – has taken what I said and shaped it into something horrible and strange. One of them hates me so much he not only wants to set me up for crimes I didn't commit, he wants to take my life and hold it up to me, to mock me with it. Do you understand? That document isn't simply a crude attempt to implicate me. The details of my life are not there simply for the benefit of the police – although I am sure they *will* be used for that – they are there because *he*, whoever *he* is, wants to hurt me. They have all the cruelty of fiction. No wonder Plato wanted to ban the poets from his republic. This character is one of those who, like a storyteller, dreams up horrors – and then enacts them. When Pappanauer heard me talking to Peter, he gave one of those vacuous smiles of his. He could see I didn't want him to hear but, now that he had heard, it was too late to stop. He hates me enough to do something like this. It's him. Like some Catholic or Communist inquisitor he is determined to make me not only suffer for crimes I didn't commit but also to make me recant my life and opinions and make the world see them *his* way.

The Carter kid was a little boy of six. Everyone loved him. He had curly black hair and eyes as big as a beggar boy in a Spanish painting. He was sweet. I never understood how it happened but he was sent back to his parents. The father beat him to death. That was one of the things I told them on the night when I made the mistake of telling them the story of my life. And, like everything else, it turns up, twisted out of shape, turned into something told by a murderer, a thief and a rapist.

I have killed no one. I have stolen nothing. I've done things I'm ashamed of – out of cowardice or misery or laziness – but I'm not what the author of that document is – wicked. It's an unfashionable word I know – but there are people who, like Iago, do things out of malice and mischief and I'm fairly sure that Mr Pappanauer is one of them.

You have to believe me. I can't believe the things you wrote last night. I love you and I think you love me. How can you imagine that I could possibly be the man who did these terrible things to you? Can't you tell, when you make love to someone, what they are or how they feel? If you can't does love mean anything at all? Isn't it a mockery as obscene as A:/AIR?

Go back over what you've written. And over all these papers. Who do you believe? Who do you trust? Say it's me. Say it's me.

Paul.

•

We were parked. We must have stopped some time ago. I realised I was still reading the letter. Paul and Pappanauer were both turned around waiting for me to finish. When I looked up I kept my eyes between them. Paul was looking at me.

"Tell me," he said, "that document . . ."

"What about it?"

"I thought it was fantasy at first . . ."

"Did you?"

He looked sideways at Pappanauer. "I mean . . . you see . . . I read it before I read your diary . . ."

I tried to keep my voice very steady. I had the idea that this might be a test of some kind. "Did you?"

Paul looked at Pappanauer again. Pappanauer had his hands on the wheel. He was staring at the dashboard intently as if he was trying to melt into it as a chameleon might try to blend into an intractable background. "I mean . . ." said Paul, "You would tell someone if something like that happened. Wouldn't you?"

I looked away from him out at the car park. A huge lorry was reversing across the rough ground a hundred or so yards away. In a dismal little shed, surrounded by puddles, the company car park attendant sat and waited for half-past five. It occurred to me that this was almost precisely the question that Peter Taylor had asked me earlier that day. "Would you?" I said.

"I can't understand why you wouldn't tell anyone about that first attack." I met his eyes then. His face seemed to have acquired the poise of his prose style. It gave nothing away.

"I suppose," I said carefully, "I might have been . . . frightened."

I got out of the car. I wondered whether he was going to start asking me whether my diary was faked. And, if he did, whether I was going to find myself agreeing with him. The pages of that hideous document – so specifically accurate in certain details, so polluted with the fantastical in so many others – had unhinged my faith in what was presented to the evidence of my senses. It was if the author of A:/AIR had managed to corrupt everything around me. And my insecurity about what was, and was not true, was a crucial part of his game with me.

I looked downwards into the carrier bag. There was my nightdress. He knew about the nightdress, that was the point. What he said about it in the first chapter of that document was for real. He certainly intended someone to find that document on the floor of the office. He intended me to find it. He wants me to read it. The way Paul wants me to read his letter.

In the nineteenth-century novel, of course, people are always handing other people journals and diaries and documents. They tend to sit back, light their pipes and wait for the recipient to read them in the sure and certain knowledge that because the thing is written down, it is liable to be true. These days the reverse is the case. Nowadays we approach a piece of writing as we might approach a dodgy piece of meat. What is its provenance? Is it really anything like it says it is? And that is as true of my diary, as it is of anything else presented to you here. Just because someone has been raped does not automatically mean they are telling the truth. If Pappanauer wrote his account of all this how would that turn out?

"There's a great girl in our office but she doesn't fancy me. That's why I raped her."

Of course, he hadn't actually raped me the second time. He hadn't even penetrated me. He hadn't even tried to do so. And, although he didn't describe himself as having spoken in the document, he had spoken, once, just before he let himself out on to the balcony. I hadn't caught what he had said clearly. In fact, at the time, I wasn't at all sure I had heard the words I thought I heard. Now, of course, I was certain that I was right. "Don't tell them about what happened before . . ." That was what he had said. He had sounded, I thought, almost scared by what he had done. And, although in the document he described himself as squeezing my neck hard, until he was almost sure I was dead, that wasn't how he had done it at all. Why should he not have tried to rape me the second time? And why should he take such pride in claiming to have done so?

Don't tell them about what happened before.

If you tell anyone about this I will kill you.

He kills the girls by the river when they fight back.

I was standing in the rain, looking out across to the company building. Paul said whoever had written it had simply taken things he had said to them and twisted them round, as if to mock his confidences to them. I knew that certain things HE said he had done he hadn't done. He lies about things over which he doesn't feel he has control. Just like Paul with his inverted commas. The way to trip him up, the way to make him angry and careless is to make me feel as if he has lost control. The way to do it is to take the initiative.

"You go first, gentlemen!" I said. With a sheepish look from one to the other they started out towards the main gate. It was getting dark now. Quite soon people would be pouring out on their way home. There would only be a few security men in the building. But, as long as I had all three of them with me, I knew I was safe. I would wait until they were all there. Then I would say it. I would watch all their faces. And then I would know for certain.

Paul had fallen into step next to me. Pappanauer was on a level with us but a few yards away. Paul looked straight ahead, as he whispered, "Did you read it?"

"I read it." I stole a glance in his direction. "Is there anything else you're not telling me?"

"No!"

We were coming up to the main gate of the building. It was only now that he managed to look back at me. His sudden dependence irritated me. I hadn't asked for any of these details, had I? I stopped as we joined the queue in front of the security guard. Pappanauer was holding up his identity card like a boy in school who is proud of his homework.

"I don't know though, do I?" I said. "I still don't really know you at all." I waited as he went through the gate, and, as we turned up towards the building finance offices I kept behind him on the rain-soaked path. I gripped the carrier bag hard and, not for the first time, began to rehearse what I would say when, at last, I found myself alone with the three of them.

16

As soon as we were in the office I went to my desk. Pappanauer started to make phone calls. As far as I could tell they were for display purposes. Paul went to his desk and sat, as he so often does, hunched over a computer print-out. Anyone who walked into the place would have assumed that we were reaching the end of another normal day. I sat staring at my computer.

"When is he coming?" I said to Pappanauer, who looked up from his telephone call.

"Any minute!" he said.

I took the computer disk out from the carrier bag and slipped it into my computer. Once I was in the document I scrolled down to the pages I had last examined. Beyond the blank space that followed them was a page on which someone had been doodling. Then, a few pages further on, was a single message on a blank page.

ARE YOU GETTING THIS, FIONA?

And then, a few lines further down.

ARE YOU BEHAVING PROPERLY, FIONA?
CAN YOU TELL WHO WROTE THIS SENTENCE?

There was nothing on the following page, but, just before his narrative started again, he had written,

STYLE IS THE MAN!

I spent a long time looking at that. And then, two or three pages further down, unannounced, HIS voice began once more.

I'M ON YOUR HARD DISK, FIONA
I'M GETTING HARD ON YOUR HARD DISK,
FIONA! CHECK YOUR HARD DISK, FIONA!

I stopped the screen. Then I pulled out the floppy and punched up the files on my hard disk. There, at the head of the files directory, was a new one. It certainly hadn't been there last week. C:/WP51/AIR.

I looked up. Pappanauer was standing by the window looking down into the forecourt. Paul was bowed over his computer. I started to shake. HE had come into the office and sat at my desk and written more of this obscene, horrible, twisted document on to my machine. His hands had tapped out this message on the same worn, grey keyboard that still lay beneath the screen. When had this happened? I retrieved the file. It sprang out like a villain in a pantomime, clear, hard white against the blue background.

C:/WP51/AIR

"HI FIONA!"

I'm writing this in the office. On your computer. On to your hard, hard, hard disk. The ultimate risk. The ultimate thrill.

I'm bored with the floppy. How can you get stiff with a floppy? A hard disk is much better for getting up someone, isn't it, Fiona? Why should a guy like me need to bother with a wilting little floppy disk/prick.

It was fairly bloody stupid of me to have brought in the disk in the first place. And a stroke of luck that, during our little seaside expedition it should have lain, meekly on the floor, in *exactly the same place*, waiting for my return. I could not understand, when we all got back, how it was that eagle-eyed Peter Taylor, the family man, could not have seen it and digested its contents. Actually I don't think he is a family man. I think he bought those pictures of wife and kiddy widdies. I think he lives in one room and masturbates just like the rest of us. In my experience, people who talk about their families all the time are probably planning to kill them. Or, at the very least, cheat on them.>

I stopped the screen. I had to try and work out when this had been written. Maybe someone had seen the man who had written it. he couldn't have written it in office hours. Surely not. We had all come back from Dartsea after the police had finished with me. Had he done it after that? Alone in this office, darkness at the windows, as now?

C:/WP51/AIR

<I'M STILL HERE, FIONA! I'M ALL ALONE IN THIS BIG OFFICE WHERE WE HAVE SPENT SUCH WONDERFUL TIMES! I'VE LOVED LOOKING AT YOU, FIONA! I'VE LOVED LOOKING UP YOUR SKIRT AND SEEING IF I CAN SEE YOUR PUBES! AND NOW I'M LOOKING RIGHT INTO YOUR FUCKING HORRIBLE LITTLE BRAIN, AREN'T I?>

I switched off the screen. I only turned it on again when I was absolutely sure that it was angled away from Paul and from Pappanauer.

It was Tuesday now. Tuesday 13th. Lucky for some. I had – in spite of protests from all three of them – been into work on the day before. He must have done this on Monday evening. I had used my hard disk to get into a file, hadn't I. Which file? Surely I would have noticed a new file, especially if – as all files are listed alphabetically – it would have come at the head of the column listing the directory?

HE had meant me to see it, of course. But then HE also knew that we never see the obvious. He had read his Edgar Allan Poe. When you open up the screen you are always looking for something specific. You're not ready for the quiet entrance from a stranger. I decided I was beginning to lose confidence in my own judgement. It must have been done on Sunday. No one would have seen him. I switched on the screen again.

C:/WP51/AIR

Has that boss you fancy so much seen this, fucky fucky Fiona? Has Peter Taylor seen it and is he thinking to stitch me up?

I think he must have seen it. I think he checked out its contents and thought, as people do in this age of information, that he would stay one step ahead of the game. He simply replaced it, hoping I wouldn't realise he was on to me. Just as we replaced the things in the Carter kid's room after we had been through them. It would certainly explain why he turned up in Dartsea with some story about "worrying about us all". For a moment I was worried he might be on to me then.

But this document, my dear little tight-bummed Fiona — you of the white panties — proves nothing. You can't be convicted on the evidence of fantasy, unless, of course, it is the fantasy of a very expensive prose-cuting lawyer. Certainly the Dartsea police, from my brief acquaintance with them, couldn't convict anyone on the evidence of *evidence* let alone supposition or fantasy.

I was fantasising, only yesterday, about what your body would have looked like in the morgue. Those big, clumsy feet of yours would have become something of an obvious statement. That wide mouth, frozen in death, would no longer have been twisted this way or that by your desire to please or offend. And those hardworking elbows would have stopped their endless dance from hip to tit. Would they have closed your eyes? I like to think so. I don't like to think that your best (some might say your only) feature should be permanently on display for policemen, forensic scientists and grieving relatives. Presumably you have relatives who would grieve? We know so little about each other, my dear. That "mother" you talk to on the phone is probably a figment of your imagination, isn't she? Is this exciting you? Are you getting wet?

I've been thinking about your death quite a lot lately. I imagine, sometimes, a complicated autopsy in which men in green aprons, wielding tools that resemble barbecue equipment, tease out your intestines like spaghetti. Sometimes you don't see the pasta. It all happens behind a raised sheet. Although this is, I think, a fragment from a police series I have seen on the television. Sometimes I see you in the funeral parlour, laid out with flowers all around you. The mourners file in and persist in talking in whispers, as if in the pathetic hope that someone who has been strangled by a psychopath is liable to be disturbed by loud noises.

Sometimes I see you, stretched out in the coffin, as it slides off towards the furnace. Because the lid's closed, and no one is going to see you ever, ever again, they have played some hideous undertaker's joke on you, and, instead of flowers around your face they've tipped crushed egg-shells and cartons of take-away Chinese food decorated with last night's cigarettes and last night's paper napkins scarlet with lipstick and fouled with the death's-heads of last night's ash.

Sometimes, this is one I particularly like, I see your gravestone. A simple affair in a suburban cemetery. It is a flat stone, set into the turf, and on almost every day of every year, it is decorated with fresh flowers — to let the casual passer-by in on the fact that this wasn't just any old-age pensioner, but a woman under the age of thirty who was *popular*, for Christ's sake. In these images I am often there, standing a little way from the gravestone, nodding and looking serious and saying things like, "How can there be such people in the world? To do such terrible things?" And then, like today, you go and spoil it all by walking into the office.>

So he *had* written it on Monday evening. It was somehow comforting to think that it hadn't been lying there like a spy all through the wastes of yesterday. I didn't switch him off this time. I simply looked away. I felt a curious sense of elation at the fact that I had had the courage to let the bastard know I was still there. I had this feeling – it had been growing in me all day – that he was, at some level, frightened of me. I met the screen the way I had met Paul's eyes in the flat and scrolled on through it. So he had written this yesterday evening. Monday evening.

C:/WP51/AIR

Rape seems to have done nothing to upset that horrible female equanimity of yours. You didn't mope in the corner, did you? You walked in and you smiled at us all in a cheery manner. There seemed nothing to connect you with the drivelling wreck who staggered round the Cliff View Hotel in the early hours of Friday morning accusing persons or person unknown of assaulting you. Not rape, you understand. You were quite definite on that subject, were you not? Did you think it was something to be ashamed of? The police seemed convinced I had shoved my cock right up your snatch, didn't they? Why do you think that was? And as I was the person who had raped you I felt quite indignant. As it was my John Thomas that had gone in and out and come right inside you, I felt you were letting the side down. There were moments when I felt like leaping into the breach and putting matters straight.

You were, actually, now I think about it, alarmingly low-key about the whole business. Almost as if you were trying to minimise it. You contradicted yourself several times as well, in a manner that would have worried even those with a less intimate knowledge of what occurred in your room than me. Your description of your attacker changed several times. Sometimes he was wearing a mask. Sometimes, it seemed, you didn't really get a look at him at all. He had just come at you out of nowhere. You never mentioned that you had been attacked earlier. In fact, after your first declaration, you retracted it several times. Didn't you, little Fiona? Were you scared of something? Were you frightened I might keep to my side of the bargain? It was almost, one of the hotel staff told me, as if you were scared that mere mention of your assailant might start him off again.

You know the rules. Don't you, Fiona?

Either that, or else you were scared that it was someone you knew. Someone, maybe, with whom you had thought you were in love. Someone who had done the love bit and the kissy kissy let's go to bed bit and tell each other our secrets and have a nice fat meal and a nice fat fuck bit. Intimacy is disgusting, isn't it, Fiona? Was that it? Did you know who had done it to you but didn't want to . . . spoil it.

It happens. A girl goes too far. She decides the man's raped her — maybe he even *has* raped her. She tells the world. She retracts. She wants to damn him. She wants to save him. I heard one of the boys in blue discussing this very question in the hotel bar but, as Miss Macmillan was still being evasive, they did not pursue it. I like thinking of you as Miss Macmillan. That's the stunt you pull on us in the office, isn't it? It's all just a professional relationship. You don't really enjoy reaching up for, say, a file and showing us the way your pants cling to the side of that tantalising cleavage in your arse.

You didn't want to have the test. They say, don't they, that the tests for rape are worse than rape itself? Well, you didn't want to take them. Which made the boys in blue even more suspicious. Who can tell what goes on in a woman's mind? Maybe she was having it away with one of her companions — several people had seen them being amorous at dinner — and maybe things had gone too far and maybe . . . We all look nice, don't we? We're all new men now, aren't we? But if you scratch us isn't there still the same old, primitive stuff?

In the end, after a lot of fuss, you did consent to be examined. There were bruises around your neck that suggested something had happened, even as if, as one of the subtle boys in blue remarked to his friend in the bar, "it was only a bit of gasping sex". And the tests, surprise surprise, proved you had had intercourse with someone that night. They took the spermatazoa away and put it in a big glass jar and waited for the man who fitted its description to give himself up. Normal police procedure.

I wasn't offering them mine. I am hanging on to mine.

The boys in blue took a lot of statements from a lot of people and looked at the window and the balcony and the lawn and your bathroom. They combed the carpet and they turned over the duvet and they interviewed your companions and the chambermaid and they bit on their pencils and by the weekend they were absolutely nowhere. I saw all this from the outside. Nobody saw what I was feeling as I watched it. But I saw what you were going through. I saw through your attempt at bravery. You didn't find your way out of it, did you? You're still scared, aren't you? I don't think, you see, that you could have found your way out of it without a few of those heavy women they have at Rape Crisis Centres. It's not enough to know you've been raped. You have to have someone else to believe your story. Otherwise it isn't true.

I wonder if you do know it's me. You certainly haven't dared to tell anybody if you do. You certainly haven't dared to tell me. The trouble is — unlike that puzzle that confronts a traveller who is faced with two doors and two guards, one of whom lies and one of whom tells the truth — you have no way of formulating a question that won't give the game away if it *is* me you ask. You catch my drift?>

It was dark outside. But the rain had still not stopped. It swept in against the wide windows, picked out by the lights of the office. A network of rivers and tributaries edged across the glass, and, down by the station, the yellow lamps picked out crazy drops of water, scudding through the blackness like fireflies. Opposite me, Paul had looked up from his computer. Dave used to look at me like that sometimes. As if he was waiting for me to tell him what to do. I didn't like it. I still don't.

When I had come into work yesterday he had been watching me, knowing he was going to plant this on my screen. He could be one of the men in the room, now, watching me read it. As I thought this, both Paul and Pappanauer, as if by some pre-arranged signal, started to wander over towards my desk. I had to struggle not to switch off the screen. But I managed not to do so.

C:/WP51/AIR

I keep going over what happened at Hunter's place. I keep going over everything and wondering whether I have made a mistake. I have made a lot of mistakes. I have left things everywhere. That's not the point. It's not what you leave at the crime scene. It's what the police are looking for that counts. Don't you follow criminal trials, Fiona?

Oh Mr Hunter, whatever will he do? Hit on a head with a frying pan, no longer as good as new . . . there is nothing to tie me to the death of Mr Hunter. As I tap this out on the keyboard, in the deserted office, with the rain driving against the windows (it's come back since we returned) I know we're into the final phase. It's back to slanted, vicious English rain, from the top left-hand corner of the sky to the bottom right-hand corner of the earth.

Some people might think that a person who rapes is not liable to be a person who murders. Some people might think that a person who embezzles money is not liable to be a person who rapes. Some people are stupid. Wickedness is an inclination. I started to steal and then I started to do other things . . . But, you see, they'd never taught me how to have an inclination to goodness. When I left the orphanage I did not know what these things called "families" — where they teach you about such things — might be. I remember walking down the front steps and looking at every group that passed as if they might hold some clue. They didn't. Families didn't seem to go around together. That man in a suit, striding along purposefully, in the middle of the pavement. Was he, perhaps, from a family? On his way to one? When people left families — the way I left the orphanage — did they carry a special secret?

Sometimes I might see a fat, bedraggled woman with a pushchair. There might be a screaming baby in it, and two or three toddlers walking behind her. Their faces might be smeared with sugar or dirt and they would be in the middle of some public row. Dad never seemed to be there. Or — if he was there — he looked as cowed as the rest of them.

I suppose I wanted a family, but not one of the ones you saw together. I wanted one of the ones that had spawned those guys in suits, pushing their way along the middle of the pavement. I occasionally glimpsed such families in glossy magazines. Usually of course they weren't really families at all but models got together for the purposes of advertising something – but these people, the ones who were seen picnicking by a river in order to advertise lavatory paper or grouped around a fireside in order to advertise a form of heating, were quite as real as the ones, sometimes featured, who were advertising nothing apart from themselves.

These real families – often the appendages of famous novelists or up-and-coming conductors – were a real puzzle. I could not imagine how they behaved when they were alone together. Perhaps they were never alone together. Perhaps they only came together in the pages of the glossy magazines. There was one family that particularly fascinated me. I don't remember the husband's name – I think he was a film director – I do remember that the wife was called Candida and the two girls were called Lucy and Fiona. I cut out the girl called Fiona – a small, fat thing with red hair – and I pinned her on the wall of my room at the orphanage. And then, one day, I don't really know why, I took a dislike to her. I scrawled a moustache on her face and a couple of crude tits on her dress. Then I stabbed her face with a pencil, over and over again. Why do you think I did that, Fiona?>

I looked up. Both of them were standing a little way away from the screen, their arms folded. I felt a moment of pure terror. The only reason I had felt comparatively safe was because – though I was no longer sure which of the three of them he was – he could not be two people at once. But something about the fixed way both of them were following the text, their expressions completely blank, started me wondering, crazily, if there might not be some hideous conspiracy at work here. Why *had* Pappanauer been given the key to Paul's flat? I looked straight at Pappanauer. He coughed and looked away. "Is this . . . him . . ." I heard him say. I didn't answer. Both of them edged a little closer. I made a sudden movement and they stopped. I continued to read, feeling their eyes on me and on the screen.

C:/WP51/AIR

The Carter kid came from a family. He had lost both parents and his sister in a boating accident — the circumstances of which always made Bill break into hysterical laughter. So, when he came to us we knew he knew something we didn't. He wanted to be one of us, of course, and so, as people like that always do, he pretended not to know his own secret. But our secret was that we always knew the people who knew what we didn't know. We had come up the hard way. And we beat his secret out of him in the end.

"I'm going home early!" she said, this afternoon. As she said this I decided that she was one of those confident people who knew what the Carter kid knew. The thing he never forgot, even when his face, blue and shitty, came up from the toilet for the last time. So that killing him was . . . well . . . unsatisfactory . . .>

I swivelled round in my chair. Pappanauer had gone back to his desk and was making a phone call. Paul was still looking at me. I looked back at him. "Did you want to have a family?" I said. He clearly didn't want to answer this question. So I asked it again. He nodded, rather feebly, in response. I looked back at the screen in front of me. The trouble was the image of the orphanage conjured up by HIM was so much more vivid and credible than Paul's. I only have to say the word "orphanage" and I see dark rooms and cruelty. But perhaps that's only because, I decided, I am one of those people who grew up in the families that were such a mystery to poor Paul.

No. No. No. It was HE who affected to find families a mystery. And HE who was telling me that all of this – the money, the girls by the river and what had happened to me, were all part of the same thing. Pappanauer looked up from his telephone call – someone (a woman? a man? a frog?) called Marky – and said, "He'll be here any minute. Shall I get us a drink?"

"No!" I said, more sharply than I had intended.

Paul looked across at him. "She doesn't want to be left alone with me," he said, in that same hangdog way. I said they could both go. Even as I said it, it occurred to me that, while they were gone, Peter Taylor might decide to show. The thought of him coming in, unannounced, through the double doors, frightened me. I said they could both stay where they were. Then my eyes went back to the screen.

C:/WP51/AIR

I'm a killer, Fiona. I have killed an awful lot of peo-ple. And there is a curious bit of me that has actually started to *like* it. I don't like indifference. I don't like, for example, your complete indifference to the work we do here.

"There are some memos about the Newsom busi-ness . . ." I heard you say this rainy Monday morning, with a roll of your eyes and a flick of those still-unanchored elbows that suggested a boredom so huge that even had I whipped out the yellow mask and tried to shag you right there on the spot I don't think you would have shown a speck of interest. That's what impresses me, you see. At some level you are completely unafraid. Or pre-tending to be so. And I don't know why that is.

There are fifty steps up from the river, up to the bridge, just down from where I swung a brick at that girl's head. And it took me seventy-two steps to get there from the shelter of the trees. But there were only thirty-five steps up over the footbridge that led me back over the railway towards Fiona Town that first sweet time, that is still our secret (isn't it, Fiona?). It is three minutes to nine. It has taken me ten seconds to write the last two sentences. I write as fast as I talk. So if I write thirty-six more sentences I will find myself at the top of the hour. But I don't have much more to say. There isn't much more to say after you have done and said everything you want to say. Except, of course, to say it again. Or to stop it, I suppose. In the end — to stop your mouth. To stop all that . . . movement. You move so! I will wait. I won't write. I'll wait and watch the clock . . .

I get scared sometimes, you see. I get scared that the beast is eating me away from the inside. I get scared that he'll burst out of my belly in a spontaneous Caesarean section, screaming "It's me! It's me!" Oh I want someone to bloody find me. Of course I do. Why else am I taking these stupid risks? I want someone to put their hand on my shoulder and say "It's all over. It's all over. Come quietly." Why else did Jack the Ripper write those notes? He was begging people not to be so stupid. He was imploring them to have the wit to find him out.

Like all good serial killers these days — you can't be a *proper* serial killer unless you can quote Wittgenstein — I am keen to let you know that I don't just go around chopping up people for fun. I think about it. I discuss it. I am aware of its philosophical implications. Murder is, in my opinion, one of the few things that gives any spice to philosophy — even if it doesn't encourage thinking of a very high order. I am a *killer*, Fiona. I killed Harold Porter as well as Al Hunter. I know I killed him, the way Samuel Johnson knew that he was kicking a stone by the way it made his foot feel. Here it comes. The time, the date, the barometric pressure.

Harold Porter always has a barbecue on Sunday night. I know, because like the rest of my office I have been there. Harold Porter needs to keep on good terms with the Internal and External Financial Audit Unit (Building Department). Principally because he is as bent as a corkscrew. None of us were asked on Sunday. So, after we had all tripped back from that lovely seaside town, I went along, unilaterally. To show the flag.

The rain that now beats at the office window seems to belong only to London. On Sunday night, at Harold Porter's house, out to the west, on the Thames, it was as hot and calm and clear as it was down at Dartsea. Harold Porter's huge house is set under a green hill, on a bend in the river near Marlow.>

Behind me I heard a light, quiet voice, say, "There is a gigantic lawn, a cedar tree and, beyond the lawn, an English flower garden, stocked with lupins, delphiniums and foxgloves. Beyond the garden is a screen of trees and bushes and, beyond that, a landing stage where Harold moors his boat . . ." It was Paul's voice. I looked back at the screen to see if he was reading the words, for his speech had the quality of a recital. Almost hypnotically quiet, it made Pappanauer look up from his desk. The words did not appear on the screen. This was Paul talking. This was Paul's voice.

"You've been there . . ." I heard myself say. Paul scuffed his highly polished black shoes on the carpet.

"We've all been there apart from you!" he said.

I remembered what Peter Taylor had said earlier that day, in the morning when he came to my mother's house. "And he's dead . . ." I said.

Paul stepped towards me. Over at his desk I saw Pappanauer

mutter something into his phone and replace it on the receiver. "Don't read that . . ." said Paul.

"Why not?"

Pappanauer was walking over towards us. I looked down at the carrier bag. It was not within reach.

"It'll be horrible . . ." Paul was saying, "he just wants to scare you, Fiona. That's all."

Why was he saying that? Genuine concern for me? Or a desire not to be thought to be like the man on the computer screen? I scrolled down on the screen and heard Pappanauer's voice reading from it.

"Why he needs a house that big I cannot imagine. Harold is, unlike me, more than a weekend homosexual. He is a fully paid-up friend of Dorothy. Don't let that big, masculine jaw, that craggy nose, those fierce blue matelot's eyes or that bonecrushing handshake fool you. Harold Porter is a fully paid-up bum banger and from what I hear he is more carpet than hairbrush and prefers, wherever possible, to be the meat in the sandwich."

There was an eerie silence. Then Pappanauer gave an odd laugh. "He does an' all!" he said.

I looked back at the text that, now, had absolutely the flavour and texture of one of Pappanauer's cruder attempts at humour.

C:/WP51/AIR

When I tied up the dinghy to the jetty, the party was finishing. It was ten o'clock. I sat, letting the water rock me from side to side, watching the dark fields on the other side of the river. Once, a lighted barge, full of brilliantly dressed people, ploughed up against the current and rounded the slow bend in the river, under the willows, until the noise of its music

faded like an unspoken thought. Over by the opposite
bank, something flopped out of the water and flopped
back again.

   Skip the description if you like, Fiona, but I want
you to read what we like to call the "good bits". I want
you to read how I killed Harold. In an ideal world I
would like you to read it aloud, with me in the room.
That would give me a real hard-on, Fi Fi! I would get
really stiff! You could read a bit and then I could read
a bit! Wait for me to come and then we'll read it
together like an old married couple! And I'll get a big
hard-on for you!>

There was a noise by the doors. Peter Taylor was standing there. He
looked ridiculously young. As far as I could see there were no policemen with him. He looked at Paul and then at me. I said, "I've been
reading this stuff!" Peter nodded slowly. I leaned forward, close to the
screen, and, out loud in the quiet office, I read the following: <People
were leaving up at the Porter house. The music stopped.
I got out of the boat and squatted in the long grass,
listening to the noises of departure. "Bye Harold!"
"Byee!" Car doors were being slammed. I heard one engine
start. Then another.>

   Peter was looking pained. He didn't ask me how I'd got hold of
the document. Perhaps Pappanauer had told him. "Don't, Fiona," he
said, "please!"

   "This is good!" I said, "it's a good bit! Didn't you used to say that
at school? This is all good bits."

   None of them said anything. I was, suddenly, very, very
angry. I got up and started shouting at them. I can't quite remember what I shouted. Something about how they must get me a
drink. They must all get me a drink. They must stay together.
They must be really quick about it. I wanted a drink. A really large
one. I wanted a stiff drink and I wanted it in a tall glass. I was very
specific about the glass. "Go on!" I heard myself yelling, "Go and
do it! Go on!"

   Paul got up first. Then, one by one, without speaking, the three of them shuffled through the double doors. They even walk the same, I found myself thinking. Same walk, same briefcases, same build, same conversational tone. It was only when they had gone that I turned back to the document and, once again, tried to look in between its sentences for the animating secret of its style.

17

The trouble was, I decided, that there was a manner common to all of us – one you could hear clearly in the document. It had started, I thought, with Pappanauer. But, although it had started life as a throw-away London drawl, a sort of natural disparagement, it had become mixed in with Paul's slightly clerkly formality and Peter's no nonsense directness. As I looked at the screen in front of me I decided that HIS voice was no more and no less common to all of them than their suits or their briefcases or their precious cars.

C:/WP51/AIR

Harold's barbecues are just as much a mission statement as his blazer, his chin, or the imitation Old Masters that decorate the grand staircase of his horrible house. They are as much a part of him as the engraved wine glasses, the excessive use of cushions, the piano that nobody plays or the fitted kitchen that is so per-fect that I always suspect the joints of meat, the pies, and the gigantic puddings that Harold serves his guests (he is a superb cook) might be made of plaster of Paris.

Harold's barbecues give the impression that he is about to do something rather more serious than lob a few bits of meat on to the grill. I always think of Joan of Arc or Archbishop Cranmer at these events – because he has a stove that could easily accommodate a

medium-sized cleric or your average French provincial
saint.>

I scrolled back through the two last paragraphs. "Mission statement".
To use that with a faintly satirical edge – that was pure Pappanauer.
The reference to Joan of Arc and Cranmer was pure Paul. And the
construction of the first sentence of the second paragraph was pure
Peter Taylor. Maybe the three of them had sat down and worked up
the whole thing together.

I had just got to this point when I realised that Peter Taylor had
come back into the room and was watching me from the door. *I want
you to know how I killed Harold Porter, Fiona. I want us to read it together.*
Hadn't he said something like that? I looked at Peter – his ginger
curls and his pudgy face. I heard him say, "You didn't say what you
wanted to drink!" Then behind him, like two sheepish schoolboys,
the other two came in. I turned on them.

"Shall we?" I said, "shall we read it together? Don't little boys
like gory stories? With which they try and frighten themselves?"

"Fiona –" Pappanauer began and I heard myself starting to shout
at the three of them as they hung back, awkwardly, by the double
doors. "Shall I read it? Would you like that?"

I scrolled down the document and, two or three pages down,
found what I was looking for. I heard my own dark, gravelly voice
say, "I gripped the croquet mallet, hard, with both
hands, and tiptoed towards him. It was hard to stop
laughing. I clouted him in the middle of his bald
patch."

None of them had moved from where they were standing. I got
up from my workstation. "You read it, Pappanauer. Go on. Read it
out loud. Isn't that what you want to do?"

Pappanauer shambled apologetically towards my workstation. I
scrolled down until I saw a paragraph I wanted him to read. I gestured
towards it. He didn't, at first, seem to understand what I wanted him
to do but eventually he started to speak, in a halting, almost timorous
voice.

"I hit him the second time in exactly the same
place. Or rather I *intended* to hit him in the same

place. I lined up my shot with a great deal more care and attention than I had ever lavished on Harold's croquet balls. But, at the last moment, he moved his neck, slowly and feebly, like a tortoise peering out of his shell, so, when I connected it was with his neck, somewhere below his left ear."

His voice faltered, gave out. I said, "What's the matter? Isn't this the sort of stuff you like?" None of them spoke. But Paul started towards me. As soon as he did so Peter Taylor moved, swiftly, behind him. I'm safe, I remember thinking, it's two against one. There's no conspiracy. It's one of them. I just have to work out which one.

I was reading now. My voice sounded different. In all my years at the office, I realised, I had never once spoken as I felt. And now, although the words I was reading were those of a pervert who was trying to kill me, my reading of them had an extraordinary confidence. I found I was assuming a slightly American accent.

"He blew like an oil well. *Domaine de Harold Porter, Grand Cru Classe*, aged in the arteries, jetted out of him like water from a fire hose."

Peter Taylor was speaking. "Fiona, please don't —"

"You want to read it?"

Peter Taylor moved closer to my workstation. This time it was Paul who followed him. Paul moved with surprising grace and speed. I noticed that both his hands were tightly clenched.

"Fiona, this man has done something really —"

"Read it!"

But it was Paul's voice that boomed out in the empty, echoing office. "He fumbled his way forward over the balcony rail and, helped by a violent thwack from me, tumbled down on to his own barbecue."

He stopped reading. I didn't say anything. All three of them just stood there, keeping their eyes on my face. I looked down at the screen. Peter Taylor was reading now. His tone was different from Paul's. He seemed to be puzzling over something as he read, as if the words contained some clue that none of the rest of us would be able to understand.

"His white shirt", he read in quizzical, Civil Service tones,

"took an extraordinarily long time to catch fire . . .
Fiona, this is all about the noise you will make when I
kill you . . ."

His voice trailed away into silence. His hands were shaking. "I'm
sorry, Fiona," he said "I'm so sorry . . ."

"Don't be!" I said with curious brightness. But his face still had
that puzzled expression, as if this piece of the text contained a (maybe
soluble) conundrum.

"Thing is," Peter said, "he wasn't burned. He was killed in a
completely different way. The police told me all about it. This is
what I read last night. What he did to Porter – the police told me this
morning – was . . ."

"Was what?" I said.

"Worse . . ." said Peter, his voice suddenly small.

So this was fiction. This was a man who had to enact horrors in
order to be able to invent them. Who was working himself up by a
complicated sequence of action and fantasy, like a demented mastur-
bator, until he reached the moment when he could do whatever it was
he needed to do to me. In silence, I scrolled down the last section of
the hideous document, now part and parcel of the machine on which
I had worked for the last five years. I wasn't reading it for pleasure. I
was trying to understand something. Something about the sequence
of events that had brought Peter Taylor to my flat last night.

C:/WP51/AIR

Have you ever tried to prise a duck leg off a carcass,
Fiona? Doesn't it cling? Have you ever tried to reduce
a cardboard box to two dimensions? Isn't it *irritating?*
There was simply too much of Harold Porter to beat out
into manageable portions and however much of him I hit
and for however long I hit it, it still didn't stop him
from being there.

But what I am going to do to you, Fiona, is to wipe

you off the face of the earth. I am going to stretch you out on the bed and I am going to rip open that white belly of yours and hack through that slender neck and dip my hands in your blood and smear it down my face and chest and I am going to do it tonight. I've just called your flat. You aren't there. But you will be there. Later.

I'll take the car this time. I'll park it some way away. I'll watch your flat. I'll see you come home. When you arrive I will follow you. Up the stairs, along the landing. Maybe I'll wait until you are actually at the door, putting your key in the lock, before I run at you. Even if you get in and lock the door after yourself I'll be patient. I'll call your number. I'll be on the mobiles, standing in the dark at the foot of those iron stairs. I'll call you. I'll watch the light go on in the front room. Maybe I'll see you as you go to the telephone and find no one at the other end. Maybe later, when you're asleep, I'll go up the stairs very, very quietly and I'll have something with me that can force the door. People think that once they have closed their front doors on the world that they are safe. Well, they're not. Even behind iron grilles and alarms and steel bars they are not safe. Because I'm out there. And I'll be out there tonight, Fiona. Waiting. And this will be positively our last night together. Maybe I'll call you a second time. This time you'll think not to answer. But no one can resist the telephone. Even a frightened girl alone in a flat late at night. You'll get up again and cross the room again and ask who is there but I won't answer. But when you replace the receiver I'll be there. So that, a little later (you won't sleep) when you hear the sharp crack of the door and you try to call out you won't be able to. All you will see is me because I will be on top of you and this time I won't be wearing the mask. You'll look on all my glory as I am revealed to you. And then I will put my fingers around

your throat and I will squeeze and squeeze and squeeze
until you are dead.

There was still no noise from any of them. The page after the last one I have given here was blank. I thought at first there would be more. There wasn't. But, I found myself thinking, that was almost how it happened. He was true to his word. I kept my index finger on the downward arrow. I was now letting the pages slide by, waiting to get to the end of the document without really looking at what was there. I only saw his last message to me out of the corner of my eye.

YOU KNOW WHO I AM. DON'T YOU?

I turned to Peter Taylor. "You didn't tell me, last night," I said, "why you thought someone was going to attack me."

"I didn't want to tell you the whole of it . . ." said Peter. His voice still sounded curiously small and faraway.

I rounded on him and heard my reply – a kind of triumphant snarl. "If this is how you knew, Peter, what were you doing in the office? And more importantly – what were you doing looking into my hard disk?"

"I didn't find it on yours, I found it on mine!"

Peter crossed to his own desk and punched up his screen. With a quick glance at the other two I went over to it. There, at the head of the listed files was C:/WP51/AIR. I almost ran across the room to Paul's machine, but I knew before I got there what I was going to find. It was on his machine as well, and on Pappanauer's.

Pappanauer sat on his swivel chair and spoke. "He planted it on all our machines, to cover his tracks. Rule of three."

I looked at the three of them. Then I said, "I want a gin and tonic. A large gin and tonic."

Paul looked at Peter, they both looked at Pappanauer. Then Pappanauer said, in a soft, obsequious voice, "I think we'd better do what the lady says!"

When they had gone, I went back to my carrier bag and took out Peter Taylor's journal. Before I started to read it I flicked through it. Someone (Peter? Paul?) had ripped out a few pages. Perhaps that was to make it seem as if Peter's narrative carried on from precisely the point at which HE had finished writing. Now I thought of it, of course, that was true of all the papers I had been sent. Someone was keen to present them as nearly as possible as a continuous story. Had someone tampered with A:/AIR? And might that explain the number of blank pages between each document?

Tuesday April 13th 6.45 a.m. (PT)

I now know that I got to the office on Monday night about an hour after he had left, but when I wandered in last night I had no idea of what I might find, and no notion that there had been anyone else there before me. It was thinking about Harold Porter's murder that made me leave home and go into the office. I simply couldn't sit at home with Anna and the children pretending that this was nothing to do with me. The violent death of someone you intensely dislike arouses very contradictory emotions indeed. You begin by trying to find in them some quality that explains the inexplicable sense of loss and genuine fellow feeling that they have, at last, managed to inspire in you. "Of course," I remember thinking, "the only thing that was really wrong with Harold Porter was that he was incredibly stupid!" But, deep down, I knew that the only real emotion his death inspired in me was the purely selfish one of being aware of our common mortality.

The other reason I came into the office was that the telephone call I had had from the police on Monday afternoon – the first I had heard of his death – had convinced me that if I didn't do something about the man who was doing these things, then he would stay at liberty for the foreseeable future. I thought I had met some of the stupidest policemen in the world at Dartsea. But they had dug up some even more spectacularly dense ones to investigate the grotesque killing at The Paddocks, as poor Harold called his riverside home.

•

I stopped the screen. Was it suspicious that Peter was in the office on

Monday night or did his admitting to being here make his innocence more likely?

There was something about Pappanauer's behaviour that was worrying me. Of the three of them he seemed to be the only one anxious to placate me. And that was very unlike him. I turned my eyes back to Peter's journal.

The idiot who said he was in charge of the case said, at one stage – "Mr Porter was, of course, a member of the gay community." Where had he read this? In some police handbook about political correctness? Why didn't he just come out with "'E was a poof! And we fink anuvver poof done it!" I think I said, by way of reply, "Oh dear. I'm afraid I didn't know that." I didn't want to hear any of the details of the case but the man insisted on supplying me with them. "Mr Porter's head", he said at one point, "is not a pretty sight. It has been completely pulverised!" At which point I felt an absurd urge to laugh. I suppose we laugh for the same reasons we cry – because we are frightened or disgusted by the world.

I don't discuss any of these things with Anna. When I walk through the door of my comfortable house in the suburbs and Jonny and Jimmy run at me, yelling "Daddy", that one word banishes the wickedness of the world. But, alone, I can't stop thinking about them. And, most of all, since I found that first, horribly anonymous document, I have been obsessed with the idea that by studying it closely I might get some idea as to which of my employees had written it.

Any piece of writing gives off clues about the author. Most people are rather dumb at spotting them. But, as I think I said earlier, it was fairly obvious to me, from the first, that the author of A:/AIR was working quite hard to conceal his or her (yes, women do fantasise about rape) identity. And my "operating certainty", to use poor Fiona's phrase, was, at the moment, that Mr Pappanauer was trying to set up his colleague. Hence, as I think I said, the unusually convenient place in which the disk had been left.

When I examined that assumption, however, it fell apart, as quickly as most assumptions tend to do. The method was too subtle. Why describe an orphanage that, as far as I could see, was nothing like the one Paul had described to me? And why the laborious, almost stilted descriptions of visits to prostitutes? They mean something to me and to Pappanauer and to Paul, in the light of what happened on our visit to Dartsea, but they are not evidence and they are not even proof of someone trying to concoct evidence in order to incriminate another. No, I had to work on the principle that the author of A:/AIR, while prepared to take extraordinary risks, did not actually want himself or anyone else to be discovered. This was a weird, solipsistic, masturbatory document that the unknown writer simply *had* to write. The only way to proceed was to analyse the content very carefully and try (literary critical theory came in handy here) to *divorce it from any local, personal, semi-biographical preconceptions as to its meaning.* The only way I was going to get a handle on who might have written it was to study it under laboratory conditions.

When I got to the office last night it was still there – where I had deliberately replaced it after first reading it last week. I picked it up, put it into my machine and, as my old teacher, Lewis, always advised me, started with a good long look at the first sentence. "If I was going to write a book about this (and I may well do so) I think I would probably call it *STALKING FIONA.*" This is a sentence that does not invite one to believe it. The deliberate, almost studied casualness induced by the conditional and the combination of pedantic precision and elaborate vagueness in that "and I may well do so", all invite us to believe that whoever is saying this is *not* the sort of man (if it is a man) who does any of the grubby things he is about to describe to us. This carefully composed unreliability, I had decided, was not likely to be deliberate. I was still not prepared to believe that my unknown enemy was prepared to go through a routine that was over-complex even by the standards of your average Shakespearian tragedy, in order to set someone up. The world has grown a lot more sceptical since that business with the handkerchief in *Othello.*

But there was something about it. That sentence at the end of the first paragraph . . . "You don't really get to know a female by leaping out at her from the trees around the towpath, bashing her on the head, dragging her into the long grass and trying to get her legs apart without even so much as introducing yourself."

Firstly there is the tone of it. It continues the impression that we are here faced with an individual who is trying to put him or her self at some distance from his or her own actions. The concessive nature of that "really" is intended to do the same job as "leaping" or "without even so much as introducing yourself". It's there for comic effect. It's there to distance him (yes, of course it *is* a him) from his actions. And then, of course, there is the question as to whether the man who wrote this really is the same person who attacked those women. Or whether he is just someone who read about it.

●

I pushed the papers away from me. What Peter was saying was true, of course. The man who raped me in the flat and who tried to rape me at Dartsea felt the need to lie about certain things. Was there any pattern to his lying? If, once I could see a pattern in his behaviour, might I not be closer to understanding which of the three of them it might be?

In the document he claimed to have raped me the second time. In reality, the only time he did – the first time – was the moment he didn't want anyone to know about. Was there any significance in that? Wearily I had to admit to myself that I didn't know.

18

It was curiously stuffy in the office. I was about to climb on the desk to open the window, when, six floors below me I saw Paul, Peter and John, standing in the rain by the door that leads into the company club. They were each carrying plastic glasses. Pappanauer and Peter Taylor seemed to be clutching pints. Paul had two glasses, one of which, I guessed, was probably mine. I could do with a bloody drink.

They didn't appear to be going anywhere. Paul and Peter were having some kind of argument. Occasionally Peter would take a couple of steps towards Paul. Paul would back off and then, a moment or two later, repeat Peter's manoeuvre back to him. It looked, from up in the office, like a curious kind of dance. Then, suddenly, Paul threw both his glasses to the ground and went for Peter Taylor. I had never seen him move so swiftly before. His hands went straight for Taylor's throat and the two of them started to rock backwards and forwards in the rain. Pappanauer grabbed Paul from behind and started to try and prise his arms apart. Peter Taylor kicked at him wildly. But it was at least thirty seconds before they managed to make him loosen his hold. For a brief while, Paul stood there, breathing heavily, and then, just at the point when I was sure he would turn away from the two of them, he went for Taylor once again. There was something almost comic about this. This time the two of them started trading punches – of the most amateurish kind. First Peter Taylor raised his right hand high in the air and did a kind of stirring gesture. Then, in case there should be any doubt about where he was proposing to land this punch, he did a kind of sketchy gesture towards its probable site. Then, when everybody was ready, he launched himself and his fist off towards the target.

Paul grabbed his arm and started to pull him off balance while thrashing at him with his free arm. Pappanauer, meanwhile, was darting in and out between them. Peter got hold of Paul's hair and started to bang his head downwards and then both of them started swinging punches and kicking at the same time. They now looked like a couple of kids in a playground. After about a couple of minutes of this they ground to a halt and stood, a little apart, panting at each other menacingly.

Pappanauer was saying something. He seemed to be pointing at the glasses, now strewn across the rain-spattered concrete of the court-yard. Peter and Paul looked at the glasses, then back at Pappanauer. Eventually, Paul, moving like a man under hypnosis, went back towards the door that leads into the club building. After a while the other two followed him. Peter seemed to be saying something rather intense to Pappanauer. I went back to Peter's journal and though, from time to time, I looked down into the forecourt to see if they were there, there was no sign of any of them. In the light of my desk lamp, I read on, keeping one eye on the door and one hand close to the carrier bag that rested just by my feet.

Tuesday April 13th 6.45 a.m. (PT)

The placing of the document where it was likely to be found was as much a part of its purpose as its style. Our murderer and rapist is not insane. He is capable of remorse. He is fully in control of all his actions. He disapproves of himself so much that he can't even put his fantasies down on paper, and instead has to be satisfied with these half-baked humorous attempts at self-revelation. All of this is borne out by the use of rhetorical devices. They are there, not to increase the authenticity of the statement, but *to distance the speaker from the horrors of his own lived experience*. This is nothing like the writings of, say, a Nazi war criminal engaged in the business of "confession". The flat, bureaucratic nature of that kind of prose, which perhaps gave rise to Hannah Arendt's phrase about "the banality of evil" is really there as an attempt to construct a world in which the things they did were possible or explicable. Our man's attempt to glory in his offence – like the wickedness of a Shakespearian villain – is there because he knows what he is doing is wrong.

He wants to be discovered. He wants people to know who he is.

Sometimes what he writes is pure fantasy. And there is a consistent tone to it. The woman he talks about attacking with a brick must, I think, be the first one he killed. But she wasn't clubbed with a weapon. In fact she died after putting up a considerable struggle, and she was, like two of the others after her, strangled. What he wants to do is simply to despatch people. But that is precisely what he can't do. He kills them out of fear. Fear of being discovered. Fear of facing what he is. I'm dealing with a guy who was best described by that unfashionable word "evil". He wasn't mad in any sense of the word. He was capable of feeling remorse and did so. He was, in a sense, rendered so unwhole, unreliable and unlike himself by guilt that his being discovered could only come as a relief.

If all this was the case then it was entirely likely that our friend had left *other* evidence for someone like me to find. Continuing his ghoulish narrative under the eyes of the very people it was designed to deceive and hurt was, I felt, almost impossible for him to avoid. He liked looking at himself. He liked, was, indeed, obsessed with the notion of being watched by and watching others.

That was when I realised that he must be using one of the office computers. He might even be using mine. None of us log our documents very carefully and there are quite often times when I find some joker has printed out a ten-page memo called BALLS or RUBBISH on to my hard disk without my being aware of it. At home, I have quite often found letters from Anna to friends I never even knew she had on my own Olivetti 286.

I went into my files in Drive C. I realised something was wrong immediately. The files are listed alphabetically. There, almost at the head of the list was C:/WP51/AIR. I pressed 1 and retrieved the document. He had transferred the whole of his document straight on to my machine. I started to scroll through it. From almost the first paragraph I thought I could tell that I hadn't been quite accurate in my earlier analysis. His narrative did, I decided, reveal a developing condition. He might start off with the same, slightly removed manner I've described above, but, as I read on, I felt I was getting a picture of a mind in the process of collapse.

I'm not a psychiatrist. I'm an accountant who read English at university. But from the little I know about the defining characteristics of madness, I would say the author of C:/WP51/AIR had them in spades. And, as I looked back at the rest of what he had written, I could see their roots in earlier paragraphs and sentences. So much for textual literary criticism. I read this document, greedily, aware that the information it contained was a matter of life and death.

The more she shows her strength the more she has to die. The more he is able to think of her as a human being the more he wants to kill her. The more frightened she is of him the more he has to think she is defying him. He is just at the point when people lose touch with the real things of the world, just at the edge of sanity. The last section was a hideous scream directed straight at Fiona, and it had been written on to my machine, only minutes before I had come into the office. Whoever was writing this stuff was obsessed with me as well as with Fiona.

All I could think about was the fact that he was, even now, probably on his way to her flat. I called her. She wasn't there. I paced about the office. Call the police? The trouble was, I was getting more and more convinced that I knew who it was. And, in a curious way, this question was between him and me. Finding his message on my hard disk was the last link in the chain. This man was jealous of me. And he was jealous for a very good reason. I can see I have presented myself in these pages, even when addressing no one except the blank page, as the person I would like to be rather than the person I actually am. I've always wanted to be the calm, paternal boss figure – good old Peter Taylor with his red hair and glasses and his oh so publicly wonderful family. But I suppose it's more complicated than that.

I think I first realised it down at Dartsea. After I got into the hotel that night when I had scrambled up the cliff after Fiona's attacker, I went straight to the door and was about to ring the bell and wake the whole place when something stopped me. It wasn't the uncanny quietness, or the fact that I was certain that the man in the mask had had plenty of time to get back to his room. I wasn't afraid of calling up the whole place and barging into both Paul and Pappanauer's rooms with a few of the local constabulary. It was the sound of Fiona's voice at the head of the stairs.

It was hearing her that made me stop and think about what I would do if I woke the whole hotel. I had absolutely no evidence that what was going on in the company was in any way connected with the attack on Fiona, apart from a document that, like its name, could have come out of the air. Before I did anything I had to talk to Fiona. And what was she calling, so quietly, up there in the darkness? I moved two or three steps up but her voice did not come again. I don't know why but I did not want to call to her myself. I trod very, very quietly as I went up the stairs.

The front corridor of the first floor of the hotel, off which the sea-facing rooms lead, is fitted with a carpet – deep, grey, reassuring – and I made no sound as I went along it towards the far end, where it curves round slightly, towards the sea. I didn't see Fiona until I was about halfway along. She was right by the last door on the right, her back to me, in a white night-dress. She was tapping, very, very softly on the door. It was only now I heard what she was saying, "Paul . . ." she was speaking so softly that he could not possibly have heard her. *She doesn't want him to hear*, was my first thought, *and yet she's frightened that if she doesn't call him she has admitted his guilt*. She brushed against the woodwork with those long, bony fingers, and called again, very, very softly. It was almost as if she were speaking to herself. "Paul, why did you go?" was all she said. And of course he didn't answer. Then she turned and saw me.

There was moonlight coming in from a window behind her head. Her brown hair was down her back. Her night-dress – square, white, demure, as modest as a communion garment – only accentuated the plunging sensual line of her neck and the untouched whiteness of the upper arms. I started towards her and she retreated, fractionally. I didn't know what I was going to say. All I did know was that I wanted her and she could see it in my face. "Fiona . . ."

She looked down at the floor. When she looked up again she was different. She looked as if she had been out in the cold. As if, suddenly, something had numbed her, so that, whatever I said or did would have made no difference. For a brief moment, there was a flicker of fear, as if she was scared I would attack her, and then an awful kind of indifference.

She thinks it's Paul, I thought, *and she's just slept with him. He's raped her and she knows it but she won't admit it. Because she's in love with him.* That was the moment I started to suspect him. But I still had no proof.

"Are you all right?" I said. She just kept on with that same dead, dull look.

"I'm fine," she said, "I'm fine."

She walked past me then as if she was sleepwalking. When she got to her room she stopped and put her hand up to the woodwork. She felt it as if it might give her warmth, comfort. When she turned back to me there was a vague, puzzled look in her eyes. "What are you doing here?" she said, "You're not supposed to be here."

There was something else about that look she gave me. It wasn't until I was back down in the bar agonising about what I should do and not doing any of it, that I realised what it was. It was pure dislike.

I thought I was feeling impartial anger at what had been done to her, but I know now that it was the product of jealousy. I know now that, when next morning she started to tell people – and she did not say anything about what had happened to her that night until the next morning – the strongest feeling I had was – *how could he inspire that kind of trust in her? When he's a shifty, tongue-tied little wimp?*

And he feels the same about me. In spite of all that old world gentleman act – the natty shoes and the crisp accent and the red hand-kerchief that's supposed to give him a nineteenth-century air, he is as crude and passionate as any of the rest of us underneath. That's why he left the document on my hard disk. That is why I was both afraid of my conclusion – and doubtful about the premises that inspired it – but also determined to find out if it were the case on my own. I was fairly sure that Fiona's reluctance to say what had happened to her, and most of all, her insistence that she hadn't been technically raped, were liable to be due to the fact that she didn't want to incriminate Paul. But I was also sure that my growing conviction that it was him – and I have tried to be fairly scrupulous about imposing that conclusion on the way I have told this story – was as much a product of my jealousy and resentment of his success with her as anything else.

Of course I'm in love with her. You will have spotted that, I am sure. I love the way she tosses her head and looks at me sideways and asks my advice. I love her big, brown eyes and her wide, jagged mouth and the way she laughs at my jokes. And I love the fact that she is only twenty-three years old and the world hasn't yet marked her the way it's marked me – with defeat and cynicism and early middle age.

But, I asked myself, and I ask you now – if it was Pappanauer, or if there was the slightest chance she suspected it was – wouldn't she have told someone? And if it wasn't Pappanauer it must be Jackson, mustn't it? Wasn't that the only thing that had explained her eerie silence? Can you really be raped, twice, by the same man, someone with whom you work, for Christ's sake, and not get some tiny clue, some noise, some smell, some gesture that tells you who it might be? I don't think so. And Paul's character fitted with my picture of the murderer. Pappanauer hasn't got the wit to be really evil. He could do something as mundane as fraud but he lacks the intensity I think you probably need to deliberately kill another human being.

That was the other problem. I couldn't fit the picture I had of the man who committed fraud and double murder with the picture of Fiona's attacker – at least as it was given in C:/WP51/AIR. The murderer and the fraudster started from roughly the same assumptions as the people who run this company. Make a lot of money and destroy the opposition. The man who stalked Fiona to her flat was, quite clearly, sick, sad, evil . . . an outsider, a loser . . . One set of crimes were committed for concealment or for gain – the others were a perverse, crazy assertion of the self – a sort of scream of pain and hatred about women in general and one woman in particular.

But then, why do we necessarily assume that beyond a certain point these two different varieties of wickedness are not interrelated? Why do we now see crime as a series of specialities as neatly tailored as a Japanese assembly line? Perhaps because we have stopped using words like "wickedness" and choose, now, to relegate any human ugliness or horror that we cannot comprehend as being outside moral boundaries. And since we have forgotten how to use morality we may be said to have forgotten what it is for.

I look out at the rain now, sweeping in across the fields. It rattles against the children's climbing frame, lashes into the sodden lawn and hurls itself against my study window. On the wall behind me is one of Jonny's drawings – a crude head, amazingly crude teeth, big, big eyes. Underneath the single word DADDY. A terrifyingly honest picture. I have to be completely honest, not only about what I think but about why I think it. And, curiously enough, confessing what I feel about Fiona has made me more sure, not less, of what I saw last night outside her flat.

When I rang her for the second time she answered. "Is anyone with you?" I said.

There was a silence. Then she said, "No. Why?"

"Something's come up . . ." I said.

What was I supposed to say? There's a psychopath on his way over to your place? Try and stay calm? She was scared enough anyway. I heard her clear her throat nervously. It was curious. I'd never seen Fiona's flat. But now I had a very clear picture of it. Thanks to the man who was probably, even now, waiting outside it, for his chance to silence those narrow, lively lips for ever.

"What?"

"It's about the man who attacked you . . ." I said, "I've found something. In the office."

I heard her gasp at the other end of the phone. I suddenly had the absurd idea that she knew about the document. That she, too, had gone into it, read through that hideous, complacent catalogue of unpleasantness and, like me, though for different reasons, was unable to tell anyone about it. Or maybe, this thought only occurred to me some time afterwards, she was *using* it . . .

Even in a marriage people can be frightened to talk to each other. If you don't want to be lonely don't get married. Sometimes Anna and I – I see I've taken care to represent us as an ideal couple in these pages – start an argument, allow it to cool into silence and then let the silence congeal into a bitterness that lasts for days and days. Sometimes the days become weeks until a chance incident – a turn of the head, a laugh – brings us back to where we were before. I suppose Fiona and I have what is often termed an "office marriage". We spend slightly more time together than the average married couple – certainly a lot more than me and Anna.

"What have you found?" she said.

This question was typical of her. She always asks one or two almost embarrassingly relevant questions. If you can't answer them she never looks angry. She just sits there, giving you an amused smile from that wide, mobile mouth.

"I don't know. It's a sort of . . . look . . . I think I'd better come over . . ." I replied.

There was a pause. I caught myself thinking – does she even trust *me*? And then I thought – *she trusts no one*.

A few weeks ago I was on my way to the school to pick up the children when I saw a young girl crying by the side of the road. She must have been about six or seven. There were three men nearby. None of them dared to go and comfort her. One of them – an older, working-class man, said, "'As it come to this?" We all knew it had. There is a habit of thought nowadays that says that all men are suspect, that no gesture from a man to a woman is innocent. That fathers are liable to be the most corrupt of all. Maybe they are. There are times when I wonder about my father. There are times when I ask myself why it was he never talked about my mother or if he did why it was always in the most slighting terms. All she had done was die, for Christ's sake.

"Look – it's like this, Fiona . . ."

She was sounding more frightened with each second that passed.

"Fiona . . . the person who did this to you . . ."

"Yes?"

I gripped the side of the desk. It was hard to keep the panic out of my voice. *Best be neutral*, I remember thinking, *don't let her know how serious it is*.

"Look, you were a bit confused . . . after Dartsea . . . and someone attacked you, you said . . ."

I swallowed hard. I hadn't the heart to tell her all of the things I knew. I certainly didn't want to start telling her about what was in that horrible document.

"It's one of the men in the office. Isn't it?"

A long, long pause. And then a very, very small voice, "Yes."

I coughed. I was almost embarrassed at being so close to someone so obviously frightened. I got a sudden, clear picture of her that, as soon as I saw it, I realised came straight from the imagination of her attacker. She was sitting on the side of the bed in the drab little flat near the railway. She had the phone on her lap. She was looking out at the street, through the flowered curtains, alone and afraid . . .

"Look," I said, "I'm coming over. Lock the door. Stay where you are. Wait for me to get there."

"Peter . . ."

"Just hold *on* . . ."

I was out on the street running for my car before I remembered that I hadn't asked her how to get to her place. Although I know her number, the first picture I had of her flat was courtesy of the author of A:/AIR. I would call her from the car. There wasn't much time. Presumably *he* had seen her go in. Presumably *he* was, even now, out there in the dark, waiting. He was waiting as he had promised, waiting until it was dark and quiet and he could climb the iron stairs and move along past the shabby front doors, and the bedraggled window boxes, with the glass above them grimed with the dirt of the city. He was waiting for his final appointment with the girl with the brown hair and the beaky nose. And this time he was not going to make any mistakes. He was going to kill her.

•

So Peter had started to suspect Paul because he was jealous. He wasn't, any more than me, going on the internal evidence of the document. He was trusting to the fact that I must know, or at least suspect, which of the three of them it might be and that the one whose identity I would be most likely to conceal would be Paul's. But that still left me with the gloves in Paul's briefcase. And those moments in the document that were so oddly reminiscent of Paul.

There was still the business of what had happened at the flat. But he could have been wrong about that. It was a dark night and, as it was tonight, foul with rain. Paul was what he wanted to see – there was no question about that. Just as he wanted HIM to be sane. That, of course, is Peter's morality. Criminals are wicked. You punish them and the wickedness goes away. I would like to believe that, but then, unlike Peter, I was the one who had turned from her bed to see that bastard coming towards me in his primrose mask. I was the one to whom he had said what, still, seemed to me the most significant sentence in all of this.

If you tell anyone about this I will kill you.

There was not much paper left. The last section of my diary. The one I had written last night. I held it up and looked at the handwriting. What would Peter say about it – if called on to analyse it – as we had both in our different ways, tried to analyse A:/AIR? I have always wanted to write the way I talk. But, more than any of them, I suspect that what I write conceals the nature of who I am. If, for example, I confess to the page that I loved my father and have never been comfortable with my mother, that is liable to be as much of a deception as the statement to the contrary.

"This is the last time I'll write this diary." I wrote that sentence in the flat after Peter had arrived last night. And it has the tone of someone saying farewell to all form of confession or self-explanation. But, of course, that was just the beginning. What I have written now makes me, as I should be, the narrator of this story, and I tell it the way I might tell it to a stranger in a bar. I wrote all of that diary under some kind of duress – and on that last night I was not only afraid of what was out there in the rainy night. I was also afraid of the man sitting opposite me – Peter Taylor.

I think I was frightened of the fact that, more than any of them, he understands me. He has that cold, patient way of looking at you that bosses seem to acquire. And on that last night he was as cool and calm and removed as if we had been discussing office politics rather than murder and rape and fraud.

MONDAY APRIL 12TH. 11 P.M. (F)

It's late on Monday night. And I am writing under Peter's eyes and for his benefit. It isn't a diary any more. It's public property. When I've finished writing this I'll hand it on to Peter – *all* of it and he can make what he wants out of it. Because I don't know who to trust any more. Don't get me wrong. I'm not giving it to him because I think that he's my Dad and that when he's read it, everything will be fine. I'm giving it to him because I've given up. I trust no one. I don't trust Peter and I don't trust Paul and I don't trust John. The Apostles are in it together. I'm so tired.

A diary is supposed to represent your secret thoughts but I'm not sure I've got any secret thoughts any more. I'm not sure that any part of me is secret. After the police department responsible for peering up women's vaginas had finished with me it was all I could do to stop myself lifting my skirts on the train in the morning and thrusting my fanny in the commuters' faces, shouting "'Adjer look? 'Adjer look?"

Fiona is public property.

I felt all the things you are supposed to feel. But I also felt something I hadn't anticipated. I still felt myself. You can be beaten and abused and attacked and still be yourself. I don't even want to hurt HIM any more. I did at first. I wanted him to be afraid the way I had been afraid. But now I don't want anything for him. HE doesn't interest me. And I suppose he's failed. Because he did these terrible things to gain my attention.

I'm writing this with the same pen I have used for all of my diary. Peter is looking at me from the other side of the room. From time to time he looks away, tactfully, like a doctor waiting for some-one to give a specimen, but I want to say to him – and I *am* saying this to him since he will read it – this isn't me. Because I have learned so well how to conceal what I am – like so many women I have been doing it all my life – that you can't be sure you are getting Fiona the Secretary or Fiona the Lovelorn or . . .

Peter you are a *nice* person and I am not. No diary is a true con-fession. Anyone who puts pen to paper begins the act of lying. Believe, or at least feel free to judge, what I say about the weather or the texture of the paper in front of me but do not for one moment assume that anything else I write isn't pure fantasy. Look – it's my life but I can't believe it when I put it down. That good enough for you?

I'll start with the rain. It's still raining. Out there, the drops of water come out of the dark, stinging your face; they are whipped by the wind. In here they make a softer sound; but they are still determined. I can hear them, wearing out the gutters, running, trickling and gushing until the water has the ominous, quiet consistency of a new flood. It won't stop – this rain. In the blackness it seems to be gathering itself for a new assault, as if it is testing the once dry earth and strict, dry brickwork of this outer reach of the city.

When he came in – sorry Peter, when *you* came in – you'd been running and you leaned against the curtains like you were in a war film and the *Russians* were out there or something. I thought for a moment you were going to get me to lie on the floor. But, if I'm honest, the thing I really noticed about you was how the rain had flattened your red hair into thick dark slabs, and how the water ran from your scalp back down your neck and on to your shoulders.

Yes, I find you attractive. OK?

•

I put the pages away. Well – that's one of the things I haven't said so far, I notice. That I have always had an eye for Peter Taylor. That some of these things described here – by me and others – have happened as if I had willed some fantasy into being. I remember as a child thinking that if I really wanted a boy, I could make him come to our street, stop outside our house, come to the door, let himself in (I could wish him a key of course) and, when everyone was asleep, will him up the stairs and into my bedroom where I was lying, alone, in my nightdress, staring at the ceiling.

I went to the window once more. They were out there again. They were carrying glasses again. This time they were talking, with some animation, amongst themselves. They didn't look as if they had any intention whatsoever of coming up to the office. I sat at my desk and looked once more at the writing of the girl I had been on the last night before I came face to face with HIM.

19

The next thing I noticed was that you were being extremely melo-dramatic. That is nothing new. When you are telling us some piece of office news, you'll quite often pace around, chew your lip and then, suddenly, fling your arms wide as if you were about to deliver an operatic aria. You turned to me and you said, "I think he's in the street." I'm afraid I didn't bother to work out what this meant.

Do you notice how the fact that I have agreed to show you this diary has altered the way I write it? A part of me, for example, wants to go back over everything I have written about John Pappanauer and say that he is nothing like that *at all*. I notice, for instance, I have left out the fact that he plays the cello.

Things like that can change your whole idea of a person, can't they?

I didn't say he played it well. In fact, on the evening when I went to hear him play in his band, who were called something like Dream Image or Firebrand (although they should have been called Big Ears because they all had them) I remember thinking that he was probably the worst cello player in the western world. His bow quite often missed the strings completely.

I've also missed out the fact that Pappanauer is devoted to his mother. He spends literally hours of each day on the phone to her, asking her embarrassingly personal questions about her health. I've left out the fact that he has a motor bike that is always going wrong and that, one afternoon, about nine months ago, I came into the office after everyone had gone home and found him slumped over his desk. I think, though I am not positive about this, that he had been crying.

247

Each detail modifies the previous detail. Each perception makes every other perception seem like a lie. If I write *you* when I talk about you, Peter, even though, now, you are standing just at the edge of the window, staring down at the street and looking more like a character in a book than anything else, your image comes between me and the page. You block my view with my feelings for you. I edge my shoulders round to the left and write the following sentence . . . When Peter came into the flat I knew at once that it was something to do with THAT. He had that fatherly look he wore when we were down in Dartsea. But I was no more able to respond to it than I was when we were down there. I think I've got to the point, now, when I have begun to feel that all this stuff isn't really happening to me. It's like I'm outside myself, watching people smile and nod and whisper to this odd little girl with the brown hair and the funny smile.

I see her lying on the floor of that hotel room for what seemed like an hour. She gets up after a while and goes to the bathroom. She doesn't wash herself. She just stands in the mirror, looking at her reflection. She is naked. She takes in her breasts, her bony hips, the dark fuzz at the base of her belly and then she reaches out to touch her own finger in the glass. There is not a sound, not anywhere, except for the distant noise of the sea. Then, with the weariness of a hospital patient, she goes back to the bedroom and starts to put on a night-dress. She picks up the telephone.

I dialled my mother. That was the first thing I did afterwards. I don't know why I did that. When she picked up the phone the first thing she said was, "Ye-es?" I could hear that she was afraid. An old lady, alone in her house. Someone calls at four in the morning. She's as scared as I am. When I think back to the things I've written about her in this diary I can see that they are often unfair. They spring from the terrible closeness women have with each other – some primitive fear of being absorbed. "Mum –" I started to say. And then I found I was crying. I only remembered after I had started crying that I hate letting my Mum see what I am feeling. Because that is always what she wants to know. But it was too late then. So I cried for that as well, for me and her and all the mistakes we've made, but, even as I cried I caught myself thinking – *these tears don't mean anything. They're just a way of getting sympathy.*

Peter looks at me as I write. He seems very solemn. He's going to say something. His red hair and snub nose can make him look a little like a schoolboy but, just now, he still is wearing the manner he adopts when he talks to his kids on the telephone. I look at his face and his shoulders and I start to wonder — *if he were wearing a mask and thick anorak and a jersey . . .*

"I have reason to believe that he will try and attack you tonight."

I liked that "try". I didn't bother to ask why he hadn't called in the riot squad. I just said, quite calmly, "If he is watching the flat he's seen you come in."

Peter nodded slowly. "I know that," he said, giving me a look that wasn't entirely friendly, "but I know more about him than he knows about me!"

I couldn't think what this might mean. I must have looked as lost and confused as I felt because he came over to me and put his hand on my shoulder, the way he does in the office if I haven't understood something. Suddenly I wanted to hear about ordinary things. I didn't want to think about *that* or *him*.

"Tell me," I said, "what you do on a weekend . . ."

He smiled then. "It's too dull," he said.

I cupped my chin in my hands. "I want to hear about something dull," I said, "something dull and safe and ordinary."

He looked straight into my eyes — something I've noticed Peter hardly ever does. As I gazed back at him I thought how easy it would be to fall for a married man. You wouldn't just be in love with them. You would want to possess their lovely homes, their sweet wives, their delightful kids — you would become a kind of ghost at the edge of their family . . . I was deliberately not thinking about Paul. I didn't want to think about him.

"Well," said Peter, "I get up. I make the kids breakfast. I walk them around the garden. We look at the flowers. If there are flowers." He laughed. I was laughing too. "I can't go on with this, it's too dull. It really is."

"I'm enjoying it," I said. "Tell me what happens next."

He thought for a bit. Then he said, "I make a cup of tea."

"Milk and sugar?"

"Milk," said Peter, "but no sugar."

I made him go through his whole Saturday routine. Honestly. Can you imagine? And he wasn't just being modest when he said it was boring. It was very, very boring. There were moments when I wondered how he managed to stand it. I pressed him for every little detail. When he told me he went to the park I wanted to know how big it was, what the railings were like, what it was called . . . When he said he went to the supermarket I wanted to know whether he always went to the same one. I wanted to know what he bought, whether his wife went with him . . . All of these little details, he could see, comforted me. As he described them I saw his life, the way I did when I went to his jacket and, illicitly, got out that photograph of his family. And yet, now, as I write this, I find myself wondering if I would have known if he had invented all of them. The tone of his voice was so soothing, as if he was telling me a bedtime story. Perhaps he was. Perhaps he spends his Saturdays stock-car racing or windsurfing. He just knew I needed to listen to something dull.

Since we talked about that he has fallen silent again. Sometimes he goes to the window. Sometimes he comes over to me and looks over my shoulder like an invigilator checking your work in an exam. When he does this I move my shoulder to block his view. He doesn't complain. What's happening, Peter? I haven't got the courage to ask you to your face. Because, of course, I don't really want to know the answer. The only thing that's happened is the telephone ringing.

That was weird. It was like he was waiting for it. He practically ran across the room and yanked it off its cradle as if the thing was about to explode. "Hullo . . ." he said. And then, neutrally, "Yes . . ." It was hard to tell if this were a question or a statement. It was only then I realised that he was trying to get the caller to talk. When he said, "Say what you have to say . . ."

"Who's there?" I said.

There was a silence. Peter shrugged in a way I took to mean that, whoever was on the line had chosen not to reveal himself. Then he said, "I've read what you have to say. I knew you were going to call. You may as well let me hear your voice. I think I know who you . . ." It sounded as if whoever it was had cut him off at the other end. His face looked grim as he replaced the receiver.

"He's done what he said he would," he said. He went, once again, to the window.

I didn't ask him to explain any of this. But, a little while later I simply said, "Is it Pappanauer? Is he the person who attacked me?"

He sat at the table then. He folded his right hand over mine. He's got surprisingly strong hands. He often talks about the exercise he does. They feel different to Pappanauer's – they are dry and firm. I let my hand go limp inside his.

"Listen," he said, "I found a diary. This man has been keeping a kind of diary . . ."

"I don't want to know about it!" I said quickly. He seemed to understand this. He nodded. That was when I started to tell him that I had been writing things down. I didn't tell him about everything, although from things he said I gathered he knew about the first attack. That was when he said, "You have to make a record of it, Fiona. You have to write it down. We have to have a case for the police. Do you see?"

That was when I got out the thick pile of papers and started to write again, under his watchful eyes. As I look back at what I have written I see that although I started on the same page I had finished the night HE was waiting for me under the bed in the hotel, I haven't told what happened. Partly because not much did, of course. I don't want to think about those policemen. But partly because of something that happened on the train, going back to London, with Paul. I'll tell it now. Because, as I said, I don't care enough about anything any more. Why bother to conceal it?

Paul, Pappanauer and I came back together on the Saturday. The police made no objection to my going. I think by then they had decided I was merely a hysteric. Peter offered to take us all back in his car, but for some reason I was adamant about going on the train. The three of us hardly spoke at all. We were about halfway back to London when the clouds built up and we saw rain coming in from the east. That was when Pappanauer said he would go off to the bar. He was gone for some time. I looked out of the window at an embankment, littered with coarse grass, and beyond it a factory and a cooling tower. I looked at Paul. He was staring at the table in front of him, a closed look on his face. "Please –" I said suddenly, "put your arms around me! Give me a hug!"

We had hardly talked since I had started babbling about the attack on me. He'd just looked at me, his mouth open with horror, saying hardly anything. The police had questioned him, on his own, but he hadn't told me what he'd said. He looked at me now, as if he was terrified of me. And then, very very slowly and cautiously, he lifted up his right arm and snaked it around my shoulders. When his hand landed on me it was like a bird settling. It wasn't like a touch at all.

"Please," I said, "hold me!"

"Fiona . . ." said Paul. He tightened his fingers on my flesh. I could feel what a strain it was for him. And then he started to cry.

Dave cried when we packed it in. I hated it. One minute he was big, beery Dave and the next minute his face was all puckered and dirty with tears. But Paul's tears weren't like that. They were dragged out of him, as if he was vomiting. Christ, I was the one who'd been attacked. But when he finally managed to look at me you could have sworn that he was the one to have suffered.

"Fiona," he said, "it's like this. You see . . . I'm a bad, bad person, Fiona . . . it's like . . ."

I was scared now. "Like what?"

"Like I'm two people. Two completely different people . . ."

I didn't ask what that meant. Then he said, "When we made love . . ." He didn't finish that sentence. The two of just stayed there, leaning against each other as the train rattled over the rails and London, with its darkness and rain, drew ever closer. The bank of bruised-blue clouds over to the east had now picked up the sun behind us and a weird, over-theatrical light caught his face. The thought that had first occurred to me when I went to his door on the previous night, came back. It was like an ugly whisper, nagging at me. *He is not what he seems.* It is because I suspect him that I am giving you my diary.

After the first phone call Peter and I were silent for quite a long time. Everything around us went silent too. There were no cars or radios or shouts in the street. Even the rain seemed to soften in sympathy – it was soft, voiceless Irish rain now, drifting out of the blackness on to the town. All there was was me and Peter and these sheets of paper. Until the second phone call.

That was about fifteen minutes ago. Ever since it happened he had been walking backwards and forwards to the window, as if he expected some monster to break the glass at any moment. The curious thing about it was that, once again, I had the impression he was expecting it. Once again he almost ran to the phone and when he spoke into the receiver it was as if he knew who was on the other end.

"Yes. Yes I'm here." The same neutral, almost bored tones. And then a change – as if he could no longer hold back his anger. "Listen –" I heard him say, "I know you're there. I know what you have in mind. And this is between you and me, my friend." He kept his eyes on the window as he said this. Then he paused. He seemed to have heard something outside.

"Did you hear that?" he said. "On the stairs?"

I wasn't sure. I listened again. This time I thought I heard a slight noise, out there in the darkness. I didn't dare speak. It was as if HE was there in the room with us. Peter was talking on the phone again. "Listen," he was saying, "I was supposed to find that document, wasn't I? Well I did. And you won't get away with it, OK? You will not, OK? This is personal, OK?"

Then he said something so quietly that at first I didn't catch it. But he said it twice. He said it as if he was saying something he knew would hurt whoever was talking on the end of the line – "No peace for the wicked!" I don't know why but as soon as he said it I remembered that somebody – one of the three of them had said that to me in the office. Quite a long time ago. I remembered it only because of the remark. I couldn't, for the moment, think of which of them had said it. But I did recall the afternoon it had been said to me. It had been raining, as it is now, and there was something about the tone of it that had struck me as odd. "No peace for the wicked." It was the kind of thing that my grandmother would have said, from her chair in the corner of the room, a reminder of the days when everyone was Christian and believed in things like wickedness. But whoever had said it to me had said it with a twist to their mouth. Who had said it?

Then I did hear a noise outside. But before I could even move, Peter had dashed to the door and yanked it open. He turned to me. His voice was emphatic and stern when he spoke, the way you might talk to a child. "Stay here. Lock the door after me!" I started towards him. "Go back!" he shouted, just before he clattered off, along the landing and down the iron staircase.

I did no such thing of course. Almost as soon as he had gone I was out on the landing after him. But Peter was too interested in whoever he was chasing to give me any of his attention. He ran down to the street and along the side of the wall, not towards the street but back along the buildings. About fifty yards beyond the back of our flats the road peters out into a patch of waste ground. Beyond that is a rusty barbed wire fence that marks the boundary of the allotments that stretch away behind us. I started down the stairs. I didn't run. I took them one stair at a time. Although the rain dripped from the steel rail, and it felt almost shockingly cold, I kept my left hand on it to steady myself. I was listening for any sound. All I could hear was footsteps down below. Peter was running away into the darkness, towards the allotments and now I was out on the silent street. I looked back up at the landing. There were no lights down here. I had suddenly lost all my courage. It was so quiet. It was so still. The rain almost sighed against the brickwork behind me.

As I stood there I heard slow footsteps coming along the street. Not from the direction in which Peter had gone. They were coming from the street that runs down from the main road. It was a slow, heavy tread. As if whoever it was wanted me to know that they were there. One – two – three . . .They stopped. There was silence again. I flattened myself against the wall, just by the bottom of the stairs. I could hear my heart thrashing against my ribs. It was shaking the blood in me, racketing around my chest like a trapped animal, so loud and strong and desperate that I was almost sure HE could hear it. And I was sure now that HE was out there in the darkness, just behind the angle of the wall.

I started back up the stairs. If HE hears me. If HE thinks I'm scared HE'll come after me. Maybe HE is waiting for Peter to come back. Or maybe HE is waiting for Peter to go off further, in among the sodden fields of the allotments, blundering around in the blackness so that HE can quietly and slowly climb back up the stairs behind me and . . . Stop. Silence again. On again. One step two step three step four. Was that me or HIM? On again. One step two step three step four. Stop. Silence again. Listen. Was that a voice? Over by the allotments was that a voice? I tell you honestly I don't know whether I was listening to the night or whether it was listening to me. Whether the only thing in the whole city wasn't my heart going thump thump thump against my ribs . . .

When I got to the top of the stairs I ran. I didn't care if that got him started again. I didn't care if the sight of me running, splay-footed, elbows out, hair plastered across my face with the rain, made him start after me like a wild animal after its prey, taking the stairs three at a time, reaching out for me in the darkness. I didn't care if, suddenly, he should be transformed into the monster he is, if his arms should shrink like a telescope, his shoulders sprout up into a hump and for the hump to give birth to huge black wings, rustling out of his skin like some obscene umbrella. I didn't care, since I thought that was the very thing that was following me up the stairs. It was too *late* to care, if his face should shrink to two bright eyes astride a monstrous beak and his feet become talons, hovering above me in the night as I beat my way to my own front door. I just ran. You know? Ran like crazy.

When I reached the door I put myself the other side of it, shut it, locked it, bolted it, put a chair against it and ran into the bedroom. It wasn't until I had fallen on to the bed that I remembered that that was where I had been when HE came out at me that night from the bathroom. As that image came back to me I knew that that was the one I had been trying to forget. Because it was the first one. How he came out from the bathroom with that hideous yellow thing on his head with his hands outstretched towards me and how those rubber gloves felt on my throat and how he smelt, sour, thick, with something anxious in it as if he was as afraid of me as I was of him. And I was thinking back, as Peter had asked me to do, and remembering things. I was picturing the scene in the office that afternoon – whenever it was – when somebody said to me – "No peace for the wicked." "No peace for the wicked." "No peace for the wicked" over and over again like a machine that has stuck in a groove.

I'm a bad person, Fiona. I'm a bad, bad person. As I write this I can hear nothing from outside. Has HE got Peter? Was HE waiting for him out there in the dark? And when HE has maimed him or killed or silenced him somehow or other will HE walk back down the street and mount the stairs that lead to my flat. There's a knock at the door. I'll call. I'll call the police.

•

When I went to look down into the courtyard, the three of them had gone. I went to the double doors and looked out, along the corridor. There was no one there. It was late now and the building was emptying. I tried to think back to last night. But I couldn't remember quite how it was. It was as if the only thing I could trust was what I had written. But, as I looked at it, I was baffled by what it seemed to say.

20

MONDAY APRIL 12TH 11.30 P.M. (F)

It was Peter at the door. I was halfway to the phone before he called through the door, "Fiona!" I was practically sobbing as I ran to let him in. He stood in the light from my front room. He was breathing heavily. The water ran from his hair, thick and sleek, and there was mud on his neat black shoes. He had cut his hand quite badly. Too winded to speak, he zig-zagged, drunkenly, over towards the table. He sat down next to this diary that isn't a diary any more. He leaned his head in his hands. Two huge drops of blood beaded out from the cut on his hand and splashed on to the very page on which I am writing this. Then he slumped forward over the table. I didn't go to him.

"I'm OK," he said, "that damned barbed wire . . ."

I waited for him to get his breath back. I kept thinking he was going to tell me what had happened. But he didn't. I thought he was never going to speak. In the end, I said, "Did you . . ."

"Did I what?" He sounded angry about something. As if he had expected something out there that had not materialised.

"Did you see him?"

"I did," he said. "I mean, he was wearing that damned mask. But I saw him."

I still didn't ask. I didn't want the answer to the question, you see. I was just glad I was here with somebody. Then Peter lifted his head up and looked at me. He shook his head.

"How much do you know about Paul?" he said.

"I don't know . . ." I said.

Peter nodded slowly. "I'm fond of Paul," he said, "of the Paul I *know* . . ."

"Yes," I said, "me too."

257

He got up then. He started to pace backwards and forwards across the room. I looked round at the furniture and the cracked walls. Nothing in this place seems like mine. I sometimes think I'll never have anywhere or anyone that's mine. Outside, in the main road, a lone car changed gear for the bend and somewhere, miles away, a siren started to cry a see-saw wail, like a baby that can't sleep.

"I thought I recognised him!" he said.

"Did you?" I said, deliberately. "What did you recognise?"

Peter shook his head slowly. "What makes you recognise someone? The way they move? Or talk? Or write? I kept thinking I could recognise the voice behind that damned document. But I couldn't. Recognition isn't like that." Peter looked up at me from the table. As usual he seemed to know what I was thinking. He didn't tell me the thing I didn't want to know. Not yet anyway.

"Who was it? Who was outside?" There was an urgency in my voice.

Peter didn't look away. I pushed the manuscript of my diary a little way into the table. It's funny. There was a time when I would have *died* if anyone had read it. And now . . . Oh Peter, when I've finished writing this last section I'll give it all to you. You'll take me away from here. You'll drive me to my Mum's and I don't think I'll ever come back to this drab flat. Maybe I won't ever come back to your office either or to any part of what my life was before. A new beginning.

"Paul," you said, "is very, very complicated."

"Yes?"

"He's two people . . ."

I tried a sort of laugh. "Schizo, you mean?" You didn't answer. You started to tap a page of this manuscript, idly, with your thumbnail. You were looking at me very intensely.

"I'm going to be asking you to think very carefully about everything that has happened. I'm going to be asking you to go back and remember every little thing about the man who attacked you and about things that have happened in the office!"

I didn't answer you, did I? I didn't need to, did I? Because we both knew, didn't we?

"Why didn't you say?" Peter went on, "that he had attacked you? That first time. In the flat?"

I didn't answer.

"Did he really attack you? Or was that just . . . fantasy?"

I still didn't answer. Do you know why I didn't? And did you guess, why, when you said, very, very gently to me, "It was Paul. It was Paul I saw out there!"

I started to cry. You crossed over to me and put your arms around me the way Paul could not do that day on the train. You told me again what I would have to do and now I am doing. I am writing this as you watch me. I am supplying evidence. I picture Paul out there in the street, perhaps waiting for me as I write and, now, I write the hardest thing of all. This is to say that I think I remember who said that to me in the office all those months ago . . . "No peace for the wicked" "No peace for the wicked." I know everything now. I remember everything about the way HE smelt and sounded. I remember everything about the way HE moved. I know what I have to say to make HIM show me the face underneath his mask. But I am afraid. I will write the last line of this diary that isn't a diary and push it across the table to you and say, once again – "I am afraid. I am still afraid."

•

I looked up from my diary. Paul was standing by the doors. In his hand he carried two glasses. One of them looked like a very large gin and tonic. He set it down on the desk next to him. I said, rather harshly, "Bring it over here!" As he did so, Pappanauer and Peter Taylor came through the doors behind him. I pushed the papers away from me across the desk. I looked up at Paul.

"It was you," I said to him, "who said that to me that time. It was you who said 'no peace for the wicked'. Wasn't it?"

Paul nodded slowly. "It's the kind of stupid thing I say!" he said. "But, of course, that doesn't prove anything . . ."

I gestured towards the papers on my desk. "None of this," I said, "proves anything. Because the man who did this to me is a liar. What interests me is why he lies and when he lies."

Pappanauer looked drunk, I thought. He had cut his lip somewhere in the middle of whatever they had been doing out there.

"You and Peter," I said to Paul, "both asked me a question. You both asked me about the first time I was attacked." There was absolute silence in the room. "It was just as he described it in the document!" I said. Pappanauer was looking across at Paul. "For some reason," I went on, "that was the thing I wasn't supposed to tell anyone. At first I couldn't understand why. I thought it was part of some complicated fetish. Why did HE lie about this or that? What made him lie about the second rape? Was it the same thing that made him lie about what he did to those women?"

Still none of them spoke. I went on, "There was a very simple reason. It was to do with evidence. The only evidence in this business was that collected – against my will – by the police down at Dartsea." I moved my foot closer to the carrier bag. Through the fabric I could feel the outline of the hammer head. Paul drank deeply from his glass. Pappanauer was blinking at me through the gloom of the office. "And the evidence on my night-dress." Still none of them spoke. "That's why he didn't want me to tell anyone about the first attack. But I'm going to. Now. And – in this bag I've got the night-dress. If it matches what the police took out of me, against my will, down at Dartsea, we'll know who it is – won't we? All you three will have to do is wank into a glass jar. Which is probably what you should all have been doing all of your miserable lives." I edged the carrier bag slightly closer to me. Outside the rain was still driving against the window.

I was starting to get annoyed by their silence. One of them, at least, must have something to say. I found I was looking, now, at Pappanauer. He seemed, as he so often is, on the edge of a smirk. Why had he brought me to Paul's flat? Because, presumably, like Peter, he was convinced that Paul was the man who had attacked me. But there was something more to it than that. It had been, when we were waiting in that weird, empty apartment, as if Pappanauer was somehow implicated in the thing. Once again, I had the strong impression that all three of them were responsible for what had happened to me. If only one of them had been issuing false invoices through Al Hunter and Harold Porter – wouldn't one of the other two have got on to him? What had they been arguing about down there in the courtyard? And why were the three of them now standing there like sheepish schoolboys?

Men are a mystery to me. They are so nervous with each other, and yet so impressed!

"I've been asking myself," I went on, "why I didn't say it was one of you. When we were down at Dartsea. And at first, you see, I thought it was all because I was frightened. I thought that if I said that, out loud, HE would come after me and find me. But it wasn't that."

Paul cleared his throat. "What was it then?"

"It was because I was in love with you of course. That was why. And I don't know why that should be the case. But it is. Even now. Whatever you are and whatever you've done."

I went back to my desk and sat down. When I spoke again my voice sounded thick, as if I was drunk. "Would you go now, all of you? Would you get out, please? Do you understand that I really don't want to see any more . . . men . . ."

My voice rose in pitch. I seemed to be screaming. "Get out!"

They went, as meekly as they had arrived. Peter started to say something, rather pompous sounding, about the police and how certain things were in motion and how it would be impossible to stop them. Paul started to reply that they shouldn't do anything until *I* had contacted the police. Pappanauer started to agree with both of them. They were still arguing when they came out into the courtyard. I thought at first they were going to start hitting each other. Then, as I thought they would, they went in by the entrance to the club. I had a very clear picture of the three of them climbing the narrow stairs. Not only that. I knew that, just before they got to the bar – or maybe just after, when they were settled and the drinks had been ordered – HE would find an excuse for leaving. "Just getting some fags!" "Got to make a phone call!"

HE knew he hadn't got much time. Because HE didn't know – any more than I know – what the exact status of the stains on my night-dress might be. That wasn't the point. The point was that I had said it out loud. I had threatened him. In front of the others. HE wouldn't be able to deal with that. I took the black-handled claw hammer out of the carrier bag and put it, close to me, under a sheaf of papers on the desk. It was quite possible that HE had had a chance to look inside the bag. I expected it of him.

I thought I knew, too, what he was feeling as he came back down the narrow stairs from the club and out into the rainy night. HE would be thinking about one thing – the way he had thought about one thing when he followed me home that night or lay under my bed at Dartsea. He would be thinking about the white silk night-dress. If he could only get his hands on that then he would be all right. He wouldn't have to worry about the money or the girls by the river or about counting the steps up over the footbridge that leads to Fiona Town.

That's why he does it, of course, I thought to myself. He does it because he is afraid. That boastful, distanced tone Peter Taylor talked about, is really there to keep his spirits up. He's not frightened of me, of course, or of that poor girl he killed down by the river. He is frightened of himself.

He's coming up the stairs now. He started off taking them two at a time and then he stopped. Because he was frightened I might hear him. He wants to come in when I am not expecting him. He doesn't know how well I know him. All he knows is that I've disobeyed the rules. I'm fighting back. Why don't they fight back – all those people who are maimed and abused and tortured by politicians and perverts? And if they do fight back why are the politicians and the perverts so keen for their stories not to be told? This is my story. Never mind anyone else's story. This is my story and I am telling it.

I could hear the footsteps now. One step. A pause. Another two steps. A pause. Very, very quietly, out through the fire-escape doors and on to the corridor that leads to our office. I listened hard to each step. It was curious. I could have sworn, for a moment, that it had the fussiness, the neatness of John Pappanauer. But I suppose I knew, long before he was standing by the double doors, his head to one side, with a quizzical smile on his face, that it was Peter Taylor who was coming after me.

He didn't speak. I noted, very carefully, the exact distance between myself and the carrier bag. And I saw him noting that as well. He is sure, I remember thinking, that the hammer is there, where it was. He even smiled slightly. He didn't look any different. It was the same old Peter Taylor. Same red hair, same pudgy, boyish charm. Murderers don't look any different from you and me. Perhaps they aren't any different. I remember meeting a friend of Dave's who, he told me later, had raped a girl, an acquaintance. No one did anything about it. It was impossible to prove. The man was anonymous-looking, perfectly charming. It was only when I shook his hand that I noticed anything strange about him. It was as limp as a dead fish. That was what struck me about Peter, as he came further into the room, keeping his eyes on my face. There was a limpness about him – an emptiness. I hadn't seen it before, of course. No such thing as character. There are only actions – and actions are the only way we can start to judge anyone. I thought he was going to stop but he didn't. He just kept coming over the wastes of the office carpet. It occurred to me that he was going to throw himself at me, the way he had in the flat that first time and, simply to avert his attention from me, I kicked the carrier bag towards him.

"That's what you've come for!" I said. He gave an odd, sickly little smile. Now I knew it was him, of course, I couldn't understand why I hadn't recognised the fact long ago. That slight wheeze, sometimes, when he breathed. And who else is as well placed to conceal financial corruption as the boss? Or to engineer a document that will incriminate someone else?

"It was Paul you couldn't stand, wasn't it?" I said.

"I saw you looking at him," said Peter, "before you even knew you were looking at him." Then he said, "You disgust me!"

"The feeling is mutual," I said. "You always lied for a reason, to make it look as if the thing was done out of something other than design. But of course you had to pretend you had raped me at Dartsea. Because anything they took out of me would incriminate Paul."

He wasn't looking at me any more. That made it easier to talk. His eyes were focused on the carrier bag. He would get hold of that first. Then he would make a sudden movement towards me. Quite clumsy. The way he had been in the hotel room. I didn't have any doubt that he had come back to kill me and that he didn't have much time. But I knew, also, that he was very frightened by what he had to do.

"Which came first?" I said. "Was it the money? Or the girls by the river? Or was it me? Or was it wanting to destroy Paul?"

He smiled then. That was when I thought of the word "wicked" in relation to what he was. It was the only thing that explained him. Then I thought, *no peace for the wicked*.

"Let me tell you something, Fiona," he said. "Let me just say this to you. I . . ."

And after that he stooped down towards the carrier bag. I moved very quickly. I had the hammer in my hand even as he was reaching out for my night-dress. He looked up at me as he got hold of the material. I don't think he can even have seen, or quite understood, that I was already swinging the hammer behind my head, because he started to snake up towards me. He looked, I thought, quite incredibly complacent – as if he expected me to stand there while he took out my night-dress and then wait, meekly, while he fastened those surprisingly strong hands around my throat.

I hit him on the side of the head first of all. The hammerhead splintered through a thin crust of bone, and for a moment, I had the weird and irrational conviction that I wouldn't be able to pull it out of his head. It wasn't until I yanked it back towards me that I started to appreciate how easily it would come free. He fell forward, although I couldn't tell whether this was due to the fact that I had hit him or whether he had simply lost his balance, long before I buried a lump of steel in his cranium.

Once I had got the hammerhead free I started to swing it wildly back on to his skull again and again and again. Blood was geysering out of him in crazily different directions and in ways that didn't seem to bear any relation to where I had struck him or to how hard the blow had connected. Once I buried it so deep inside his head that I did have to work it this way and that before it came back into my hands. But then, I remember, there seemed to be hardly any blood at all – only the eerily definite noise of cracking, shattered bone and a sort of wheezing sob that seemed to be coming from behind me but was in fact being gargled out of his throat as he fell, heavily, across the carrier.

Once he was on the floor I hit him in the face. I didn't want to have to look at his face. I wanted to smash it back into his skull until all his features were as smooth as porcelain. I stooped over him as I worked my way round every fragment of relief in that smooth, complacent boss's face and, as I did so, the blood gushed up out of him on to the white of my jersey, into my face, over my hands, until it seemed as if every inch of the face I presented to the world was sodden crimson. I was saying something but I didn't know what it was. It was something I should have said to him that first time or that second time or all of the other times when I wasn't ready for him. I was ready for him now all right. "No peace for the wicked!" Was that what I was saying? It sounded like that. If it was that I seemed to be saying it again as I swung the hammer down above his eyes and his hands clawed the air in front of his eyes, curtained with fountains of his own blood. "No peace for the wicked!"

He was saying my name. How was he managing to talk? Would he rise up off the carpet, like some headless ghost in a revenger's tragedy and come after me, still reaching for my neck? How could I stop him saying my name? I hit him again – on the cheeks, on the scalp, in the mouth, below the ear, in one eye and then in the other eye. I hit him until I didn't know any more what it was of him I was hitting or whether the noises coming from his throat could, any more, be said to be anything to do with him. Surely it couldn't still be Peter Taylor calling to me? "Fiona! Fiona! Fiona!" And if it was him how could I make him stop? How hard did I have to strike him with the bloodied steel head of the hammer until I was absolutely sure that he would never, ever get up again?

It wasn't him. The voice was Paul's. It was coming from the door. When at last I dropped the weapon in my hand, back on to the carpet and looked across at Paul, I realised that, not only was the noise coming from him but that it was quite a loud noise. He was yelling at me, his fists screwed up into a ball, his face tight with tension. And the noise only stopped when the hammer was next to where Peter Taylor lay, silent now, not breathing, with only a bloody, inert, pulpy mass where his face used to be.

"I heard everything!" Paul was saying.

"What did you hear?"

"I heard him confess!" said Paul, "I heard him say what he'd done."

I wasn't sure that I had heard him say anything of the kind. But, with two of us to swear it was true, it might well be the kind of thing that the police would believe. I stood there, breathing hard. I looked down at my white sweater. It seemed to be a different colour from the stuff oozing out of his head and on to the office carpet. I couldn't, somehow, connect my hand with the hammer that lay, just next to Peter Taylor, below me. There was something I wanted but I couldn't think what it might be. Still Paul didn't move from the door. I looked at his face, long and hard. Then I remembered what I wanted to say.

"Come here!" I said, in that thick, drunkard's voice, "Come here now, would you?"

Paul's head was nodding like one of those puppets you see in the back of cars. His hands, I noted, were poised up by the lapels of his jacket, as if he was about to make some point in a committee meeting. I looked away from his hands. His eyes weren't as pale as I remembered them. They were alive, almost excited, and when, reluctantly, they met mine I could have sworn I saw the distant shadow of pleasure somewhere within them.

"You're supposed to be in love with me, aren't you?" I heard myself say. His head was still bouncing this way and that. I thought he would never move from the frame of the door, as if he, too, was frightened that Taylor might climb up from the carpet. It seemed minutes before he began the long journey across the floor towards me and even then he stopped a yard or so away. There was blood, I realised, on my jeans as well. On my shoes, on my hair, on my face, and on both of my hands. My hands were shaking uncontrollably.

"Will you put your arms around me?" I said, as Paul stood there looking at me. "Will you promise you'll never leave me? Will you say you love me the way I love you?"

Paul looked at me. It seemed as if the distance between us was getting longer and longer. As if time, too, was stretching out in front of us and that his voice, when next he spoke, would be slowed, too, like a tape winding down. If he did speak. Perhaps, I thought, all of these things would grind into a glacier's halt and that neither of us would ever move or talk or make any attempt to start the rest of our lives. In the end – and this didn't happen until I became aware of other footsteps out in the corridor – he did speak to me. "Yes," he said. "Yes. Yes. Yes."

Then, bloodied and shaking as I was, he came to me and put his arms around me. Like a couple of wounded soldiers, helping each other away from a scene of devastation, we walked out of the office, into the corridor and past the rain-flecked windows, towards the waiting world outside.